Hot Thots

by
Hitachi Choparazzi

Book 1 of the Hot Thots Series

HOT THOTS
Book 1 of the Hot Thots Series
BY HITACHI CHOPARAZZI

Editing and Interior Layout by Urban Book Editor
Cover Design by Bowman Artistic Designs

Published by Chop-A-Style Publishing, PO Box 391212, Snellville, GA 30039.

Printed in the United States of America.

ISBN-13: 978-1-7320886-2-7
ISBN-10: 1-7320886-2-4

Library of Congress Control Number: 2021908894

10 9 8 7 6 5 4 3 2
First Edition

Acknowledgments

I'd like to give due praise to Allah. My G-Ma Lawson, may Allah bestow peace and blessings upon you all your days. My Unc Dale, G-Pa Lawson, Lil Bro Pierre (Peppy), may y'all rest in harmony. My Day1 Souljahs, rest in sync. My kids, Kolany Jr., Pierre, Kylan, and beautiful, intelligent daughter China: Daddy loves y'all unconditional. To all my fans and fam city-to-city and lockdown society, I do it for y'all. Teflon luv!

Also, special thanks to Urban Book Editor for not discriminating against incarcerated authors and independent publishing companies.

#IncarceratedLivesMatter
#FreeHitachiChoparazzi

Contents

Prologue

Teasing Tasha checked her DM on the Gram. She had 92 direct messages. They couldn't get enough of that pecan Puerto Rican-Jamaican breed. She had jet-black silky hair with an island accent. She was sassy and snappy like a Puerto Rican. She scanned thru some of her DMs, but they weren't talking her language—MONEY!

As quick as she deleted them, more DMs came. She hated when they were stalking her Instagram and playing, not paying! All winking emojis, and no dollar signs.

"Ugh—shit! SMH—OMG!" Teasing Tasha screamed as she signed out, annoyed. Then she went to check her Snapchat. She thought she found a potential nigga tricking big and played his Snapchat. She saw all his big ice…

"Hey, sweetness. I dig what I see! If you feeling me? And like what you see? Hit Denver JD! My Instagram is the same—Denver underscore JD. I'm a local rapper, but I'll fly out there just to meet and greet you! I look forward to hearing back from you via Snapchat and seeing that exotic frame," Denver JD the rapper. He turned on his seductive charm, hoping to lure Teasing Tasha into his Ritz-Carlton bed.

Bingo! Teasing Tasha's eyes lit up like lightning. She wet her hair and greased it down so her fine baby hairs would curl up. Then she got butt-naked, dropping her cute red lace thong on the edge of her bed. She went to the bathroom, sat on the toilet, and hit her pussy clean 3x with the pink Bic razor. Then she rubbed it smooth. It was soft as stewed sweet pork.

Next, she grabbed her Mr. Rabbit sex toy, placed it on 3, and then put it on her clit to get it wet. She let out a few soft moans as she closed her eyes, took a deep breath, and relaxed her mind. All she could feel was the vibration stimulating her clit, sending small waves through her body. It sent intensely pleasurable waves to her head and back down to her swollen clit. When she felt her pussy contracting and legs trembling, she seized, snatching the Mr. Rabbit toy away to regain control. Still, it felt like a magnet was trying to pull the toy back under her tiny clit.

She shook it off and pulled herself together to give an impeccable performance. Then, she grabbed her selfie stick to return a Snapchat to Denver JD, the rapper.

"YASSS…You see this sweet pretty pussy? Yeah, look at all this pretty pink-pink…See how tight this pussy is? You couldn't put ya pinky in this pussy, I bet? You gotta work it first. Let me rub this small love button for you and watch me gush! See…O-O-O…Ooo…O-O-Oh-Ooo-Owee-Oweee…Oh-Oh shit!" Teasing Tasha whispered soft and sexy, seducing him right back.

Then she did another Snapchat to send him a Part 2 after she squirted like a cat fast on her bed. She bent over from the back and showed off her pretty asshole.

"Yeah, Denver JD, you ain't neva seen a bitch ass pretty as this! Huh? I'm with all that licky-lick Kevin Gates shit all my holes and between all my toes! I hope you 'bout that life! Go head and jack ya dick to this…" Teasing Tasha said, panting as if she had dashed from the car to the apartment.

She spread her ass cheeks, tooted her ass all the way up for the selfie stick to get a bird's eye panoramic view, and massaged her pink asshole with K-Y Hers spray. Then she glided her own thumb in-and-out of it slow motion.

Denver JD's mind was blown! He instantly went straight into the bathroom and got one off! He skeeted to her sexy sweet voice and audio alone! Then, he felt like Weezy. After he came, he came to his senses.

He was a rapper, not a trick, and he had almost bit! Fuck this Snapchat hood rat! he thought as he sent her a Snapchat back, shaking his head. She was a hot THOT trying to come up on a few knots or for someone rich to save her and take her to the top.

Fifteen minutes later, Teasing Tasha got her nut off, too. She squirted all over her sheets, laid up in her own flowing juices. Her pussy was still pulsing when she received the Snapchat back from Denver JD. She smirked devilish and played it...

"SMH—You Snapchat hood rat! You lil nasty hot THOT! I skeeted and deleted cha THOT ass! So, bum bitch, beat it cuz you been cheated!"

Teasing Tasha's eyes burned red as she cursed "Mother Fucka!" and threw her Galaxy Note.

Hitachi Choparazzi

Chapter 1
"Snapchat Hood Rat"

Teasing Tasha sucked her teeth as she picked up her Galaxy Note4 that she had chucked at her apartment wall. The screen had cracked, and she was super on fire hot. She wanted to kill Denver JD the rapper for putting her on blast, calling her a Snapchat hood rat!

He was already putting her on blast all over the Gram, which is where it counts because that was where she would fish and catch all her big tricks and vic them to tricking off first if they wanted to taste and see that pretty pussy.

She could care less about the book of life because it was mainly for family and friends now. Plus, she saw herself as Instagram Hot, not a THOT. Besides, she wasn't sexing or freaking all them ballers and shottas anyways; it was just a little sexting and Snapchat pussy shots or play sessions where she busts it open as a token of appreciation for choosing to trick on her. But she knew it was just high anticipation, which led to a big ol' cash-out!

However, occasionally she had jerks and childish-ass niggas that had a social media frenzy for spotting and blasting—HOT Thots. Then they try to let the whole world know, but still follow her on Instagram and hit her right back in the DM. She shook her head. Niggas be on fleek!

Teasing Tasha stood 5'4, 135 lbs. with perky B-cups, and a 19-inch waist that complemented her frame and gave her the bee shape just like a Coke bottle. She had curves, thighs, hips, and a phatty bottom! She teased cats by twerking it gently and making it clap in silence, which made their jaws drop, "Ds" stiffen, and hearts stop. She knew that she had a pretty pussy like Pretty Ricky sang about, and how super tight it was due to the fact she couldn't take no real "D."

That was Teasing Tasha's biggest problem. She couldn't keep a man because he would only hit it maybe once to twice a week. They had to chase her because she'd run from the dick and she would scream bloody murder, waking the neighbors up, calling the police. She'd use her hands to intervene. They would be all in the way, and she had a cold method she used so you couldn't kill her shit. She wasn't going for that. She came with a sex filter and some more shit. She would claw up your back like she was possessed with her gouging talons.

Them scratches were deep and called hater marks, because they'd get a real playa caught up by his main thing, had him once again caught up for playing with them thots on the Gram again.

Teasing Tasha was a crazy mixed breed of Jamaican and Puerto Rican so she was a crazy cute one with an attitude. She was the true definition of exotic and erotic. She could move her hips wind and grind better than some of her Jamaican cousins in Kingston. They loved her teasing ass in the clubs and after-hours spots, too, especially when she twerked something like the twerk team and did the dirty wind, twisting her neck and flicking her hair ratchet as her ass cheeks bounced one at a time from left to right. It was mean dirty dancing on the scene.

She always made the club look like a strip club with her gyrating seductive pussy-popping hot THOT moves. Girls couldn't stand that bitch and would be attached by the hips with their dudes, clutching them like a handbag by the arms as they shook their heads and making slick comments, hating while pointing her out, saying, "Ugh…Look at that hot thot! LOL #FlaminHotThots!"

It was typical envy females, just jealous hating on a bad bitch. Even if she was a hot thot, Teasing Tasha still was super bad. Usually, they didn't have to point out Teasing Tasha, because their dudes would notice her with their lustful cutting bulging eyes anyway. And there's no feeling like when a female sees that her man is moved by another female right in front of her, especially by a hot thot.

That was exactly what Tasha specialized in, breaking up a good thing. She'd leave you broke with no hope, and take you down there with blue-blue nuts! She was vicious and an expert at her webbing craft.

Teasing Tasha was from Chicago, but had been born in Queens. Her mama was a Puerto Rican from Chicago that got involved with Tasha's crazy Jamaican dad in Jamaica, Queens, New York City. Tasha's mama used to go visit her Nana and Puerto Rican family back in Queens every summer. Her mama was a hot Rican thot, too, back in the early '90s, running around Queens chasing her daddy.

Her dad was first-generation Jamaican straight from Kingston. He got deported twice by the U.S. Marshals. The second time he got sent back to Jamaica, he never made it back.

He was found dead at his own mother's house with his throat slit ear-to-ear style, lying in a pool of his own stale blood. Tasha had only seen her dad twice in her life, but she couldn't remember him because she was a toddler at the time.

Nowadays she was too busy to worry about family ties. She was too grown at the tender age of 21. It didn't stop her, though, because she had been playing grown ever since her teen thot years when she was coming out of her shell.

Teasing Tasha was interrupted playing with her

cracked screen by a familiar light tap knock on the door of her southwest side Chicago apartment.

"Bitch, hold on, let me throw some clothes on! You know how you like to bring strangers over my crib with ya ass, too. I keep telling you dis ain't the SPOT! Or a damn trap!" Teasing Tasha said with her West Indies accent.

"Oh, bitch please, ain't nobody with me! Please, this a bando cuz you know ya teasing ass don't hardly pay no rent in this Section 8 muthafucka. Hurry up, it's cold out here! And open this damn door up before I leave," Teasing Tasha's BFF said.

Teasing Tasha popped up half naked with just her thong on. She unlocked the door, then ran away, switching her ass to the bathroom as her BFF opened the door, letting the chilly breeze in.

"Bitch, you act like nobody ain't seen you naked before—Jo! And hurry up so I can tell you 'bout cha hot thot lil selfie…" Tasha's BFF said in her south side of Chicago accent as she saw Tasha holding her arms over her nipples.

Tina from the south side of the Go off 59th, the low ends. Everyone called them Tasha and Tina, a.k.a. Teasing Tasha and Tina da Cum Cleaner. Tina was a real city hot thot, too, just like her BFF Tasha. Both were unemployed. They couldn't keep a job, mainly because they were too lazy to work. They would just get a paycheck and then quit, no-call, no-show. Besides, they partied hard during work hours, then slept during from 9 to 5. They were night owl thots.

When Tina saw her Tasha's IG going ham, she was on top riding the "D" and checking her iPhone. She saw a nasty video message being passed around the Gram of her girl and told that cheap-ass nigga to drop her off at Tasha's crib, leaving him rocked up still, hanging and holding his meat in his hand. She sucked her teeth and rolled her eyes and kicked him out. She couldn't even get no L-Train money from his tight ass and felt like, fuck him. In Chicago, they always wanted to fuck and blow a bitch back out, then wet a bitch ass up and don't have shit, no dollars!

Tina was 5'6" and caramel brown with a honey glowing glaze. She had a cute face, dimples, big booty, and little waist. They were the perfect thot duo. She and Tasha didn't need a crew. You know most thots don't get along with other thots, especially square bear bitches, because they believed in a fairy-tale dream that a "real" man was supposed to save them and marry them into a rich family. But they were doing the most and getting down for their crown, then once they break up with their ex, he would clown them and drag smut their names all over social media, too. Them bitches were fucking for free—a promise ring, but ended up with a broken heart, empty-handed with mileage and luggage.

Tina knew her BFF couldn't take no damn dick, either. They had gone on a double dinner date and rendezvous at Tasha's apartment to "watch Netflix" with two niggas from the wild hundreds on the Southside of Chi-Raq, spending hundreds.

Teasing Tasha was fucking with Lil Weedy that night, and Tina was messing with Lil Weedy's folks, Big Cuzzo. How Tasha was hollering and carrying on that night? Damn! Who would believe she was serious and not acting out?

Tina herself messed with Lil Weedy a few times before. He didn't have no damn king cobra, but she knew he was alright. And Tasha ass deserved and earned her name because that title fit her perfectly, Teasing Ass Tasha, with her fine China doll-looking ass. Then she had what every dude on the Gram called it "dat Ri-Ri voice," that Barbados Island accent just like Rihanna.

Tasha's Instagram went hard just like India Westbrook except she wasn't getting paid or no endorsements. She guessed they didn't endorse thotery, but she had stupid men followers, all stalking, hunting and preying on her prowl.

That same night Tina discovered her BFF was shallow with the pussy like J. Cole say. Tasha had the shakes like she needed a Newport smoke break and some more shit. She was shaking like she was freezing cold inside her room after only 30 minutes of her and Lil Weedy teasing session. She slept for 10 straight hours after that like a baby brat.

Tina wouldn't ever forget that night. She even tried to help Tasha out and told her to start trying to use small dildos to break herself in and train herself to take the "D." However, that really didn't work. It seemed worse than the real thing, pain, not pleasure.

Tasha was set in her ways and didn't care too much. On top of that, a lot of cats would say she was a dime piece for nothing, a straight waste, because not only couldn't she take "D," she couldn't suck "D" neither. She was whack! She hated it, too, and knew she was horrible in that department mainly because she was so traumatized by the "D." She would give you more of a hand job the whole time and breathe on it. She would barely put her mouth on it. She was just too scared to choke on it or for you to skeet-skeet down her throat and in her mouth. Yuck! She had a "D" phobia. It repulsed her, but she wasn't gay into girls, though. She was known for leaving a frog in a nigga's pants, especially when she was thot twerking.

Teasing Tasha finally came out the bathroom with just a plain white tee on, like she was dressed. Tina could see her erect full pink nipples thru the light Hanes shirt. Plus, it cut off at the middle of her ass cheeks. It's no wonder she never wanted company and hated whenever her BFF Tina popped up with all type of dudes.

"So, what up, Jo? You a hot mess, bitch! Dem fools on the Gram crashing your page and thot'n you around, once again all thru da ground," Tina said, slick shaking her head but really hating because Tasha's bad ass was still trending and she knew really niggas loved thotery and thotness.

"Gurrl, I ain't stunting them. They broke social media niggas stunting and frontin' as ballers and moguls. They know I'm a bad bitch and none of them never had this tight pussy! They wish and could only dream of this, Tina!" Teasing Tasha said nonchalantly and shrugged her shoulders.

"Please, Tasha, you know ya ass got a bad review. They got you on Snapchat Yelp! They going to ban you from Snapchat for being a hood rat, bitch! This like, what, the fourth time a nigga put you on blast and literally exposing ya ass? Showing off ya naked ass and you busting it open every time," Tina said, astonished, shaking her head with her hand on her hip. Tasha was still her girl, though.

"I'll just say my Instagram was hacked and change my account, again...ya know, start a new one on them ho ass niggas, spread'n pics like bitches anyway. Messy mouths, ugh," Tasha replied. Her island accent thickened the more aggravated she became.

"Bitch, how many times you done that now, huh? And every time you switch profile pics and names, they all know it's you and find you throwing more dirt than shade. You need a social media break. Just take you some damn selfies for a few days straight. And please, no more making videos of ya lil horny play sessions. These dudes ain't worthy. And if ya daddy was alive, he would been done killed ya lil narrow ass!" Tina replied.

Tasha just waved her off, then changed the subject.

Tina asked, "You have any more weed left from the other night?"

"Yeah, go get the sack out of my panties top drawer."

Tina told her, "Ughh, Bitch, but you gotta roll the cigarillo."

They smoked the eighth of green crack kush they

had left as they got dressed. They could fit into each other's clothes. Even though they were a size or two different, you couldn't notice too much. And every night, they got stoned before they went out sex on the city, Chicago-style.

Tina decided to take Tasha to the new hookah lounge off Lake Shore Drive. They were about to prance thru downtown Chicago, too. They both wished the Taste of Chicago was going down right now. They had the munchies and Tasha never had anything to eat or cook in her place. Neither couldn't cook anyway. But out of their Chicago little pussy pound clique, none of them couldn't make shit to eat either. All of them were a bunch of eat-out bitches that enjoyed fast food Whoppers, White Castle, gyros, chicken wings and fries dates, typical thot food and plenty of soda.

After they got dressed, Tasha created another IG account and another Snapchat. "Snapchat is where it's at. I want all the Snapchat points, trophies to unlock 'em all." Tasha said.

She had 36 trophies so far. She knew how to use and work certain filters with the right emojis to make her light bright self pop out more vivid than light.

Tina was a black and Italian breed. They called themselves the BFF Triple B's—Bad Bitch Breed—club. Except Tina was a caramel honey complexion, so you would have to look close to see her half-breed side, like her curly fine jet-black hair and pointy narrow Italian nose. Then she had that Italian Jersey Shore shit come out in her ass, too.

That was part of where she got her handle from, too, Tina Da Cum Cleaner, because she would get drunk and get loose as a goose off Grey Goose. Tina was a thot that they called drunk pussy. All you had to do was drink with her for 30-40 minutes and turn the heat all the way up, but you could only give her clear liquor. That dark brown would make her sick and throw up, but the more Cîroc she drank, the wetter her panties got. Almost every time she would roll her panties off because they would be so soaked and sticky, it would annoy her to the point she'd melt inside-out, wet, which led to her getting flipped every which way and gang-banged by the famous Chi-Raq cliques. They had her all on video around town. It was rumored that she even licked Chief Keef's feet. So, they started doing the #IGT hashtag all over the Gram, which stood for Instagram thot getting tagged team and choo-choo trained.

Teasing Tasha was a true Snapchat hood rat, but her BFF Tina was a hot Instagram thot, so when they went out on the city, every man tried to get lucky.

Tina was scrolling down the Gram, waiting on Tasha to finish setting up her new accounts and profile pics, when she stumbled across breaking news…

"Damn it, bitch—check this shit out! I got Denver JD in a pic tagged with his old ass daddy with a Cubs hat on in front of the Cubs stadium! You know what that means, right?"

"Of course, duh, Tina—some Snapchat get-back!" Teasing Tasha said, cutting her BFF off. She was turnt-up.

"Yeah, he gotta be close and in the go, Jo!" Tina replied deviously. Her Instagram was Italian underscore Chianti. Chianti was a dry red wine from Italy, since she loved alcohol and to blame it on the alcohol like Jamie.

"Oh, yasss! Bitch, I'm 'bout to hit him in the DM and Snapchat him the same one as his son, if his lame-ass son didn't sent it to him already. But yeah, bitch, I'ma tell him look at all this young tender flower that ya son was too immature for. So, if we can keep it private, he can eat some sweet finger-tight warm wet bomb ass pussy for a personal 1500-dollar cash fee. Then once he eat my pussy, have him lick my ass and make him stick his tongue all inside my booty hole. Ha-ha-ha…give a bitch a colon cleanse…and have him taste all colon, then tell him to go give his son a kiss on the lips for me—LOL, bitch! Fuck Denver JD. He'll see me post some selfies of his Dad eating me out from the back with his face and nose all in between my ass—like a dog! Watch…and I'ma hip his old ass Grandpappy–Daddy to this new generation where you got to lick a bitch and play with a bitch ass to make us cum!" Teasing Tasha said, turnt the fuck up as she was thot clapping both her hands together in sequence ratchetly.

They both giggled and passed the green crack kush back and forth as they choked and wiped their mouths. Teasing Tasha was rejoicing in her evil ploys with a vengeance conscience dancing devilish inside. That was that Jamaican side of her manifesting. If she had her way with him, she would throw his messy mouth, funny-looking ass straight into Lake Michigan mafia-style with concrete shoes on his feet at the bottom of the lake getting eaten by the fish and crabs, then make his daddy lick her booty juices after she had an anal-gasm, just straight raunchy and disrespectful. Now that's what she called some Snapchat get-back! The kush had her mind blown.

She looked at her BFF, curious. Tina was sexy and a bad half-breed bitch, too, she had to admit, but she just wasn't a redbone. And that's what all the guys bi-costal on the Gram loved, went ape-shit bananas, and lustfully sought for. She knew Tina was slightly jealous and would throw shade on other redbones calling them thots, even the married ones modeling and promoting on the Gram as an independent hustle. She couldn't blame her, though, because Tasha knew her shit jumped like some jacks.

The weed had her horny and moving her legs in an open-and-shut, motion creating friction between them as her clit hardened up. She knew Tina had been in a few ménage-à-trois on the West Side before. Tasha knew Tina wasn't into girls either but was drunk A.F.! She heard all them bi-sexual West Side thots putting Tina on blast and slick comments all over the Book and the Gram. They were saying how she gave bomb lesbo ass sloppy thot top when she bubbly like she did it before. Plus, they were inside joking, giving her the Thot Top of the Year Award during the ratchet Facebook Awards where everybody would shout out and give out all type of ratchet awards like Trap Queen of the Year award, the Gangway Gun Play of the Year Award, Thot King, Juke Squad, Twerk Team, and Bando Bands of the Year award. It was too much. Right about now Tasha would've let Tina eat her pussy out and bust a nut all over her tongue and sexy juicy-ass lips, too.

"OMG—Bitch, WTF? Why you looking at me like that? You all rubbin' ya thighs, opening and shutting your legs all hot in the ass…Bitch, I don't want to see ya hot-ass pussy, bad enuff it's all over social media. Ugh…now let's go to that new hookah lounge and downtown to eat. I got the munchies for a Philly cheesesteak. C'mon! Tasha gurrl— let's go, Jo!" Tina said, stoned, as she shook her head. Her BFF was trippin'!

Hitachi Choparazzi

Chapter 2
"Teasing Tasha"

Teasing Tasha walked into the hookah lounge first like she was a superstar. Tina was behind her and envious at her for once again stealing the show. She mumbled out *ugh* as she sucked her teeth, hating. She enjoyed all the attention but hated on Tasha when she stole the spotlight like right now as she watched Tasha working it and her magic all over the lounge.

Tasha wore an all-black velvet cat full-body suit that showed off her full erect nipples protruding like raisins. Her sexy, perky B-cups accented a phat pussy print with a 2finger-size camel toe. Her booty giggled as she walked, switching from side-to-side. Everyone could tell she wore no panties. She had lied and told Tina she was wearing a thong from Victoria's Secret.

Every dude in the joint grabbed the hard lumps in their pants as Teasing Tasha walked past. They blew out big clouds of hookah smoke as they choked. She made dicks jump as her ass waddled swaying side-to-side like a duck. You could tell Tasha had cakes from the front when she walked, too, because all you would see is her ass fishtailing side-to-side and her rear end trying to catch up with the front. Her Puerto Rican hips and thighs complemented her Jamaican curves and tiny waist. She truly was blessed with the best of both worlds.

Teasing Tasha wouldn't please; she was just a sweet tease. The more she said no and held back with her legs shut, the more ballers broke themselves tricking off and throwing big bands at her toes, begging for a sniff. She'd get naked and strip, then dance, twerking soft and slow. She'd let them lick her ass and pussy long as they tricked off. She didn't have any specific amounts; long as she could count it up in her hands, she won and got paid to cum. She only would flat back if she absolutely had no way out, and that was a task within itself.

Tasha had been putting on this same walk since she was 15, a hot little thot with her Puerto Rican cousins in New York at the Puerto Rican Day Parade. She would take Tina with her every summer, too, being NYC marching thots with their ass cheeks hanging all out white skimpy spandex and tennis skirts.

As they went to get seated at a table, the music in the hookah lounge changed up…

"Let me rock, put you back to sleep, girl—I just posted my landing…" Chris Brown's hit latest single went off, which was the thot anthem so far for the year.

Tina started singing along with Chris Breezy. She really had vocals and could sing her butt off. Then Tasha was dancing slow and seductively, once again being the center of attention while getting a few dudes in the place in trouble, slapped, and checked on the spot. As always, she smiled and pretended to be oblivious to her show-stopping and stirring up the place.

"Girl, that's my shit and number 1 on my playlist! You know Chris Brown my baby daddy, bitch!" Teasing Tasha said, still bobbing her head as she sat down and grabbed the hookah stem.

"Girl, please, you know that nigga Chris Breezy is a M-thot and ain't none of ya BD. He not saving ya Hot Thot ass if he didn't save Ri-Ri or Crueche Tran either," Tina replied as she pulled on the hookah and puffed the scented smoke.

"Bitch, please, my baby daddy Chris Breezy ain't no damn M-thot. Shit, Ray J is a M-thot," Tasha proclaimed turnt up, all light-headed from the hookah.

"Unh-unh…Oh, hell nawh, bitch. Don't be talkin' 'bout my man Ray J! I don't care if he is engaged, but he's not an M-thot! Now, Justin Bieber is a real M-thot, LOL," Tina said as she did the thot clap with both her hands, expressing herself.

"Oh, hell yeah, true-true. You ain't lying, bitch. He a lil hot M-thot, lol! C'mon, let's hit the hookah together. I like this mango shit, bitch," Teasing Tasha concluded, all mellowed out from the flavored sweet smoke.

An M-thot was a Man-thot, a guy that was out there, too. Basically, a man ho! Men were hot in the ass, too, just like some of them thots. Somehow it was a basic rule of thumb that a woman could sleep with 2-4 guys and be labeled as a bona fide ho! But a man could do the same thing and was considered a king, and the man, a pimp and player with good street cred.

There really wasn't a difference what the M stood for. East Coast and Down South both used the M for Man-thot. And the West Coast and the Midwest used the M for Male thot. Either way it still meant and was used for the same thing, a man whore.

The meaning of thot varied from coast to coast; some people say the meaning is That Ho Out There. Other say That Ho Over There! Still, meant she was hot in the ass, just like a hood rat.

Tina and Tasha saw a party of four females grouping up, giving them dirty looks and hard mean mugs on their poked-out jealous faces, which they were used to being in the triple B club. They just waved the other envious thots off.

Then two guys made their way over to Tasha and Tina's table. They finally built up the courage to be the first guys to approach the table and asked if they would love to join them for a double hookah date to celebrate the grand opening of the new trendy hookah lounge off Lake Shore Drive like they really owned the place.

Tina looked away as Tasha sucked her teeth and blew smoke in both of their faces disrespectfully. She couldn't believe their lame-ass game and that corny stunt, like they were going to bite. She shook her head and dismissed them said, "Oh, we Gucci ova here, Jo!" She shot them straight down in front of everybody, which discouraged the rest of the little players around the joint.

Bad bitches had a way of intimidating cats and bruising their macho man egos because it didn't matter how much money or clout you had. All good game could get you was a good smile and blush. A bad bitch had to basically just choose up. You had to really be their prototype or just dressed out lucky.

Tasha's phone was going off. She was getting DMs like crazy. Tina peeped her joint going off, too. Then Tasha's page crashed and got shut down once again! All they did was post a few pics on the Gram from the hookah lounge blowing big clouds of smoke, then did a few Snapchats, too. Tasha's page been shut down before on the Gram from haters reporting her pics and shit. She was hot because she just built that page and switched her profile and username for the 10th damn time. She shook her head in defeat.

Tina slid her the phone and saw that Denver JD was back at it again, stalking her new page and putting on blast, leaving slick comments: *Some thots try to switch it up and fool the public posing as church and schoolgirls, but are public disgraces. And the Snapchat Hood Rat of the Week Award goes to...Chicago Triple B's.* Then it was a screenshot pic from Tasha's Snapchat, which had all her and his followers along with all their followers and friends, too.

He had a screenshot pic with her holding a selfie stick from the back with her sex toy playing. He had a filter of Hello Kitty cats over her private parts exposed and sex toy, but you could still tell she was doing an explicit act. It got her kicked straight off the Gram. Tasha been kicked off the Gram more than the celebrities! She was that hot but a trending thot! Denver JD was really starting to piss her off now. She DM'd his Pops once again quick with Tina's IG account. She was ready to let the Hunger Games begin! All the Puerto Rican and Jamaican came out of her as she got turnt-up and eyes bloodshot-red, clenching her nails in her fist.

She shook her head and sighed out as she cursed Denver JD. Then she mean-mugged them bitches at the other table, like WTF, bitch?

Tina just watched her BFF get right back on that ignorant B.S. once again. She swore it was that West Indies in her because Tasha was like a damn Gemini: cool as a fan one second and then hot as fish grease the next second, from 0-100 quick like Drake. The cold part about it was being a light-skinned half-breed from Chicago, Illinois, you had to learn how to fight and slice growing up, especially with the jealous bald-headed chicky-tails of the Go. And Tasha and Tina both could fight. Tasha had hands and would square up and fistfight like a dude. Really all the bitches on the South Side of the Chi-Raq fist fight. Those windmill and clawing scratching days were over with back in the early 2000s.

"Sup, bitch. You gotta problem with ya ratchet ass, huh?" the alpha female of the little weasel ho pack said as she stood over Tasha with her knuckles cracking.

"Oh, hell nawh. Who you calling ratchet, Jo? Only ones we see ratchet up in this hookah joint is y'all lil weasel hos, bitch!" Tasha replied as she and Tina stood up in unison.

"Hey-hey, nope! Not in my new establishment. I'm sorry, no cat fighting! No cat fights allowed! Take that junk down Lake Shore for all I care, for Christ sakes!" the short, pudgy Italian manager intervened and got in between.

The party of four weasel hos backed up, nodding their heads up and down like, "Yeah, bitch, we got y'all soon as y'all come outside." Tasha and Tina knew they were about to try and jump them, but as soon as Tasha hitachi'd one of the bitches with her infamous wooden handle Jamaican ratchet, the rest of the bum project bitches would run down Lake Shore and get somewhere. And Tasha specialized in slicing faces up like Pizza NYC-style buck-fifties; she was known for striking bitches' faces with that blade around the Go. They knew she Go!

Then suddenly, Tasha heard one of the bitches in the crowd yell out, "Stupid thot!" which really set her smooth the fuck off. Her blood was already hot from Denver JD's childish ass. Now, it was really boiling. She turnt all the way up like Remy Ma and Fat Joe! She grabbed the whole hookah up off the table and slung that bitch at the bitches.

It clocked one bitch in the head like a Redd's Apple Ale commercial, then bounced off and hit the other bitch in the lower back. The hookah water flew all over, catching one of those weasel hos and the pudgy Italian manager. Despite ducking, he still got splashed. He was hot! He didn't want the bad opening reviews; otherwise he would've called the Chicago PD on Tasha's crazy ass. He couldn't believe how strong she was and how far she launched the two-foot hookah.

This was the bell that set it off! A thot fight! They started jumping Tasha and Tina, swinging wild out of pure emotions. It was typical biting, scratching, shirt-ripping, and weave-wig snatching brawl. Cats had their phones out. Fuck Worldstar, this was going on Snapchat ratchet thot brawls.

Tasha was kicking like a donkey in a trunk to get them bitches off her, trying to get into her Prada clutch bag for her blade. And Tina was in a two-way hair lock as them bitches were working her. Tasha warned her about wearing her curly hair all out like that, especially without no grease, all dry and shit.

By the time Tasha started swinging, connecting them bitches to the chin, she saw they whooped Tina out of her halter top and her double D's were hanging out all over the place, bouncing for a nice peep show for all the guys in the joint. Even the manager was being a pervert. No wonder why nobody helped or tried to break up the cat brawl. Then she saw they had Tina's mouth leaking as they worked her to the ground.

Tasha went berserk and got to slashing bitches like tires. All you heard was burning screams. She really was surgical with that wooden island ratchet blade. You could tell she used it before. When the little pudgy manager saw that and all that blood splatting all over the place, with girls running away crying, trying to hold the flaps of skin on their face together, he had to call the law and report her crazy ass. She was a raging lunatic and seemed possessed. Shit, she even made him jump.

She told Tina to get up off the ground and grab her shirt to put over her titties. Tina covered herself with her ripped halter top and spit blood out her mouth. Then she held her bleeding nose as they hit the front door, fleeing from the law. They ran down Lake Shore Drive. They knew to hide until they found a ride. Tasha used her Uber app to call a cab.

Tina was holding her pointy nose pinched up in the air. She kept sighing out and shaking her head. She told Tasha, "Damn, Jo—OMG! Ugh!" Tasha told her that next time don't flop on the ground. Then they heard sirens, but it sounded more like an ambulance or fire truck than Chicago

PD. They decided to move out of hiding.

"I ain't tryin' ta see no part of Cook County jail. Fuck that!" Tina said. "We can go to my mama's spot on Wentworth."

Just then, a car with tinted windows came to a screeching halt. The BFFs flinched, startled.

"Aye, Jo, sup? Y'all need some A.A.? We seen y'all getting down in da hookah lounge…Y'all know he called the law on y'all? And two of them thots faces leaking bad, too. We was the two niggas puffing all the way in the back. We can drop y'all off, tho. We was just on our way to Harold's Chicken right now. Y'all better c'mon, Jo!" the tall one with the dreads yelled out from the passenger side of the Charger.

The girls both looked at each other for validation, both paranoid and afraid to go to jail. They hopped in the backseat of the black-on-black Charger. The driver smashed the gas, opening the hemi hot-boy style as his tires peeled out and pressed the girls into the backseat, stunting and fronting, beating that new Kevin Gates in his four 12-inch subs. They sparked a sour diesel kush cigarillo and passed it around the car rotation a few times, listening to the thump and music in silence as they smashed thru the South Side passing everybody by in traffic and on foot. If only these niggas knew they weren't getting lucky or no digits. Just hi, bye, and thanks for the high and RIDE! They went to Harold's Chicken and ordered the girls some chicken, and then dropped them off at Tina's Pop's house on King Drive. Once they saw the top-notch thots wasn't going, they told them that they had to make a run on the block and it was BD territory. So, if anybody started shooting Chi-Raq fashion no questions, then they didn't need no girls getting popped or snitching all up in their bizz. Tasha and Tina couldn't care less about all that street inner-city beef. If they dropped them off, it saved on their Uber cost.

Tina's Dad was an O.G. He went to a south side H.S. with her Italian Mama. They met sophomore year. He did time in Joliet back in the '90s for shooting somebody over a dice game, which led to the end of her parents' relationship. Plus, her Mama's Italian side of the family wasn't really feeling that interracial dating back then.

Tina's Pops opened the door and saw his daughter's bloody nose and ripped-off shirt and immediately knew she was out there fighting all over the city. She was such a tomboy he didn't even have to jump and go get his gun.

He called Tasha "Miss Trouble Girl" and told them to come in. His wife was cooking fish and spaghetti, his favorite. It was some straight hood shit, but Tina and Tasha's high asses ate it with a whole bunch of Red Devil Hot Sauce along with her Pops.

Tina had a room in her Pop's two-story house since she was a little girl, so she had ample apparel there. After summertime fights and block parties, she would go straight to her Pop's house with Tasha. Pops knew his half-breed daughter was a hot thot and mess all over social media and the city. He learned to live with it long as no man put his hands on his only baby girl.

Tina called her boy toy Keith, a.k.a. K-Smooth, for a ride. Everybody around the Go knew K-Smooth. He was a pretty-boy fly player. He was 6 ft. with deep Caesar waves. He was known on the southwest side of the city for flipping cars, CDs, air fresheners, and scented incense. Plus, he was a thug-rat, what they called a thug nowadays in the Midwest.

She had him drop them off back at their cribs. They dropped Tasha off first. She knew KSmooth had a thing for Tasha and that he wasn't shit because every time they would go to the Evergreen Plaza Shop Center, he would be blatantly eyeballing Teasing Tasha. And Tina was already envious of Tasha and wouldn't trust or bring certain dudes around her or to her house. It was some typical jealous hot thot shit.

K-Smooth took Tina back to his spot on 95th where he was trappin' out of, to bend her freaky ass over and sip on some apple Cîroc to trick her out of her panties once again.

That night Tasha saw she had a DM back from Denver JD's Daddy. He was JD Sr. and he told her, "Sorry, young lady. I'm married, but thanks anyway, and my son has plenty of woman problems already. Have a beautiful night, gorgeous." Teasing Tasha exhaled and rolled her eyes. She logged straight off her Instagram account that was back up and running, despite the haters putting her in the penalty phase.

The next day Tina kept hitting her BFF up at 4 p.m. Nothing! She knew and hated when Tasha would put her phone in airplane mode from snoozing all day like a nocturnal fruit bat. So around 6-ish Tina caught an Uber cab over there. She beat on the apartment door for damn near 10 whole minutes, trying to get her BFF up.

She started yelling, "Bitch, get ya trifling ass up! You sleeping all in the evening like ya a prego thot! C'mon now, Tasha, you know it's freezing out here, Jo!"

Suddenly, the door opened slowly. It sounded like she was struggling to unlock the locks, slow playing. She saw Tasha looking high A.F.! Her eyes were bloodshot red slits.

"WTF, bitch. Why you just standing in the door half-naked with a wife-beater on? Are you gonna let me in, Jo, or what? Dang, what you on? And I smell all that skunky kush—move, bitch, and let me in," Tina said, annoyed as Tasha stood holding the door like she was blocking a million-dollar safe. And she had a dreamy look on her face like, Oh well!

Tina blew past her BFF and saw K-Smooth ass with his shirt off and retro J's number 10's in his hand.

"Ahh, hell nawh—nope! Bitch, that's how you

getting down now? Really, Tasha? And you, Mr. Dirty Dick, you been liking my girl Tasha, too. I shouldn't have never let you drop her off, period. I knew better. Ugh!" Tina said in shock with her eyes wide and jaw jacked wide open, too.

"Man, Charlie, you know what it is…we just smokin' and chillin'. She was giving me a back massage straight up so I smoked her out. Plus, you ain't my bitch, last I checked. We just smoke, get drunk and fuck," K-Smooth replied, high as a moose.

"Gurrl, you know we ain't fuck, he just ate my pussy all morning and this ass, too," Tasha intervened like it was just harmless fun.

Tina yelled, "You thot douchebag!" Then tried to rush her. Tasha stepped on the side of the couch and snatched her wooden handle ratchet and told her BFF she wasn't exempt either. Tina nodded her head in disbelief. Her BFF pulled out a blade on her as she back pedaled out the door, then ran downstairs.

Chapter 3
"Nasty Neesha"

Snapchat LA—All Day! —was the most poppin with no other city stoppin! Nasty Neesha was a Snapchat Hood Rat, too, but was the Backpages queen. She also was the queen at catfishing cats, especially while soliciting on the Backs. Nasty Neesha was a network-swindling hot thot!

Money made her cum. She was a pimp's worst nightmare. Nasty Neesha had the sweet science of renegade hookin' down. She owned it. She would tell niggas and other bitches that nobody fucked her without her getting paid. They had to pay to play. She was a throbbing thot because she thrived in selling more ass than an LA booty plastic surgeon.

Nasty Neesha was a black girl from East LA. She grew up out there around the Mexicans, especially during all their gang rival beef and black versus Mexican turf wars. She managed to make it out, but you could tell she was raised around some Chollas. She wore heavy make-up and painted her eyebrows on with a dark shaper pencil, but sworn her shit was on point and looked like her idol Beyoncé. It was so not hot, though.

She was a BBW—a Big Black Booger Wolf. Neesha was a plus-size thot. She was built like a warthog from *Lion King*, like an upside-down pineapple cake—funny built, and with the face of a gargoyle, a chiseled clay face. You couldn't even be mad or hate on Nasty Neesha, though. Just get it, girl.

She was keen and slick and would catfish ya ass quick! She just would post ads on Backpages and sit in a room next to the McDonald's down the street from LAX streaming live. Once dates arrived at her hotel room, they would see her and frown. She would tell them she knew she was a little round, but looked like Beyoncé laying down! A little round? Obtuse was more like it. Neesha had to be a cheesecake away from 230 lbs., obese, especially being 5′4.

She would tell them she could squirt and make her pussy muscles dab and twerk all on the "D" while offering them half-price off the listed $300 per hour. She also lied about her Kim K round booty, too. It was more like a hippopotamus ass—a straight buffalo booty. Talking about she on a dick diet? All straight dick and water. No food permitted, not even liquid soup.

The tricks usually traveled thru that LA heavy smog traffic for at least an hour trying to meet up with Nasty Neesha with a Photoshop triple filter profile ad pic, only to get catfished and tricked. Just about all of them would see her and about-face with a heel-spin turn military-style. She had almost a 99.99 percent straight turnaround rate. She would entice them with a sweet Beyoncé put-on voice she had down pat as another impressive vic trick to pitch herself, and then sprayed herself down with Beyoncé perfume.

Pimps say you could put a wig on a pig! But a Scottsdale plastic surgeon begged to differ. He thought, *What the hell?* Neesha looked like a pig with a freakin' wig on with make-up on, painted terrible like a clown. He had an hour-and-a-half delay at LAX before his scheduled flight to Arizona. He told Neesha that he was terribly sorry and he had gone to the wrong room and he was looking for his wife.

"I'm not your wife, but I can be other than your wife—for the next hour at a discounted rate of one-fifty? I promise it will be worth ya while and I'll make you cum and smile…" Nasty Neesha pitched, sank, and hooked with her sexy Beyoncé voice.

"Look, I'm sorry, you basically misled me and you put on your ad that you had a real Kim K booty? An authentic ass that wiggles and jiggles. I figured I could get some twerk dancing in and some doggy-style off the bed action before I charter my plane at LAX?" the Scottsdale plastic surgeon replied in disbelief, disappointed for her lewd actions. He wished he could have reported and banned her from Backpages right there on the spot.

"I could twerk! I'm just a lil overweight—it's called baby weight. But I guarantee I can twerk better than Amber Rose and get you off right after, else your money you'll get back. C'mon in, give a plus-size girl one solid chance to please you. Don't judge this thick ol' book by the cover. Let me welcome you to LA the real way?" Nasty Neesha said seductively as she ran game and seduced him into the hotel room with a challenging charm as she held the door open, inviting him in. All that could be heard was the hotel door shut, lock, and Beyoncé's "Drunk in Love" playing throughout the room. Nasty Neesha was once again successful at her craft and spinning webs, catching and luring tricks into the room. Once she solicited them online, getting them to stay and play was easy. She had that East LA game. She sold more ass than a skinny bitch and than a white girl! She had the perfect vic trick and pitch.

It read: *Before you leave LA, come play. I'm right by LAX and promise I'm LA's best. My review rate says it all. If I'm your fantasy type, call 310-760-4860. Avail. 24/7. Best Netflix in-house dates.*

Nasty Neesha was a beast and Backpages queen. Every now and then she would run into pimps online posing as tricks to catch a bitch out of bounds. She was good at distinguishing them. Sometimes it would even be pimps calling from prison that had cell phone access trying to knock a bitch, too. She seen it all. Half the time a lot of cats wanted to talk, play, and bullshit. She didn't even have time for all that shit, though. So, she switched up from posting her free ads to paying for her listed ad. This also would put her classified ahead of the rest of the thots on the Backs. She even saw some of her homies she went to school with, actual Moms on the Backs soliciting dates, too, in their late 30's and mid-40's. She never snitched or put their bizz out in the streets because she knew how it was. Most of the scheduled appointments, the dates didn't show. That's how she knew they wasn't vice squad or the police because they would never come to you. Police always made you come to their rigged-up surveillance grounds.

Neesha had several thot sisters, too. None of them were as smart or bold like Neesha to sell ass and put out an ad. They were the type you could throw a quick dollar at and flash some cash and just have weed and liquor. They would go that easy. Neesha couldn't stand how good they all looked and body was all blessed intact, not fat like her. They all had four-plus kids with four different baby daddies from all over LA—Pasadena, San Bernardino, Compton, Santa Monica, Wilmington, etc.

Neesha could name at least 10 cities and subdivisions in LA and O.C., too, where all her sisters had dudes and baby daddies with a million headaches and heartbreaks but no paydays. She just believed her sisters were damned simple-minded and played themselves short.

When things would be very slow in LA online, she called them her slow time and usually had some of her sisters come chill, smoke, and drink with her. Neesha truly was the black sheep of the family, the ugly outcast. She felt she had to charge the entire world for everything, basically because she was fat, ugly, and broke. She had a fairytale dream wedding and her prototype of her Prince Charming, too. She knew it would be a plus-size white wedding dress but she could pull it off, though. Everyone else could kiss her ass, especially her hating-ass sisters. When they got drunk, they'd talk all slick and usually Neesha would kick them out her room, crying.

They'd call her all types of nasty thots who will fuck and suck for a buck and bird crumbs all over the worldwide web, letting the entire world know, putting themselves on blast with no shame in their game. Her sisters called her trifling.

And the nasty part was from when men asked if she a BBW that BB? She would say yes and would do it if the cash was right. She was playing a deadly game of Russian roulette with her life, throwing her life and health right on the gambling table. BB stood for bareback, meaning raw, no rubbers. Somehow it was sick to say, but most of the creeps online wanted to BB and going in deep with no hands or hats.

Nasty Neesha would let everyone know she only been hoeing for five months when she had been selling ass online and streetwalking at the end of Sunset Blvd. for over five years now. She had what they called snap-back! And it wasn't from her being fat! Her pussy would always snap back tight right into shape, no matter how many dates she'd catch and turn. Then she knew all types of tricks to make her clients cum fast and hard. But making her pussy dab, then squirt was her secret weapon and it always did a number on her dates. She was the fat girl who really would rock your world, but you didn't want to be seen or caught dead with your dick in her, period. It would sure end relationships and lead to quick divorces.

Nasty Neesha had low self-esteem but she stayed representing the Beyoncé team. She was obsessed and even drew the Beyoncé Monroe mole on her, too. She was

Beyoncé's number 1 fan, like Eminem and Stan.

She would get all types of likes on Instagram and people following her on Snapchat. She would really wake up in the hotel and Snapchat every little thing like she was a celebrity. To her, Snapchat was her version of her own reality show. She didn't get a lot of hate like the top-notch bad bitches would. Her followers were more real and loved to see a healthy sister win and get theirs. So, she had an ardent fan base, the BBW Club, with a blonde Beyoncé wig on. She was famous for her Snapchat videos because she would go in live and own it. Very bold, loud and proud with good captions and emojis and lots of views.

Today her sister, Sugar Baby, was coming to kick it with her at the room. Sugar Baby was light-skinned and skinny with 3 little boys, all back-to-back, ages 6-5-4. She didn't really have too much free time to get out and away from her boys to cool out and smoke. Nasty Neesha was paying for Sugar Baby's Uber from Huntington Beach, as always. Her sister brought the alcohol.

Sugar Baby was a single mama of 3. Her first baby daddy was her heart and first love. He got struck out in the penal system back in the days from Cali 3-strikes laws. She married him in LA County Jail and she got pregnant with little Darius at the prison during a conjugal visit.

Her second baby daddy got killed by some rival gang members in Watts. And her third baby daddy was a straight smoked-out bum! Just a sorry excuse for a Dad. He didn't care about his son, just his next weed sack or where the kush was at. Last she'd heard, he was smoking crystal glass meth out of a pipe. She didn't care, he didn't call anyway. She would run into him at different spots and a few times on the Shaw trying to get at other bitches to impregnate them, too. He was a sorry-ass M-thot.

"Heyyy—Sis! What's gud, girl! I see ya Cali Swagg…

with ya skinny ass. You need a meal tho, Sis! Ha-Ha-Ha...
Let's trade some weight? You can have some of these pounds.
Oowee...I like ya shoes and ya weave, girl—oh shit, own it
with ya ashes ankles and elbows! Come on in, let's chop it up
and catch up!" Nasty Neesha said, excited to see her favorite
sis and having company besides her special house guest.

"Aye-aye, lil sis. I luv and miss your crazy thot ass,
too. Neesha, ya nasty ass get hot thot of the year for 3 years
in a row. How hot you bust it open! I love ya, tho! And we
'bout to kick it, girl. My girlfriend watching the boys. You
know all them still bad and just all copy and follow each
other. Ya know them. But c'mon, let's get it cracking, sis!"
Sugar Baby replied, eager to lean back and get faded with no
worries about her babies.

They started smoking and drinking, turning up early
broad daylight. Neesha heard her song come on she had
streaming thru her phone from Google Play Store. It was
that latest Mystikal / Trinidad James song, "She Ain't Fat,
Bro! She Just a Lil Thick!" Then she started rolling her neck,
popping her gum, fixing her blonde wig till her favorite part
came along on Mystikal's verse.

*"She just a lil round—but she looks just like Beyoncé
laying down!"*

"Hey, Sis, this my shit—and that's my favorite part.
That's what I be telling these tricks I catfish," Neesha said,
all with her head swollen from her own wicked excitement.

She was interrupted by a knock at the door. She
jumped and stopped mid-sentence. She ran to the peephole
with her wig in her hand. Her heart fluttered with nervous
nerves. This was the first time she had company and company.
How embarrassing. How would she do this? Tell her sister to
go wait outside or hide? Maybe send her to the McDonald's
next door?

She quickly told her sis the news and gave her the

rundown so she could be up on game. Then they quickly scrambled like New York City pigeons, putting the drink and stuff up while fixing themselves. Nasty Neesha kept yelling out, "Hold on—hold on!" Neesha patted down on her wig, adjusted her titties, and cracked open the hotel door.

Sometimes Neesha would schedule tricks to come within the same hour timeframe because not all of them showed up. Sometimes she would have scheduling time conflicts, but none of them bumped heads at the same damn time. She didn't think this guy was serious because he didn't seem interested.

"Oh hey—how you doing today? I actually didn't think you were coming today. Aren't you about to miss your flight to Florida? You know LAX. You have to be there an hour and a half early to check in and board your ticket. I fly out to D.C. every month. I got an arrangement worked out back there. He pays for my flight and hotel accommodations. So, sup? What are you trying to get ya self into right now? I could make my sis bounce!" Neesha said, out of breath from dancing prior and scrambling to put herself together while packing a pound of make-up.

"Umm...ummh...Damn—you put on ya posted ad petite? Girl, you all big like Mo'nique! Then you got a pound of make-up on, looking like the bride of Chuckie and shit! I'm good. I ain't paying for your time. How ya sister look? Is she hookin', too?" the Sarasota, Florida man said, dismissing Nasty Neesha for acting like she was a bad hooker on demand. He could hear that Mystikal and Trinidad James song playing in the background. He was disgusted. Fat girls repulsed him.

"Girl, he didn't just call me Mo'nique? Check this out. I'm a lil fluffy thick. These is what you call curves, FYI! And Yasss! I do really look like Beyoncé laying down!"

"Pspph...Please, you don't look like no damn Beyoncé laying down, standing up, or sitting ya big ass down! You doing what's called catfishing cats. I'd rather go spin or donate my money to McDonald's than on you!" he said, cutting Nasty Neesha off, not believing how she was disrespecting Beyoncé as a woman, not an artist.

"Hold up, Blood! You not going to be disrespecting my lil sista and shit. You mess around and don't make ya flight, homeboy! Nigga, you in Cali—LA! All I got to do is make a call and they will beat you to the stairs!" Sugar Baby snapped as she intervened, opening the room door wide.

He told her to calm down and no need for all that and calling all South Central! Then he peeled his pockets back and tipped Neesha a hundred-dollar bill for her troubles, basically for a pass. Then he powerwalked to the elevators, pressing the buttons in a frenzy.

Neesha shut the door and laughed as she gave her sister the hundred. Sugar Baby skinny couldn't fight no damn man, but she surely talked a lot of hardcore gangsta shit she had picked up from her different baby daddies. All her sisters were hot thots and they knew it, too. They finished drinking the Hennessy and fired up some I.E. Kush.

Suddenly Nasty Neesha got another knock-knock at the door. It startled them paranoid, especially since they just punked a trick out of his money. They thought he could have snitched and called the police. Or just sitting like some pond ducks in a hotel suite, soliciting clients is still hot and illegal. And the door can get kicked in any second, which was why Neesha switched up rooms every weekend. She'd get the rooms hot like a trap spot. One time she solicited a retired Lt. from the Cleveland PD. He wasn't snitching, just tricking and tipping. He told her don't mind his status, he loved to pay for it and to getting what he wanted. Plus, he had a mistress from Toledo, Ohio, he would bring out to LA to play.

The knocks at the door increased with some harder impact behind them. Neesha took a deep breath, fixed her blonde Beyoncé wig and went to answer the door as her sister Sugar Baby ran to hide. This time they had paused the music.

She opened the door to a corky white middle-aged man with a bald spot eagle's nest on top of his head with red-frame glasses…

"Heyyy, my lil Beyoncé! Are you open? Or is it bad timing? I could swing back around if you have company right now?" the old man stated sharply.

"Hey, my honey dip! Old Man Jimmy, how did you find me? You know I switch rooms every Friday! And how did you get here from West Covina? Did your wife drop you off again, huh? Come on in, Old Man Jimmy, before your wife kills you and catches you with this fine black diva, honey," Nasty Neesha replied in her Beyoncé voice, using her charm as she batted her fake eyelash long curly extensions.

"Oh—yes, yes I found you, my love. All I did is smell you. I smelled your sweet Beyoncé fragrance. My wife could die all I care—marriage is just a financial statement. But shall we…" Old Man Jimmy said as he extended his hand out for Neesha's, then tucked it into his arm like they were walking down the altar as they walked thru the room door together.

Sugar Baby came out of the tall hotel curtains, nervous and still paranoid from her little stunt she pulled earlier with that scare tactic. She saw the little shriveled-up old white man and laughed. She thought to herself Neesha big ass would kill that poor skinny senior citizen. He'd have a straight heart attack! Not from the pussy, but from her big sister squishing his old ass. Ugh, Neesha was such a hot thot!

"Oh, excuse me, sis. This is my Old Man Jimmy. He is a regular and this won't take long. He spends the rest of his time playing cards and listening to music with me. And Jimmy, this is my thot trot sista, Sugar Baby," Neesha introduced them. Sugar Baby greeted him with a Hi, then she excused herself to the bathroom. She was about to leave because her sister had her fucked up if she really thought that she was going to sit there while Neesha turned a trick, especially fucking that hairy old man—ugh!

"Hold up, sis, let me grab that shower curtain first out there, real quick. I'll be done by the time you get done." Neesha jumped up from the bed.

"Hey-hey. Wait. Excuse me—Umh, sister! Can I call you Solange, Beyoncé's little sister? Well, I'll pay you double for your services, too! Right, B—tell your sister it's cool. I don't do no touching and pay on the spot!" the old man said as he stripped off his clothes.

"WTF! Oh, hell no—This Solange ain't fo sale, old man. Please...you couldn't pay me like that or a nuff! OMG, would you please put ya clothes back on until I leave? You're sitting in the chair in your church socks! Matter of fact, Neesha, deuces, sis! I'm out of this bitch, blood! I'll use the bathroom at McD's next door!" Sugar Baby turned her nose up in disgust as she grabbed her shit to split. The old man's saggy pirate chest and curly gray body hairs had blown her high.

Nasty Neesha called to her, "Wait up, sis! Old Man Jimmy is a special. He wants special peculiar requests. All fetishes are double, period."

LA was home to all the 50 shades of gray fetishes. You would think it was creeps coming straight off Venice Beach to freak. Some people would want to get tied up and beat like a bitch, spanked, and spit on. Some would have whips and paddles. Others wanted to be walked on with high heels poking their flesh. Some men got off to the weirdest shit. Corky—raunchy.

"Old Man Jimmy's fetish is to get pissed on, Girl, he loves it and pays me a lot to pee on him. He just offered you 300 cash to pee on him, too. The only catch you have to be butt-naked, too, so he can see you peeing on him."

"Ugh-ugghh…Damn, bitch. That's some nasty ass shit! That's not thotery, that's straight raunchy and heinous, bitch! —But shit, for 300 cash I'll piss all over his old ass, on Piru! But this don't leave the room, Neesha, else—owwee, I'ma kill you, sis…But you go first, tho!" Sugar Baby said, nervous and ashamed of her doings.

Sure enough Nasty Neesha unsnapped the shower hooks and snatched the blue curtain and placed it on the floor by the vanity mirror and sink. Old Man Jimmy laid down.

Her big ass squatted like a bullfrog and released a fast, drunken jet stream. It was more like a flow. Sugar Baby closed her eyes and turned her head as she frowned. Ewwe… she thought to herself and she couldn't believe how Neesha nasty ass was pissing all over this old-ass veteran like she was a man. She never seen or heard a female pissing like a man, as her sister was doing. Neesha had to be pushing super hard! She always knew her sister could squirt and make her pussy do the dab, but damnit!

She turned her head back around and took notes as she watched Nasty Neesha hobble trot up and down Old Man Jimmy like an escalator as his arms fidgeted and body went into a frenzy like a tranny at the Gay Pride Parade!

"Damn, Neesh—That long ass Austin Powers piss! You nasty as fuck! Ugh…Well, let me go to the bathroom and get ready real quick. So, hold on, Old Man Jimmy, while I pump myself up. And I need a drink, too! Now all of a sudden, I don't got to pee. Girl, this shit is ludicrous! And look at Old Man Jimmy. He like that shit for real, huh? He over there gloating all in piss, ugh…" Sugar Baby said in shock as she shook her head and hit the Yac 3x. She took another deep breath and went into the bathroom and shut the door.

It took her a whole 2 minutes before she came out. Neesha lit up a Newport and Old Man Jimmy was still wallowing in Neesha's excrements.

Old Man Jimmy looked up to see a beautiful young flower. She couldn't have been no more than 24 years of age. He was at least 3x her age. She walked up and stood right over him. He could tell this was her first time and she was a virgin to peeing on people because she was standing there stuck without a single drizzling drop of urine. She was very skinny and petite but she had a pretty phat pussy. She had a sweet plump Georgia peach. It stood out like a mound and her sexy little gap she had in between her legs complemented her clean-shaved pussy. It gave it a nice V shape and made it pop out and being the center of attention. She'd do excellent and see all dollar signs at a fully nude strip club in LA.

Then he saw her cover her whole face as she hid with her 2 hands. He got super excited because he knew the golden shower was about to begin! She screamed like OMG! as she twinkled like a toddler.

Sugar Baby pushed with all she could down her bladder and her little short stream stopped. "Fuck!" she cursed out loud as she tried to coax her nerves.

"Bitch, you better do the finger in ya ass trick!" Neesha said quickly after seeing her sister freezing up, making a rookie mistake.

"Unt-unnh...Hell nawh, Sis. You know I got these damn nails on!" Sugar Baby replied, still standing midway over the old man.

"I'll help you out, Solange!" the Old Man Jimmy blurted out as he grabbed both Sugar Baby's ankles.

"Oh-owwee-ahhh...shit!" Sugar Baby screamed as she immediately started peeing from his cold-ass hands shocking her nervous ass. She really was scared and peed from his touching grip. He let her go and kept telling her go higher—higher!

Sugar Baby was Gucci now, so she slowed her flow

down and decided she might as well be a thot for a hot second, too, and have fun while getting paid for it. So, she went up and down like a roller coaster to the Tupac beat she had playing in her head. He was loving every minute of it. She decided, fuck it, and to pee all over his face, mouth, and hair, too, with his nasty old ass. She would give him a golden shower he'd remember in his casket.

Nasty Neesha called her sister a natural as she watched her doing her thing, shaking her head. And Old Man Jimmy quivering in excitement, growing a boner.

"Damn it, Jimmy. That old thing ain't never got up with me peeing on you! My sista arouse you that much, you old farting billy goat! Fuck!" Nasty Neesha yelled out, envious.

"Oh-oh. I'm sorry, Honeybun…I still love my sweet Beyoncé…I'll be back on your slow Sundays, B, I promise. You know I can't get enough of your strong showers, my love," Jimmy replied, feeling like a bachelor all over again as he acknowledged his erect half-staff penis. He hadn't seen it in over a decade straight and forgot he even had color in it. Sweet!

Sugar Baby was done! Her bladder was completely empty. She was ready to drink some more. Embarrassed after finishing, she ran back into the bathroom and slammed the door as she giggled. Getting dressed, all she could do was think about how easy that was and how none of her baby daddies never even gave her $300 before or after fucking, so her getting paid 300 just for peeing—damn! She would do an arrangement herself with Old Man Jimmy once every few weeks or post an ad, too.

Once Sugar Baby came out the bathroom fully dressed again, she saw Old Man Jimmy's half-stiff penis was now gone and soft as baby oatmeal. She sucked her teeth and shook her head, then told Jimmy to get his pissy ass up and give her money to her, then leave, because it was sister time and they were about to rejoice.

Nasty Neesha told Sugar Baby to shut up, bitch, and roll another blunt while she helped Old Man Jimmy up and get dressed, still drenched in his golden showers. He loved every single bit of it. Sometimes Neesha would call an Uber for him and pay for it on the house because Jimmy loved to catch the bus and his old wife would be worried sick about him. Plus, she treated all her clientele with kindness.

After Jimmy got on his feet and cashed them out, they cleaned up, smoked and drank. The room still smelt like pissy waste. Sugar Baby was complaining about having the serious munchies. Neesha explained to her sister she was serious about being on the D-Diet—strictly dick and water. No food! She claimed it was just water weight from too much water building up in her joints, then seeping into her fatty cells expanding her to the maximum, but Sugar Baby knew that was a bunch of the poop emojis!

Then after another 30 minutes, Nasty Neesha had another knock-knock at the door. This time Sugar Baby wasn't shocked nor startled. She just told Neesha, "Damn, for it to be a slow day, ya hot ass thot trap is jumping! Rolling-rolling-rolling…"

Neesha waved her off as she slowly checked the peephole to see an unfamiliar white man. She opened it up slowly. It was a trick from yesterday that was a no-call, no-show for the same 4 p.m. time slot. She asked what happened and to come in. He frowned and told her, "Hmh…wasn't what I expected." Then he saw her sister and got aroused because she looked more like the Backpages ad pic. And Neesha's measurements were off by far. He told them, "Geesh, it smell like pee in here!" They both giggled and blamed it on a stray cat they had brought into the room trying to rescue.

Neesha saw him looking over at her sister as she was

talking to him. He still couldn't take in getting catfished. He thought it was a prank and Sugar Baby had to be the one for sure on the Craigslist ad. Neesha didn't care if he was salty or more attractive to her sister. She didn't need a freaking glam squad. All she needed was her filters on Snapchat and her Galaxy phone. All her Snapchat pics were perfect fitting filters. She would screenshot other girls' selfies and trick their pics out! Even they wouldn't know it was them or their original selfie.

The trick immediately asked Sugar Baby her price, too. She snapped her neck and rolled her eyes as she sucked her teeth and told him, "Please, I ain't open for bizz…umh… talk to her. I'm just here visiting, not partying or playing! Besides, you couldn't afford this! I don't care if you came from Rancho Cucamonga in a Benz, you not getting none of this Blackberry juicy fruit, white boy!" Sugar stood up and got ratchet really quick.

"Well, actually, I am from Rancho Cucamonga, and that white 600 Benz outside the window is mine, too. So, money isn't a problem, but it's okay. I'll pay you to spectate. I've a special request anyways—isn't that right? She'll tell you…" the Rancho Cucamonga trick said nonchalantly.

"Oh shit…Yes, that is you! Damn, I almost forgot! You're the special from Rancho Cucamonga requesting onlookers, an audience. But most of all, my pimp! I told you I don't do no pimps! I'm strictly independent like Beyoncé. I'm self-driven and ran. Oh no, sweet. Sorry. That's one Neesh can't fill. Sorry! Now if you want to get laid, I'm cool with that long as I get paid my hourly wage!" Nasty Neesha stated, overwhelmed but not really trying to turn down money. It was already bad being on the D-Diet. She was missing meals.

"Oh…for Christ sakes, y'all have pimps…C'mon, all y'all always have a pimp! I know—know the routine and protocol! Silence and secrecy is mandatory. But hey, I'll pay for my special fetish! It's what gets me off—to mount you from the back in front of your pimp while looking him square in the eyes. I think pimps are all low-lifes that prey on vulnerable less fortunate women…C'mon, just call him. I'll pay double for y'all trouble and for his time, too," the trick replied desperately.

"Damn, what you, the fucking police? Vice or something? Why you coming off so strong requesting a pimp's presence? My sister would gladly watch and look at you, not me, for a hefty fee, shit!" Nasty Neesha snapped.

"Oh no! No! No! I'm not the freaking LAPD or not with any agencies! Here, pat me down, take my keys, check my Benz…I'm just a freakin' ortho doctor, for Christ sakes—C'mon now, give a white guy a break, OK?" he pleaded desperately again.

"Wait a minute. I'm lost—So he saying he wants you to call your pimp? And then pay double and all us for our time? Let's hear him out, Neesha girl…So how much is double and for our trouble?"

"500 right now, cash!" he shouted, cutting Sugar Baby straight off.

Neesha shook her head no! And then Sugar Baby said it was too low. So he offered them a stack! Neesha told him hold on while she talked to her sister while they both excused themselves and locked themselves into the bathroom, whispering in a low tone.

"Damn, bitch, what we gonna do now? Shit, that's a whole band, sis! Can you call anybody?" Neesha mumbled.

Sugar Baby shook her head no! She couldn't even think of a nigga in LA that was down with that type shit. Plus, she didn't want that thotery to be tied to her name all on the Gram and cats blasting her out there. Neesha, on the other hand, could care less about her name being out there because her reputation was already shot.

Then Neesha asked her about her dude—Ol' boy Trinidad?

"Who—Trinidad Slauson? Girl, he ain't none of my dude…I mean he help me with the boys and coming around, but that's it. And we may play around every so often? But that's it and you know I can't call him, sis. He ain't wit no ratchet shit! You know he selling all gold everything like Trinidad James right at the Slauson Swap Meet," Sugar Baby whispered shyly.

Neesha pumped her up to call him anyways, saying it was a whole stack up for grabs and Trinidad was their only chance. Then she told her how to game him up and if he still said no, offer him 500 and they will split the other 500. Sugar Baby said, fuck it, and warned Neesha she would put it all on her to Trinidad Slauson as she scrolled thru her phone to find his face and number stored.

Trinidad Slauson got his name from selling all gold at the Slauson Swap Meet. He had his own stand and would do cash for gold all wholesale and sell retail prices for whatever you had in your pockets. He even sold gold for EBT food stamps. They would follow him in the grocery store with his shopping cart. He had this place in Compton where the Koreans gave him half-off all chains. That's where he got his name and from being like Trinidad James' song, "All Gold Err Thang!"

"Dis Trinidad, Slauson Swap Meet where I'm posted at—Sup?" Trinidad Slauson answered with his catchy little jingle.

"Boy, you need to cut it—LOL, you know it's me and see my pic and number pop up, fool! Anyways, do you want to make a hundred dollars real quick? All it requires is your presence. And it involves my sister—You know, Neesha lil thot ass," Sugar Baby said in a sweet tone like she herself was hot and horny for him, that 'please don't tell me no' voice.

"Man, I ain't no hundred-dollar real-quick type nigga! It's slow but not that slow. And what I gotta do, dude? Nasty Neesha big ass always on sum straight ratchet shit! I would have helped any of your sisters, but her, baby—"

"I'll pay you 500 to watch her get turnt by this white pencil dick trick. We get 250 apiece! Ya know a bitch need that doe, nigga. So, sup, fuck with a bitch, blood? We by LAX, that hotel next door to the McDonald's. You know them cheap-ass weekly rooms. Sup, tho?" Sugar Baby said, turnt up as she cut him off, going hard.

"Hell, yeah—I got ya, baby…for 5-hundo I'll shut down shop and catch the bus!" Trinidad Slauson shouted thru the phone.

"Hello—Trinidad. Heyyy…How you doin', Big Bro? I hope you taking good care of my sis and being sweet to her. I hear you playing step-daddy and all that sprung ish, LOL…Ha-ha, she got you pussy-whipped, huh? That sweet good-good, huh. Heyyy, the power of the P! Now you see why I don't jus give away my pussy. I charge a fee! Anyways I appreciate you helping a big bitch like me out. I got cha and will slide you 500 dollars. He wants y'all to watch and for you to be my pimp. So, don't come down here all smiling and goofy, bro…Please pose as a pimp. Knowing you ain't got no damn pimp bones in ya body, saving all these damn hos, LOL…Hurry up, Big Bro, tho," Neesha snapped slick.

"Oh, say no more! You want pimp, I got cha. My daddy was a pimp or player. I don't know that sorry bastard wasn't there with his cheap suit and tie-wearing ass. I'm on my way, Neesh. Let me get dress and close up shop—BET!" Trinidad Slauson replied, pumped up and ready to pose as a pimp! He was overly excited. He went to pick out some pimp strings at the Slauson Swap Market. He was about to pick out

Compton's finest!

The girls left the bathroom and sat with the Rancho Cucamonga trick after delivering him the news with an ETA of about an hour. They smoked and drank some more. The trick was getting restless after a whole hour and a half went by. Neesha told him she would knock off $50.

A whole two hours later it was a light tap-tap at the door. Then Sugar Baby got a text from Trinidad. She texted him back the 100 emoji and the wink face.

The trick asked was that their pimp? And Neesha told him, yeah and shh…not to talk loud or piss him off no more and that he was lucky her pimp showed up for this bizarre act of yours. Then she opened the door slowly. OMG! WTF? she thought as her eyes dilated as she was shocked.

Hold up, wait a minute. Let me put some pimpin' in it! Oh, no he didn't! This fool Trinidad been watching too much Friday After Next. He looked like he bought his pimp clothes from Money Mike's Pimp and Hos Crenshaw store.

This fool showed up looking like Sugar Fly, a straight retro pimp with loud colors and shit. He stepped into the room with a fake limp and a cane with a small white feather brim. Neesha wanted to snatch that damn cane from him and turn him right back around and kick him square in his ass as she kicked him out of her room. And she could have sworn that was one of them Slauson cane/swords with the silver duck engraved handle. She shook her head.

Sugar Baby tried to keep from laughing, too. She knew this nigga picked out everything from the Slauson Swap Meet he could find under $5.

"Sorry I'm late. You know this Los Angeles traffic…" Trinidad Slauson said with a put-on high-pitch pimp tone all proper with his loud cross-colors.

Neesha's blood boiled like a volcano! What pimp ever apologizes and said sorry or talked proper, saying Los

Angeles than just LA? She couldn't take no more of Trinidad play pimpin' stunts, then asked everyone were they ready to get the show on the road? Then told sis and Trinidad Slauson to take a seat in the chair facing the bed and asked the Rancho Cucamonga trick did he have condoms? Like it really mattered to her. It was just company around and an audience sitting and watching. He told her yes, he had some XL Magnums. Neesha didn't believe his pencil dick ass, but saw the gold condom wrap.

However, once Neesha big ass got naked and bent over on all fours on the bed, the trick had a trick of his own. He pulled the 12-inch rubber dildo he had tucked between his legs and spread some lube all over the top of it. He had on a strap-on piece with the rubber dildo attached. He was about to have some fun and give Neesha a run for his money while taking out all his self-hatred for a pimp in front of a pimp.

He got started and went slowly. Neesha noticed his slinky dick was cold but huge. She didn't mind because she knew most tricks didn't last longer than 15 minutes. Then his pace picked up as he went deeper and harder. Neesha's moans began to turn into screams.

Her sister at first thought Neesha was putting on to make the trick cum quick because she doubted he was working with a monster like that, or his stroke was that Trump tight, till she really saw Neesha's wide-eyed face of terror. She was making the harshest ugliest faces ever! As if he was sticking a whole plunger up her ass. Especially when she noticed Neesha sweating like crazy all over the place and the Rancho Cucamonga trick's menacing face.

Trinidad even noticed this hostility and the odd tension in the room. You could just feel it in the air. The trick started to talk slick and saying little remarks while looking Trinidad Slauson dead in his eyes. At first Trinidad didn't catch on to who he was talking to or referring to. He looked around side-to-side and just figured he was venting his daily problems and had issues.

But when he started talking all that slick bashing a pimp shit? Trinidad knew he wasn't no damn pimp—however, he knew it was disrespecting a pimp. That white man better respect his play pimpin'. Even though he was truly posing as a damn pimp, the trick still was going to respect his temp pimpin'.

The trick started getting more vulgar and obnoxious while looking directly at Trinidad with a screw face. Trinidad saw him turning up and talking slick all indirectly but still felt him shouting directly at him. So, Trinidad Slauson started fixing his posture, sitting up straight. He wasn't leaning back like a Mac no more. He started adjusting his pants and fixing his shirt as he slightly cracked his knuckles. He even fixed his shoes and sighed out harshly.

"Take—Take it, you filthy whore…Yes—take it loud and proud, huh? You hear her? Squeal like a bloody pig. Yes! C'mon, you're not done yet…You can take some more of this vaginal beating—I'm going to stretch you for the limit today and get my freakin' money's worth! We just getting started. Hey, you—Hey, you low-life pimp. You see your filthy dirty fat whore squealing? You can't save her. She's all mine for the next hour, damn it! I pay the cost to be the real boss around here! Right, pimp? Money moves you all? All you scummy pimps preying on vulnerable young women, huh? Yesss! Shut up and take your punishment, you felt whore! I'ma screw you till you cry and dry—Sweet!" the Rancho Cucamonga trick said in a devious trance with a treacherous racy plot. Even Sugar Baby wanted to check him and stop the session. She saw her sister's eyes rolling backwards like his "D" was ripping thru her cervices and into her stomach awfully. But Neesha didn't say nothing and Sugar Baby figured she'd have a safe word? If not, just simply say stop or help? Neesha's screams got louder like she really was drying out in excruciating pain. Her pussy kept farting like a flapping flat tire, embarrassing. Maybe from all Neesha's heaping and hollering, it triggered something in the trick's mental as he started to tense up and reach a climax without any real penetration. It was just from his psyche so aroused to a cumming peak that it manifested into a stimulating exploding climax!

"Oh-oh sweet hell yesss! Oh-yes! You filthy whore— you fucking low-life pimp! You fucking N—" The trick came all over Neesha's fat inner thighs as he slipped up and said the N-word! The music stopped and the CD sounded like it skipped. Trinidad was the first one to take off! He flew across the bed and over Neesha's sweaty ass and cold-cocked him dead on his chin, folding him. He'd been wanting to check the trick's temperature. Sugar Baby was right behind him. She had picked up his cane and started cracking the trick upside the head, knocking him unconscious as Trinidad A-Town stomped on him. They were fucking him up and kicked him to sleep, then ran into his pockets. They peeled him back for five stacks! Neesha turned around, pulled herself together as she wiped her eyes dry. She saw the strap-on 12-inch dildo and went berserk. She got down and ground and pounded him with her fist. They had to pull her off him and ditch the hotel room ASAP!

Chapter 4
"Notorious NaeNae"

Welcome to Hotlanta, GA…Home of the sweet Georgia peaches. In Atlanta, they take sex serious like a death. The Freaknic days were long gone and over. Nowadays it was the ass-eating generation. They were all Freaknic-conceived babies from the '90s anyways.

S.W.A.T., Notorious NaeNae was waiting to pick up her sister from work at the WalMart where all the thots shop. She sat in her pussy-pink Chevy two-door box on 22-inch choppers. She was playing with her iPhone and click-clacking her tongue rings like a freak. Them perk 30's had her wet and horny like a bitch dog in heat. Ughhh…she hated when her dude played these little stop, drop, and gos. Drop her off some pills to get her to stay still, then get right back into heavy traffic like he was cross-country trapping. She knew he was just riding around the A, chasing hot thots, but she could be slick and a hot little thot, too. She was texting and messaging cats trying to play house that was DTF and roughhouse.

Just as her sister came into the Chevy and slammed NaeNae's heavy-ass door, they went berserk as they heard their song playing on V-103 FM station.

"He gotta eat my booty like groceries—He gotta eat my panties…Oowww, if he wants me to expose the Freak—He gotta eat my booty like groceries," NaeNae and her white sister sang in harmony Janae Aiko's part of her featured song with Omarion and Chris Breezy. Janae Aiko had the whole South turned up and out. Now everyone could eat an ass out. It was trendy and the new norm. You could toss a bitch salad and not get clowned. However, it wasn't just guys eating ass inside out. Nope! It was females now tasting ass, too.

And that's exactly how Notorious NaeNae felt, like every bitch had to eat her ass like groceries and taste that swirling tongue all over her booty. NaeNae was into girls, too. She loved to lick and bump pussy, too. That sweet soft peach taste and shape drove her into perpetual ecstasy. She been liking girls since she was 12, but she was infatuated with the "D," too. She couldn't get enough of it, and it drove her crazy when she indulged the best of both worlds. She had to have her cake and eat it all, too. So, of course, she was down with a female companion to guest star in her bedroom with her dude. She believed regular sex head up with a guy had to be spectacular or else it was too bland. The girl added the spicy flavor to the relationship. She didn't have no problem letting her family or anybody else know she was bisexual and into bitches, too. She thought all women were hot and sexy as hell. She even had her upper earlobe and bottom lip pierced like a lesbian. They all had hidden meanings and green lights in their underground lesbo world.

Notorious NaeNae was a redbone with a banana-yellow sexy complexion. She was a half-breed, too. Her Mama was white. She had a white sister and another half-breed sister, too. NaeNae had red dyed hair. She was one of those thots that kept red hair no matter what she had on. She didn't care if her outfit didn't match her hair color. That shit was red-hot and fly and you couldn't tell her nothing. Guys and girls loved it. It attracted more fly-bys than shit. Some cats even would call her Banana Red like the MD 20/20 fruit drink.

NaeNae was so notorious they named a dance after her and had the whole ATL and world doing the NaeNae like—Heyyy! Aye-Ayye!

She was notorious for being a few different things including a set-up artist, too. She would set you up to get liq'd quick. She'd send some Decatur where they jacked greater—jack boys right to your spot to hit your stash and safe, ASAP-fast. She was the type of thot you had to take to the telly, not the crib or to Mama's.

That's how she got her condo on the South Side of ATL. Last season when the Warriors came to Atlanta to play the Hawks, she clipped one of the starters in the lineup at the hotel downtown for a chunky link and 2k earrings. She got cashed out by one of the ballers in the city that was a trap-a-holic superstar in West Atlanta. The other ice she gave to her dude.

Notorious NaeNae was most notorious for thotery, being a bona fide thot. She was the P in promiscuous. She fucked all the major ballers in the A and a few celebrities and cats in the music industry, including R&B singers. Her pussy wasn't a honey pot, it was a hot melting pot. They were running thru that thot ho like Pepto Bismol. Everybody didn't wait their turn—they had their fair turns. It was a huge difference. Sometimes her pussy would be so hot and super soaked that she couldn't even shut or cross her legs. She felt it pulsing and jumping with throbs of sexual anticipation. Her mouth even would get watery and super slobbery to where she would click-clack her tongue ring back and forth across her bottom and top teeth seductively. She knew and admitted she was a straight nympho and had to have sex every single day. She claimed she suffered from nymphomania. The popping pills, smoking, and drinking just intensified and increased her sex into freaky double overtime. Her pussy had long frequent flyer mileage.

NaeNae looked at herself as an Atlanta porn star. She was camera-ready and wasn't scared to get down on film. It was her showing out and off her skills. She felt like Nicki—the best—and loved to perform her magic tricks that she knew the next bitch was too proud or ashamed to perform. Not NaeNae, though. She would get down for her Thot Queen of ATL crown. There was no damn shade or shame in her game.

NaeNae was from South Side Riverdale, where they gave 'em hell! She was on her way to East Atlanta to drop off her sister that she called da white girl. Her sister could dance for a snow bunny. She would get ratchet and thot-pop and twerk like a sister straight out the projects, but looked more like Miley.

East ATL was home of da thots, not da Braves. It was the land of the NaeNaes, KayKays, LayLays, ShayShays, TaeTaes, and all the baebaes!

NaeNae was proud to be a thot and knew it. She owned it and was really the queen thot. She was versatile with girls and guys. She was what the Bible called a harlot, a bona fide harlot. It was speculation that was where the word 'ho' came from harlot; it means the same thing anyways. And thot came from ho. All words had similar letters in them.

"Nae, you see dat? There goes your hubby being slick over there in the McDonald's. Dat niggah ain't shit, SMH!" NaeNae's sister pointed high as hell as she passed the blunt back to her.

"Oh, hell nawh, ughh…I thought this fool was suppose to be out in Bankhead, not the East Side. I'm 'bout to text him and pull right up on his bumper, watch! And he better be ova here selling pills only, shawty!" NaeNae said as she sat up, breaking her neck over at the Southeast McDonald's, staring at Sirachi's Hawks dunk, popping her gum ratchet. Then she texted him and she pulled off and flipped a bitch, wildly cutting off oncoming traffic. She was fabulous at texting while driving.

Sirachi looked at his Galaxy S7 messages from his main thang; he ignored her ass. NaeNae didn't want shit! She was probably trying to creep with another nigga or bitch. He knew she was treacherous and would get down scandalous and shit, but steady pointing fingers at him and shit. He had to watch NaeNae because she was deadly from both ways.

NaeNae texted him again, asking why he was ignoring her when she could see him and was directly right behind him with all type of set-tripping emojis. As she was looking up into his Hawks dunk, she could see his snapback cocked hard like T.I. She knew he was more than likely waiting on a little East ATL hot ratchety thot.

Sirachi had a pineapple haze Cutlass with a red Atlanta Hawks emblem on both doors and a 21 Hawks jersey for Dominique Wilkins on the hood and trunk. It had six 12-inch Audiobahn subs slumpin' like six dead men and a Gorilla six-inch lift kit with the wheel wells cut dumb to drop some all gold 26's to the rubber on some 50 series tires. This was his second pair of 6's. NaeNae slashed and tore his first 26x10 pair up when she was drunk on that bullshit. His goldish tint matched his mustard Hawks yellowish-colored dunk with that pineapple wet glossy dripping haze.

NaeNae saw a bitch's head pop-up and went nuts. She jumped straight up, turnt up! She pulled her wavy silky hair back into a tight ponytail and wrapped it up as she held the scrunchy band in her mouth. It was going down.

Sirachi pushed the little hot thot bopping deep on him viciously like she was for apples with no hands or coming up for air. He felt her tonsils and epiglottis, that flap of cartilage that opens and closes on the windpipe during swallowing every time when she engulfed his "D," making it disappear. NaeNae couldn't swallow so deep; she would gag and her eyes would water like she was about to throw up all over the

"D." It took her a half a minute to calm her nerves, relax and reset to finish the job.

"Yeah, you busted, niggah! Sup, bitch. Get ya funky ass out of my dude's whip now or come catch dis fade, lil hot thot! Sirachi, tell her, niggah, what it is? Tell her bye. Gohead...Bye, hot thot! Oowee, this niggah got me so fucked up fa-real," NaeNae said at Sirachi's door ready to fight.

Sirachi knew this East Atlanta thot would get him into trouble one day, but fuck it, she was worth it because she had thot top out this world. Super head couldn't write enough or have shit on this local East ATL thot. He couldn't get enough and never needed or wanted to fuck her chocolate big booty ass. Besides, she had 3 kids anyways.

"Man, NaeNae, stop trippin, lil mah...I-I-I was just selling her some perks, dats it. Shawty ain't on nothing. Plus, she married, duh. Stop trying to start all these thot fights. Err body don't want me in ATL, NaeNae!" Sirachi checked her .

"Please, OMG, Sirachi the M-thot king himself! What thot hasn't had my dude in ATL, huh? Niggah, you the thot king. Please...miss me. Anyways, come on, bitch, fa-real, shawty, get up out my dude's whip else I'ma pull ya ugly duckling ass out of the whip myself—"

"Oh, hell nawh, you the thot, Miss Nae fucking Nae, OK? The whole world know ya da real bona fide hot thot! And FYI, I been sucking Sirachi's dick for 3 months now and just got thru before you rudely interrupted us! He drives all the way to the East for this long deep-throat beast! Now, if you bitch be gone—and move right along. Right, Sirachi?" the thot yelled back, cutting NaeNae off.

"Oh...OK, bitch, let's get it. Come on, I need that. Bring yo ass—bring dat ass! Come here, bitch!" NaeNae said, turnt up, thot clapping and snapping, trying to infuriate her threatening opponent. Sirachi knew NaeNae was just talking big hog shit and wasn't really going to bust a grape, just only intimidate. She was too cute to fight like a blue pit bull. He didn't know if she could really fight, but she could talk big shit though and scare a ho up off her.

"Look, I'm sorry, you gotta go! Bye, bitch! Get out my shit," Sirachi said viciously with no regard smashing hard, dissing her with sweet pre-cum still in her mouth.

"Oh word—like dat, Sirachi, huh? OK, bet dat up! And you know what, fuck you, too—and ya lil hot thot bitch, too! I wish she would run up…I'll knock that light-skinned and her half-white sister both out," the thot said as she slid down out of his dunk, hot as venereal piss she got dismissed.

"Yeah, LMAO! Bye, bitch. Walk you lil thot giving up head in the McDonald's parking lot. He so rude, huh? Couldn't even take a bitch thru the drive-thru and get you or all them damn kids some food! Bum broke bitch, sucking dick on the strength, giving thot top—Bye, bitch. Walk! — And you, Sirachi, you on probation. Fuck dat IPS, niggah! And you dumb cheating on me when we can fuck thots together! You better follow right directly behind me to drop my sister off and straight home! I'm serious, don't even try to be funny or stunt playing with me, Sirachi. No yellow lights or stopping for lights trying to turn off. You better run all stop signs, too, and keep up with me. And don't send me none of them sorry texts and emojis, Mr. Sirachi. We got bizz at the crib. So, come on, Boo-Boo," NaeNae said, trying to hide her happy feelings.

As Sirachi pulled out the McDonald's lot, pushing behind NaeNae, he burnt rubber on 6's showing off his turbo twin cam 350 rocket getting sideways. Then he heard his car get hit with some of them little McDonald's rocks. He hit the brakes to see that thot run into the McDonald's to get close to call the law for help. NaeNae stopped, too, and texted him—WTF? C'mon! You better not stop and turn around for that thot!

He tailed her to her sister's house. After they dropped her off, NaeNae jumped south on the 285. Sirachi and NaeNae were smoking and pushing their classics in and out of traffic like they were playing freeze tag dangerously. NaeNae drove like a nigga from the hood, all gas. Sirachi kept texting her the heart and winking emoji, then saying sorry over Snapchat while hitting the blunt and blowing the smoke out of his nose like a Chicago Bull.

NaeNae kept replying IPS probation, BAE. SMH! And the I Love You, Too emojis. She would only let him go anal on her despite how horny in heat she was because she knew Sirachi was her heart. And every baller in ATL knew Sirachi was her hubby because she had his name tatted in fancy script on her chest like a real hood bitch. They had a hood love story and they were the perfect thot couple that couldn't remain faithful in any significant way. They had an abnormal love affair. They were each other's only, as long as they were around each other. It was too funny because they felt like each other's favorites.

Sirachi felt that no matter how much his wifey was out there or roamed, she would always come home and break him off or bond him out of Dekalb County Jail. Every liq or come-up she always tore him off. She was his stylist, too, and would stay buying and draping him in the best from Lennox and the Underground Mall. Plus, the condo in Riverdale on Woodlake Drive was in his Auntie's name. NaeNae would pay most of the rent, but some months Sirachi would put up, too. He didn't mind and figured it was the best investment.

Sirachi was from West ATL—Bankhead. He was one of them light-skinned red Atlantans. Him and NaeNae were both light-skinned with her banana high yellow ass, too. Usually you didn't see two bright-skinned couples in da South together.

Sirachi and NaeNae had met at the Velvet Room back

in the days. He told her when they first met, "I bet cha gonna luv me," as he pictured the lustful ways he would bend and twist her.

She told him, "And, niggah, I bet cha gonna luv me," like she'd throw it right back on his ass, too. The rest was history. Their horny, kinky, and freaky chemistry met its match. The queen thot and M-thot king Sirachi himself were too much for Atlanta and that spoke volumes. NaeNae's freaky ass had a sex swing in her master bedroom that Sirachi and she practiced on other people behind each other's backs. Sometimes they'd have threesomes incorporating the swing. She also had a boudoir spraying toilet installed in her master bathroom that she even got Sirachi into using, thinking he was a thot pimp.

They had an open hood relationship. They named him Sirachi, like the hot Chinese sauce with the rooster on it and green top, because he was a hot M-thot. Sirachi was hot in the ass and knew it, but steady blamed it on his crazy ass Cuban BM. She was from Jacksonville, FL. He had a little boy by her. He also blamed her for him not having any more kids, too, after his little incident.

One New Year's in 2015 he went super hard with NaeNae and his Cuban BM caught them in her bed. Her crazy ass went to her Papa's tool belt and got an actual carpenter's long 4-inch nail and snatched his dick while he was snoring and drove the nail repeatedly down his pee hole as she jigged it around like she was stabbing him while cursing in Spanish. NaeNae was knocked out.

Sirachi felt a stinging hot burning sensation, but whole body felt paralyzed like it took every ounce of energy away. He woke up as his heart jumped and passed right back out from shock! NaeNae woke up and saw his crazy BM run out the room and Sirachi's eyes rolling in the back of his head while his joint was hemorrhaging dark blood like crazy.

She threw straight up and rushed him to Southwest Baptist Hospital. NaeNae couldn't stand his Cuban BM and blamed her for them not having any babies. She wanted a baby boy. She already had a baby girl out in Buckhead at her Mama's house.

After this incident, Sirachi didn't piss or nut the same. He pissed like a lion of the Kalahari Desert and when he busted a nut, he skeeted out both ways at a sideway angle that NaeNae loved because that warm gooey protein would go all over the place, her hair, face, and ear. All the thots loved it, too. But this was why he went hard in the paint. It was like chasing a first high, he couldn't get that same feeling back after he climaxed. His BM tainted him for life.

He also been shot by his high school sweetheart right in his ass with a .32 pistol. NaeNae shot at him twice before with a .380 handgun, too. Sirachi was known for his bad karma and ratchet dog ways with the raunchy ladies.

Sirachi had a face tatt on his cheek bone of an all-red ATL Hawks emblem. NaeNae would clown him every time she got mad at him, saying that was for a chicken hawk, chasing all them chickens and hawking them, too. She'd call his dunk the chicken coop. Sirachi loved thots just like ratchet T.V. superior and loving ratchetness. He didn't care if they were thots or ratchet. They were all still freaks. Nor did he mind being a thot king or M-thot himself. He wore his crown because it was fit for a king.

NaeNae popped another perk 30 and dry swallowed it with her saliva from her watery mouth. She decided to call her hubby Sirachi and tell him she forgave him, but he was on punishment and grounded to the Woodlake Drive condo. He had to park the chicken coop for a whole week, too.

"Aye…Hello. Sup, my luv? Damn, I can't lie. I miss you, Nae," Sirachi answered.

"Awhhh…How sweet! Bae, I love when you tell this

redbone something sweet. I hope you know you grounded, niggah, and gotta park that chicken coop in the garage, too! You sleepin' on the couch, too. You're not 'bout to be slick creeping in the bed late night—Oh hell nawh, Sirachi! I know you ain't. WTF! You thot texting on me. I hear you texting on ya other phone listening to Kevin Gates like I can't hear that! And I was just about to forgive you, too. Ughh—You ain't shit and so disrespectful! Bye, Sirachi." *Click.*

NaeNae sucked her teeth, swiped her call off to the right and tossed her phone on the passenger seat after putting it on airplane mode. Sirachi was blowing her up. He flashed his high beams on her twice. She tapped on her brakes to scare him and get him up off her bumper, then she sped up doing 20 over the legal limit, trying to shake him as she zipped and weaved down the 285. Everyone was watching them drive erratically thru 285 traffic.

NaeNae got off her exit and she was flying thru Riverdale running stop signs with Sirachi running them, too, right behind her. It was all part of their little games and sick relationship.

She pulled up on Woodlake Drive and quickly hit her garage door opener. She jumped out with her compact Glock 17 and pointed it up at Sirachi's dunk. He hit the brakes and flinched because she was known to bust that thing. Her country wild ass popped her gun at him before so he couldn't take her bluff nor call it. But he did love it how hard she went over him. He loved any attention regardless of whether it was negative or ratchet attention. When she didn't shoot and he saw her hesitate, he jumped out, too, and snatched the Glock from her as they wrestled over it.

"Watch out, dude—Fa real, shawty, move—Sirachi, OK. Give me my gun back fa real, niggah—Move. Get off me. You know what? Don't you even come upstairs tonight, else I'ma shoot you dead this time! Ughh...I can't stand ya dog ass. Bye—Good night, Mr. Cheat on his wife err night," NaeNae said as they tussled.

"Shut up and stop frontin'. I'll sleep on da couch, shawty, but you ain't 'bout to keep pointing guns at people, and don't use it with ya cray-cray ass! You need help, bitch! And them perks just got you all turnt up horny and hot. You need sum sausage, dats all!" *Smack!* Sirachi said as he bear-hugged her, squeezing her extra hard, then smacked her on her booty with intense sexuality.

"Niggah, don't be smacking my ass like that, either. Cuz you not getting no cut-up! Matter of fact, you not 'bout to cut shit up for a long time, so betta call one of ya thot tops," NaeNae said as she punched him hard in his chest, causing him to lose his breath. Then she switched her ass into the house. He followed behind like a puppy dog.

NaeNae took off her heels and cut the air up, then ran up the stairs and slammed her room door. Sirachi went to the refrigerator, grabbed the Kool-Aid pitcher, drank out of it, put it back and grabbed NaeNae's grapes. He sat on the couch and went thru his phone and streamed Gucci Mane's late single "1st Day Out the Feds" from SoundCloud.

"I had a dream three killas came in my cell to get me, and if I don't feed my wolves they would turn against me."

NaeNae stripped down and peeled off her sticky cherry thong. She sighed out, cut on her flatscreen, and sparked her blunt roach up. Then she went thru her phone to activate her playlist thru her wall-sized flat screen. The first song that played was the thot anthem of the summer, that Chris Breezy "Put You Back to Sleep" song. NaeNae rolled her neck to the beat and sang along as the kush blew her mind. She was bored and antsy.

Next the Weeknd song played, which was another anthem that had the thots going cray-cray.

"I got you touching on your body, I'm touching

on your body—to say we in love is dangerous...I got you touching on your body," The Weeknd sang in a high pitch that sent a cold chill thru NaeNae's body. She felt her clit swell and tingle. Then she shook her head and grabbed her box of toys under the bed. She hated how she couldn't listen to that Weeknd song without wanting to touch on her body.

She jumped under her satin sheets and rubbed it around and around her clit, then in and out her hole as it vibrated the studded beads inside her.

Not even a whole two minutes later Sirachi came busting in the door while she was on Fantasy Island moaning to a cumming climax.

"Boy unt-unh...Nope. Bye, Sirachi! You slick and I know you must have smelt all this wet-wet bomb ass pussy all the way downstairs wit cha cock hound nose, ugh... Bye!" NaeNae said, frustrated from Sirachi killing her vibe, bugging her.

"Please, love, I jus came to give you ya gun back and to apologize for hurting ya feelings...at the end of the day you who I come home to and vice versa. And FYI, I'ma red nose, not no damn cock hound. I see you with dat between ya legs. You sure you don't need help lu—"

"Nope. I'm one-hunnit niggah! I told you dat no pussy for you tonight. You grounded IPS. You gotta do community service work if you want to taste and smell this pussy anytime this week. Now, bye, Daddy. Shut my door, please..." NaeNae said as she cut a pleading Sirachi off. She couldn't give in like many times before. She had to show Sirachi she was serious and had control. She finished five minutes later but her climax was just that, a simple climax. All it did was relax her whole body for a few minutes, then that feeling went straight away. She watched her show on Netflix, then jumped in the shower to end her night. She had to work early the next morning anyway. She had her pink scrunchy scrub with Chanel bodywash. All of a sudden, the bathroom door opened and she flinched, startled. It was Sirachi. She sucked her teeth hard and stared at him even harder.

Sirachi came in, sliding on his bloody knees. He was trying to pull a stunt to win NaeNae over. That couch wasn't so comfortable after all. He told NaeNae to just hear him out for a second. She said OK, if he got off his knees first unless he had a ring in his back pocket. Sirachi jumped up quick after that statement nervously.

NaeNae shook her head. Sirachi was from West ATL Bankhead. She looked at him for the first time today. He was a sexy daddy. You could tell he was a Bankhead nigga from how he was dressed. He had an all-gold grill with chocolate diamonds in his mouth. He had retro chocolate Jordans matching his chocolate diamonds in his teeth with a gold-stitched Jumpman hat complementing his all-gold teeth. He had a black pair of pants on with chocolate stitching and a shirt with gold and chocolate on it, too. NaeNae's nipples got hard like raisins.

"Bae, I'm sorry. I jus wanna make it up to you and for you to cum on my tongue tonight. Can I put you to bed and make you oversleep for work tomorrow, huh, love? You know you my fav—who Daddy's favorite bitch?"

"I am! I better be…Now Sirachi, you could come to bed, I guess, but Daddy, no touching, either. You know my gun still loaded, too? Now bye—go to bed and let me finish washing up. I'm too tired for this ish, Daddy. Please," NaeNae said as she had a change of heart from Sirachi's charm.

Sirachi dropped back down to his knees and army-shuffled on them to NaeNae in the shower. He kept reaching out for NaeNae's legs and rubbing her thighs as she swatted his hands telling him to move and watch out, resisting temptation.

Sirachi straddled the tub for a brief second, then crossed all the way over still on his knees. He started kissing on her thighs and nibbling on her ass cheeks. She loved when he bit her on the booty because it was pleasure and pain.

Then he put his head dead in her ass, stuffing his face like a turkey. NaeNae told him to stop. He is getting his outfit wet and messing up his new fit, and she would be the one taking it to the cleaners as she moaned.

Sirachi started to eat her ass out viciously as she went ham. He'd swirl his tongue clockwise around her bootyhole with hard thrust of the tongue, then reversed it counter-clockwise with light presses of the tongue softly, then he would suck on her bootyhole until it retracted from slipping from his pussy-eating lips. Then he'd pull suck on it again. And he'd be extra nasty and jam his long tongue into her ass after working his thumb while sucking on her pussy, too.

NaeNae was facing the shower head and wall as Sirachi ate her ass out and rubbing on her clit with them light and hard fast presses, which drove her berserk into a gushing orgasm as Sirachi made her squirt all over herself fast and hard.

Then Sirachi spun her around still on his knees facing him. NaeNae had a sexy ass tatt of a green leaf and a peach shape outline below her bikini line on her bottom v-shape of her pussy to make her pussy pop and look like an actual fruit. It was a pretty phat peach. She blew motherfuckas' minds. It looked like they were eating an actual GA sweet peach. Sirachi loved it sniffing them Mollies and would kiss all on it, going hard.

She moaned more and more, saying, "Oh…Yasss—Yasss!!" as Sirachi got down for his M-thot crown. Sirachi always said he had them pussy-eating lips and would suck on her luscious pussy lips with his juicy lips. She looked down at him with his eyes closed, sucking on her phat pussy as the shower water sprayed down all over his face. She didn't see how he could even breathe, but her boo was so talented and she'd kill a bitch over this head and how he made her nut! Straight-up!

Sirachi knew how to eat her pussy and mastered eating it better than a bitch. He knew how to put his face in it, not just lick and flick on the clit. He had this way of licking on her pee hole that tingled and drove her bananas from the sensation that made her toes curly and thighs tremble from pure ecstasy, talking about knees weak.

She loved when Sirachi put them chocolate diamonds and gold grill all over her phat wet pulsing pussy. Super nasty and kinky is how he does it, smacking pussy.

Then Sirachi started putting his fingers in, working both holes viciously, freaking NaeNae like crazy. He was fast rubbing on her clit and massaging warming her asshole up. NaeNae's ass got wet just like the pussy and she'd cream every time from him eating her ass out with no clit stimulation. NaeNae had talent and tricks. She was in tune to her sexual side. Really, she was very familiar with her body and knew how to make herself cum and squirt at the drop of a dime.

"O-O-Oooo…Oh Daddy—Sirachi…Yasss. I love you…O-O-Oh…I swear I do. I'm 'bout to squirt. Hurry and put ya face in it, Daddy…Please. Oh, I can't hold it, Daddy— Oh, SIRACHI!" NaeNae said as she squirted in the heavy gushes all over his face and tongue. Sirachi had to catch her after that because her knees buckled. He knew NaeNae was out of gas, drained. He turned the shower nozzle off, then picked her up butt-naked with both of them dripping wet and carried her to their king-size bed. She was kissing all his neck and whispering she loved him. She'd almost lost her voice from her screaming orgasms.

The next morning the house phone was ringing off

the hook. She told Sirachi in a groggy voice to get the phone, but he was over there snoring heavy off them Zanny bars. She jumped up to find the black cordless under the bed...

"Hello!" NaeNae answered, annoyed.

"You have a Securus pre-paid call from 'CHOP-CHOP!' at the United States Penitentiary, Beaumont, Texas. To accept, press five now. To block all future calls, press nine now," the automated operator said.

"H-Hello, NaeNae. Sup, gurrl? Where dat nigga Sirachi lying ass at? Talkin' 'bout he blasted me three hundo," Chop-Chop answered, turnt up.

"Oh, hey, Big Cuzzo—Damn, it's early. That fool sleep and you know he tight wit his money with his cheap stingy ass. Oh—shit! I'm late for work. It's almost 10 o'clock. I was suppose to be at work at 9. I told Sirachi ass. And Sirachi, wake up, ya Big Cuzzo Chop-Chop on the phone, hurry! Sirachi! I gotta get dressed for work real quick and Sirachi snoring like a baby. You know the whole A not the same without you and Chi-Money. I heard he got caught up at Victoryville and they moved him to ADX Florence, Colorado? You know I keep bitches wit dat shit if you need sum. You got lil Mill and all his followers wit money signs and money bags all tatted on their face like you, too, talkin' 'bout money gang! Then it's a lot of O.T. niggas coming to the A getting' knocked off left and right. You know these jealous Atlanta niggahs be hating heavy still. How ya leg feeling? Dat shit was crazy. Ya ass lucky you didn't catch a body that night, too. Crazy ass shootout. Time flying, you almost out, Big Cuzzo. You still in FCI-Phoenix?" NaeNae ranted on like a female as she was shuffling to get dressed.

"My leg Gucci, jus a pimp wit a limp now. Hell yeah, send sum broads my way, but none of them ratchet thots you be wit. I been hearing 'bout cha lil ass, too. Nae—slow down! Sis—all these O.T. niggas that been to da A tell me they know you."

"Please…OMG, they wish they really knew the one and only Banana Red, aka NaeNae—Fuck! See, nope, I need to jump in the shower. My thong is soaked. I run thru them like pads, changing them two to three times a day. See, tell ya peanut head ass cuzzin 'bout this good-good he keep fuckin' up on, Chop! Matter of fact, SIRACHI! Get up and get the phone. Plus, you gotta take me to work, BOY! Ugh…" NaeNae said, cutting Chop-Chop off, then threw the phone on Sirachi's lap hard, hitting him dead in the nut sack. He jumped up, coughed and snatched the phone.

"Sup, Big Cuzzo?" Sirachi answered as he heard the automated voice saying good-bye. The call timeframe was over. Chop-Chop would call back another day, he was sure, and sparked a blunt as he watched a naked NaeNae taking a ho bath in the sink quickly.

When she got done she twerked her yellow ass soft and slowly for Sirachi watching, then smacked both of her own ass cheeks as she stuck out her gold tongue rings, teasing him.

"Janae Anne—if you don't stop playing I'ma punishing you and blow ya back out and get you fired! Fuck making you late. Besides, you better call Uber cuz I gotta go to the studio and lay these vocals down, get my Drake on."

"Boy, whatever…and you know you can't rap, Sirachi, please. Now, Daddy, take me to work. Please stop playing," NaeNae intervened with her seductive swaying hips and soft sweet voice.

"Nope!" Sirachi replied slick.

"I'll give you sloppy thot toppy all the way there. Bring the baby wipes and come on, Daddy…Oh yeah—I bet that made you move, huh, fool? Ugh, ya ass get on my nerves. Only reason I'm asking cuz I don't want them niggahs to steal my whip and wheels. You know a smoker will get a bitch in the A," NaeNae said as she slicked her hair back.

NaeNae worked for ATL Hot Wives Mimi. She had her own cleaning franchise service in ATL that all the thots worked for because they didn't do backgrounds and you didn't need a helluva résumé or credentials to clean. A lot of them been to the federal joints for trafficking. Some had charges for everything from boosting to prostitution and soliciting to bad checks. You name it. NaeNae would work to pay for the condo rent and her goodies and bills. She couldn't rely on the tricks and ballers or the sweet liqs that drop in her lap. She couldn't depend on Sirachi's stingy ass either.

She told a baller at Strokers after trynna pay for it, "Oh-no! Sweety, I don't sell pussy—No thotery here." But he could give her $1,500 to go on a dinner date and she may tip him for the night if he was lucky and his game was tight. Then told him matter of fact, 2 bands. He was a trap star and looked like he had ten bands racs-on-racs, on-racs.

NaeNae worked at CNN full-time cleaning and Phillips Arena part-time. She would be smoking weed half of her 9-to-5 shift and texting the other half. All them ATL thots were hip to the skip at work and had each other's back despite their social media beefs and brawls over the same trap stars and baby daddies.

"OK, Daddy—I love you, and please be here on time to pick me up at 5. And don't be bringing bitches in the condo or fucking thots in my bed, Sirachi! Fa real, dude, you play too much, shawty…I told you we can run thru these thots together, but you want to creep, be selfish, and cheat, dummy. Niggahs don't think, period! Bye, Daddy," NaeNae said as she jumped out his chicken coop, adjusting herself for work.

Sirachi leaned back, adjusted his fly and cut his Kevin Gates back up, beating around the city, checking his two phones. Kevin Gates was the M-thot's anthem over the summer.

Sirachi was flying down Martin Luther King and spotted a thot in heels with a mini-skirt on with a mean ho stroll like she was working. He bust a hot ass U-turn playing Yo Gotti-Law song. He rolled down his electric Cutlass windows.

"Say, shawty—Sup, lil Mama. Damn, Martin Luther King had a dream. You walking and working for the wrong team! Dis ain't Peachtree, gurrl," Sirachi was poppin' and choppin'.

"Please, ain't nobody working! My dude jus kicked me out so I'm on foot wit his sorry ass. But what's good? You gonna offer a bitch a ride to the West End or what?" the walking thot said rolling her neck with her hands on her hips.

"I mean, damn, shawty, rides in the A ain't free. You see ya dude gave you the boot, so U DTF and DTH [down-to-ho], too?" Sirachi said slick, trying to get lucky both ways. NaeNae told him stop asking thots if they were DTH and if they wanted to be a thot for a day or night. And pimpin' was by blood, not relation like Jay-Z said. She told him he was related to a pimp. Chop, his Big Cuzzo, was a pimp—not him. Then she would get on him, saying she never seen a pimp in shorts or swim. He couldn't swim. He would doggy paddle, but what pimp swims at public pools in the summer in Atlanta?

The thot shook her head and said, "Hell no! A double no!" Then she noticed his red Hawks emblem tatted on his face. "No, I'm Gucci. I know you NaeNae's dude."

She gave him the brick wall and kept walking with ho struts down Martin Luther King. Sirachi flipped her off with two middle fingers and peeled out, cranking up that Gotti so she could hear and feel him beating super hard. He popped two perks to start his sunny day in the A.

Five o'clock came quick and NaeNae been blowing

Sirachi phone up sick. He was somewhere fucking off. She was sure of it. Talking about he was with Big Tricky, another one of his M-thot boys. She couldn't stand Big Tricky black ass or his ratchet BM Rika from East Atlanta. Her phone only had one text from Sirachi all day, saying, BAE, I'm on my way. That was at 4 p.m., an hour and 15 minutes ago.

NaeNae wasn't trippin'. She had one of her fuck buddies named Cheesy pick her up in his 2015 black-on-black Camaro on stock rims. They called him Cheesy because he had some low dreamy sex eyes with a Kool-Aid smile always cheesing. She hated every time she encountered him how he always tried to fuck. She told him every time he couldn't smash and she would call him when Sirachi was gone away and she could play.

When Cheesy pulled up, NaeNae was pissed off with her arms crossed with a fuck-off nasty attitude. He knew she wasn't in the mood. He tried talking to her but she was mute, still frowning and texting a mile per minute. He handed her the green crack kush. He told Nae he had to stop to get diapers for his BM at the CVS. She sighed out, knowing Cheesy had 4 different BMs with 6 kids. He had them long pretty braids like he was cut with Indian and some good dick too, she'd always admit.

"Jus hurry, Cheesy, please. I'm all sweaty and trying to get home and relax and wash up. Uggh, I'ma kill Sirachi sorry ass. I know he out there laid up with a thot and not answering his phone, dogging his main thang, once again!" NaeNae spit with venom.

Cheesy said, "Is that right?" as he put the Camaro in park, then leaned in and kissed NaeNae all over her neck hitting her sweet spot. She brushed him off and punched him, but they both liked that roughhousing shit. After Nae kept telling him no, not now, she sweaty and he didn't want no sweaty work pussy because he knew her golden rule. He had to eat to beat that plump wet pussy up! He started fighting her over her pants, unbuckling and unzipping. She would fasten them back up until he got his finger on her clit, working it with slow massages till he felt it swell to a full inch, and her legs relaxed as they gaped open. He hurried up and snatched her pants down and bent her over the seat from the back. All he saw was yellow ass—no panties on and a fresh shaved pussy. Nae told him put a rubber on real quick. He ignored her, saying, Shhh…as he went into her warm wet sweaty crevices like a madman. No mercy! She kept telling him slow down. This pussy ain't going nowhere. She couldn't believe how he was going hard smashing. She couldn't even catch her breath. He was smacking her ass super hard and yanking the shit out of her half-breed hair by the roots as her head kept bouncing off the windshield. She was panting like a dog and ribbiting like a frog as she came back-to-back! She felt his dick pulsing and throbbing hard inside her as her pussy got super soaking wet and sticky. She was happy his wild ass was finally done, but mad he skeeted in her and not on her. She wasn't ready for all that hard fucking and he caught her off guard. She told him now for nutting in her to go inside to buy her that Plan B morning-after pill, too, as she attempted to catch her breath and saw Sirachi texted: WTF, where you at? I'm here! NaeNae giggled and texted him back with all emojis, the eye, heart, and winking face. She lit up Cheesy's blunt and fixed her hair in the rearview mirror, thinking what a bitch got to do nowadays in Atlanta for a ride to and from work? Head to work and ass from work after slaving at CNN all day. She was tired of niggas and was ready to go lay up and play with a bad bitch and flick her tongue ring on some pussy and ass to hear a bitch moan and scream. She loved it.

Sirachi knew NaeNae would call one of them niggas paying her bills to pick her up. He was at Strokers with his best partner Big Tricky, infamous Big Tricky from ATL.

The name speaks for itself. He was a big trick on thots. He was 6'4, 240, a big ol' teddy bear Hershey Black and always wore a red shirt. He wasn't no Blood, but always thought red brought out his purple-black color. He had a long fluffy beard like Rick Ross. After Sirachi's mama was caught by one of the homeboys from his hood in Bankhead on Craigslist selling pussy and the whole projects clowned him with a million and one Yo Mama jokes, he didn't want to be around crowds or niggas. But Big Tricky was his dude that never even commented on his mama's Backpages trife. Big Tricky had a 4-door box Chevy all flat black, an Atlanta Falcons dunk with the red, white and black Falcons on the sides. They called it Ashy black in ATL. Big Tricky had a table at Strokers tricking off all his trap money. He sold weed all the doe in Riverdale. All the strippers knew him personally. They pulled out back-to-back with some freaks to creep.

Chapter 5
"Slutty Shelly"

Sleepless in Seattle, WA...Slutty Shelly was a platinum blonde stripper with long sexy legs. She was 5'10 with bright sea-blue eyes. All her hair on her body was naturally blonde, eyebrows, lashes, and her pubic hair, too. She had double DDs naturally and a slender frame with pretty pink nipples, lips, and toes. Shelly was an all-time favorite; they loved it.

She was a 30-year-old stripper who looked no older than 21, barely legal with her baby face. Most clubs she worked at forgot all about her age, really, especially with her being their main cash cow. She would take home after the house, DJ, and bar close to two grand a night. She had all crowds tipping her heavy, making it rain with chances of them getting lucky to take her home or pay for some action.

Shelly was an alcoholic who loved to drink and get loose. She just loved to party and live on the edge. She knew she was hot, though, and men had her so spoiled even when she wasn't working the pole naked. They offered her rides, opened doors, and asked to take her out. She set the standards around Sea-Town on how and when she wanted to work. Or else she'd go to another place to dance and have her spoiled prissy ways.

Slutty Shelly could really twerk. Miley didn't have shit on her. She could make her ass clap and bounce and roll like the rest of them. She was Seattle's favorite snow bunny.

She loved bourbon and drinking whiskey. Even Jack Daniels and Coke wasn't too much for Shelly. It was hard for her to keep a boyfriend and be in a normal relationship because all of Seattle knew she was a slutty stripper. She did a porn tape black market for 10 grand and she believed that the shyster independent porn company marketed a million or grossed the high 6-figure margin. All it left her with was a bad reputation.

All her boyfriends and relationships wouldn't last longer than six to eight months due to her stripping and late-night lies, major jealousy, and some would even hit her or act emotional like a female and bash her car windows out or egg her car. That made Shelly say she was thru with younger guys and she started to mess with older guys. However, it was the same outcome, all short results. She started messing with black guys. They all fucked her and used her or tried to pimp her out. She wasn't with all that and just wanted to simply live life and party.

She was always DTF without reserve. She had a teardrop booty which gave baby phat on her bottom. The catch was she had a beefy twat. Shelly had them meat curtains that hung down droopy. It was far from a pretty pussy, but them extra-long lips made her pussy feel like it was sucking your dick, no lie!

She was what they called Becky with that good hair. She was the white girl where Plies got Becky from. He really meant Shelly and forgot her name because the head was so great and phenomenal. Shelly set the standard for thot top. She had the whole nation competing with her amazing head jobs. She didn't need no hands, but when she used two hands, God bless you. She made a married man want to leave his family and abandon his own flesh and blood. Her head game was that vicious, thot top the three S's: slurp, slobber, and swallow.

She was the myth that most of the sisters heard about how white girls gave head way better than a black girl. It was true if you knew Slutty Shelly with her vicious vacuum suckers and deep-throating non-gag reflex tricks. She worked wonders and did magic with your stick. Now you see it, now you don't. It would disappear while she was giving you direct eye contact. She was heating up Seattle like it was Phoenix. thot top, she owned it!

Seattle was number one for things to do and places to go, but also number one rate for suicide. It rained nine months out of the year, but a light drizzle most of the time so it stayed gloomy, which enhanced her drinking and slutty behaviors.

On this gloomy, rainy day, Shelly went to work feeling depressed and PMS moody. Her dad was in Edmond calling her all types of whores and sluts, arguing with her over the phone. He was an alcoholic, too, and most likely where Shelly inherited her nasty liquor habit,. She couldn't stand how her own father bashed her and put her down. She had a bad enough time with the assholes of men in-and-out of her life now, let alone her dad knowing she was the slut of Sea-Town. He wasn't the same after her porn tape. The whole family west of the Mississippi knew, including her grandparents in Idaho. Even her own mama wasn't on speaking terms with her. She was disappointed in Shelly's actions and ashamed of her daughter's lewd acts because Shelly had been raised Mormon. Her Mom was a push-over, though, with her Dad abusing her and the bottle. This all forced Shelly in isolation.

At work, she had an older bald-headed manager they called Steve because they said he looked like Steve from the *Jerry Springer Show*. He had been bitching at her for being at the bar too much and he had to call her to the stage three times for the past two turns for her stage routine. They exchanged some words, then she spit at him and told him to fuck off. She quit. And she stormed out one of downtown Seattle's elite strip joints that the Seahawks attended frequently.

She felt like she had the whole weight of the world on her shoulders. She took her heels off and ran to her Kia Sport bubbly as she stumbled thru the aisle in between the parked cars. She fumbled with her keys and dropped them twice in the heavy rain.

When she finally got into her car, she opened the glove box and swigged the bourbon hard with two deep guzzles and wiped her mouth as she tossed the bottle into the back seat.

She started the car, put it into reverse and slammed on the gas, backing up into the pole and fence. Then she placed it in drive, peeling off, sideswiping Steve's SUV, telling him… "Fuck off, Steve! You old dirty bastard!" in a drunken scream. She roared some more… "I hate my life!" as she thought about jumping on the Pacific Coast Highway and traveling straight to California. She was on her way to her house on the northeast side of Seattle when she was on Federal and got T-boned from her speeding mad and not paying attention. She was blessed to have her seatbelt on.

The car hit her on the passenger's side and smacked her into oncoming traffic from the impact and slick streets of rain. She slid right under an 18-wheeler. The semi slammed on his brakes hard and caused the truck to do a jackknife ugly. Shelly was wedged on its rear wheels with them crushing most of the KIA Sport like a monster truck grave digger.

Shelly was alive and in a coma for two weeks. She suffered from three fractured ribs, four broken discs in her back spine, and multiple lacerations. But the main thing wasn't the huge ugly scar on the side of her neck. Nope! She could live with that. However, the bombshell when she came thru was she lost her right leg from being impaled by the semi-truck so long they had to use the Jaws of Life. The Seattle firefighters saved her life. They gave her a prosthetic leg. She was 5'10 on one leg and 5'3 on the other leg, give or take. Shelly didn't even have a right knee anymore. It was just a stub where you could feel the hardy bone gristle. She was devastated and fell into a deep depression.

That was five years ago . Nowadays Shelly looks close to her actual age, like she's been living in the crackling desert for the past 20 years and it did a cold crackling demo on her face. It was the stress, alcohol, and depression that caused the change. It was hard for her to adjust. She just couldn't cope.

They gave her a help dog that aided her with her disability. The dog came highly trained. It was a Golden Retriever. She named him Jax. She used Jax for many useless things and would yell at him like he was human. She needed someone to take all her anger out on.

She was also pissed they revoked her license and charged her with a D.U.I., when she was the one that got T-boned. Whether she was speeding or not, the other driver still blew thru a yellow light. Yellow meant slow down and hit the brakes, not speed up.

Poor little Jax would get scared and hide every time she'd get drunk because she'd beat on him, punching him with her fist, kicking him, and smacking him in his nose with the newspaper. She was abusive and it was animal cruelty at its worst. She fell into the same abusive footsteps of her father.

She was collecting $600 a month on disability for the first three years, but since the changes in Obamacare and Trump got elected, it got cut to $320 a month. She was pissed when they said she could still work and had another leg along with her prosthetic one. People in the military did it and with fewer limbs. She couldn't believe the Social Security place. She was legally handicapped and even had a blue handicap parking sticker.

Nowadays Slutty Shelly made a living as a phone sex operator, and she would do live Kik videos streaming her playing with herself for credit card charges of $2.99 per minute. It would help with the bills when it wasn't slow. FuckBuddies.com would even have down time. She was catfishing guys, too, with her one leg. She'd have her legs spread wide out of camera shot. Then she would show off her one pretty, long leg, and most guys, being perverts, didn't catch on. She just played into their blonde fantasy. She still was sexy and hot just with an older thirties look to her.

And just like her stripping and not being able to keep a steady man, being a hopping woman on one leg made it that much harder. You'd be surprised how many guys knew she had a fake leg and still smashed but would hit and quit like they had that in their bucket list before death. Check!

She even placed a classified ad online for all the guys with peculiar fetish, especially with women that had one leg. And out of the whole Seattle metropolitan area she had a hit of 42 guys. Most of them were bullshit, and the other half were clowning, being very disrespectful. They weren't serious and she couldn't get anybody to take her seriously. She finally forgave her dad after he had a mild stroke but it paralyzed his right side, including half his tongue. He slobbered when he talked and would drool all day. Her mom kept him in a bib like a baby and became his caretaker. At least he had one. All she had was a dirty smelly dog. But she found it in her heart to let it go and matured after slowing down from her accident.

Her phone sex operator was her daily life. It got boring and annoying. She used to love talking dirty over the phone at first until she started making herself hot and horny. The phone sex game turned on her. It did a reverse from her being lonely and horny many sleepless nights in Seattle. Rain, rain and more rain poured down long and hard night after night. Since she was connected thru some private phone sex company they had a 1-900 number and people would be calling internationally from Japan, UK, Mexico. All businessmen cheating on their wives. Plus, she'd get calls from New York and all over the U.S. at all times, day hours, night hours, and wee hours.

She'd be in the kitchen working online and cooking/ eating like she was pleasuring herself but eating brownies, moaning from the good taste. Besides, she had the munchies. She picked up a weed habit and laid off the bottle as a lesson, especially since Seattle legalized marijuana. She had her medical card but didn't need it.

They even had her going to physical therapy and rehab, but she hated both. Her therapist was a pervert and would push her too hard. He knew even though she was 30 she still was an emotional wreck! And the accident and loss of her beautiful long leg was fresh. She needed time to adjust. And all he could do was feel her up and play it off, then force her to balance on one leg and shift her weight. All his pervert tricks of stretches and wannabe yoga exercises were plain out ridiculous. So, she started training herself. Now she wished he'd come by and fuck her consistently. She needed to get laid bad and was long overdue. And this is what sparked her slutty overdrive, especially to stoop so low and desperate, too.

One day she was doing her regular phone sex operator job in the kitchen, shuffling around baking and cleaning. And this couple called in and requested her to kiss on his girl's ass and cunt. Then other things led to other things. When she sparked the couple with that crazy fire they desired, they thought they hung up but didn't. She heard an intense sexual session that she ignited herself. She hurried up and put them on speaker thru her T.V. while eating Jiffy peanut butter with a spoon.

As the guy ate his girlfriend's ass out, she began to really get turned on and was sucking on the peanut butter spoon like it was a big cock, slobbering all over the silverware and glued peanut butter. She had her hand rubbing it fast on her enlarged clit but kept getting frustrated as she'd lose her grip and focus. This just wasn't cutting it.

"Ohh…Fuck! Damn it! OMG!" she yelled, frustrated, scaring Jax once again. She saw Jax dart into the backroom and that's when it clicked to her. She called Jax back in her sweet friendly voice when she needed something from him to go retrieve.

Jax inched closer slowly with his head down, wagging his tail, afraid. She encouraged him to come to Mommy, still with a pleasant voice.

Once Jax returned, she spread peanut butter all over her clit and vagina region, then told Jax to lick and eat the peanut butter as she patted on her pussy, welcoming him to an eating treat. She knew they said you couldn't teach an old dog new tricks, but she could retrain his ass to obey. She smeared his nose in it. Then he began to lick it a few times and backed up, looking up at her with his tail between his legs. She told him to go ahead, boy! After that she couldn't keep peanut butter on there fast enough until she came. He knocked her over, dry humping her good leg as his pink popped out…

"Jax—Heel…Heel, Jax—Heel, boy!" Shelly yelled, demanding he sit and knock it off as she sat upside down on her head from falling backyard off the La-Z-Boy. Jax was in a humping dog frenzy from her climax and pussy scent under his nose, super excited even though he was neutered. He licked the peanut butter all clean down there. She couldn't keep it on the spoon fast enough and started gobbling it down there as her toes curled and she could still hear the couple over the phone in the background still foreplaying.

She needed help up as she shoved Jax back and away. She felt very relaxed and whole body relieved of pressure and stress. The terrible thing about it was she didn't even feel guilty about it. She bit down on her lip and grinned, which turned into a devious giggle as she blew her hair up off her face in relief.

She knew that she just committed a bestiality act and didn't care nor mind. As a matter of fact, she would mostly like to do it again. She was already second-guessing herself being a little slut and nasty with an actual animal. If the State of Washington found out, they would take Jax and charge her to the max. Jax's tongue was warm and he licked with a long thrust. Each stride was a pleasurable tickle. It was better than all the men she encountered. Plus, all men were dogs anyways, so what was the difference? And Jax didn't talk back, give her flack, or steal her money. She would wake up and he wouldn't be gone or creep off like a thief in the night. Shelly wasn't thinking logically or sanely. She let her thotery get the best of her and used a dog as an excuse for a man's absence alibi. She had issues and was about to make doggy clit-peanut butter licking part of her routine at least once a week. Besides, nobody could see what she did or how she got down behind closed doors.

She needed to take a trip to California and catch her a young boyfriend that didn't mind her fake leg or damn near cougar age. It seemed like the older she got, the hornier and in heat she became. She wanted a black guy!

Chapter 6
"Pandora Da Explorer"

Teasing Tasha sat back playing in her DMs, checking them with a big head as usual. OMG—WTF, Jo! she thought as her mouth dropped. It was a DM from Denver JD's Daddy! Yasss!

He told her she was so beautiful and his PYT (Pretty Young Thing), his Chi-PYT, and he had 300 cash for her services and not to tell his wife or son. She was shocked, shaking her head. Normally, she wouldn't jump at a few funky hundred that she'd burn at the mini-plaza on knick-knacks. But this was more of a vengeance thingy. She would gladly oblige and replied to his DM and accepted his offer immediately. No counteroffers or special requests needed. This was personal. She felt insulted overall, though.

Tasha missed her BFF Tina. They were the bad bitch breed girls and where you saw one you'd see the other off tops. But since their fallout over a dude and Tasha crazy ass pulled out a ratchet knife on her, they began beefing tough like 50 and The Game were. She would see Tina on the Gram flexing and throwing super shade. She wouldn't forgive her for her loose lips and fronting. However, she did miss her girl and day one BFF. They were two bad bitches together, thot or not, even though Teasing Tasha was in denial on her thotery still and being an actual thot like her BFF Tina thot acts. Regardless, they were hot. Bad to the bone.

Then she put all her focus right back on Denver JD. She was happy to finally get some get-back on Snapchat after he called her a Snapchat hood rat and passed her video around on Snapchat and blasted her on IG, too. Vengeance was all hers and it wasn't no fun when the rabbit got the gun. And it wasn't nothing like a spiteful bitch gunning for you.

She gave his Pops her number and told him to call or text her. They set up for the weekend at the Marriott downtown. He would get a suite for them. He would text her thru the week with that old ass '80s corny game. But she would play along into his game to keep him on her hook till the weekend. Then she would block his old ass.

Once the weekend came she showed up at 7 p.m. sharp on the 3rd floor. He texted her and said excuse his tardy but he was in the lobby talking to his snooping wife on the phone. He had to play it off like he was still in Denver with little JD. She couldn't believe his old ass and would really make him pay for it. For sure!

He came up to the 3rd floor walking all slow with a played-out retro stroll. He smelled like a bunch of cheap stale cigars. Ugh, she wanted to pinch her nose in disgust. He grinned devilish at her as he opened the room door for her to enter first. She wasn't scared but hoped he didn't try to put his old-ass dick in her or want his nasty shriveled-up nuts licked either. Else he could keep his funky $300.

He ended up being cool and respectable. He did think he was slick, pouring her drink after drink. She kicked it off first because she needed to use the bathroom. She danced slowly and stripped butt-naked twerking slow, bouncing and clapping her voluptuous ass. Eye-filling his heart fluttered how sexy her curvaceous body was put together. And every time she would cat-crawl on her knees and slide in reverse on them, she would spread her pretty pussy open, exposing the pink tight walls to her love tunnel. His old ass would down a shot of liquor every time until she made his old-ass dick hard.

Once she saw it pop up like a toaster, she threw her thong on him and told him to sniff it and not to lose her bomb-ass pussy scent! Then to rub it all under his nose, too, while she continued to dance. She kicked her left leg over his shoulder and told him to taste her pussy. She unzipped his pants and freed his old "D." She spit and slobbered down on it as she gave him a rapid hand job, rough and no lotion. Tasha had soft suave hands and didn't need lotion anyways. She kept slobbering and yanking as it made a lot of swoosh noises.

She was already cumming on his tongue and held his face closer to her pussy on her clit even though he had his tongue everywhere. It's true what they say about dirty old men. They knew how to eat a bitch pussy out thoroughly from years of prior pussy-eating experience.

After she came out of wind, she quickly sat down on his lap and rubbed his "D" back and forth on her warm-wet twat, teasing him until she felt him about to cum. She stood up from her squatting position and yanked on his "D" hard like she was milking a farm cow. He busted a Grandpa big ol' nut! Ewwehh…she thought, letting go. She ran to the bathroom and threw him a hot towel and told him to clean up! She knew the show was just beginning. It was her turn next.

She came out the bathroom after rolling her some kush up and asked if she could spark it up? He said sure as he slid her the 3 hundred-dollar bills. She told him it wasn't over, to keep drinking, and she was about to make him feel super young again. She already saw he was fatigued after that first nut, but could tell from his pride he didn't want to be a poor sport. She wondered if she could get him hard again? But then again, she didn't need him to be.

They drank until the bottle was upside down in the trash can, Tasha being in control of her liquor limits. Denver JD Pops got the bottom worse half. He was already bubbly mumbling after an hour. She told him to shut up! And it's time to let the games begin. She pushed him back on the bed, took out her phone and recorded as she sat on his face and rode it the long way.

Soon as he was gaining control and getting into his rhythm from her smothering him with the P and her weight, she stopped…jumped up and yelled at him as she flipped him over and demanded he get on his fucking knees on the bed!

She bent over on all fours, still recording, looking back, telling him to eat her out from the back and taste her ass, too, until he was chin deep into her ass. All the phone showed was her ass with his Pop's eyes closed drunk going ham. Teasing Tasha's moans grew louder and rapid as she told him to stay on her booty and keep swirling his tongue just like that.

She flipped the phone to get a face shot of herself, then back around to see her throwing it back on his tongue. He had to grab her by the waist to hold on and keep up. She then twerked her ass cheeks slowly, getting loose, showing off for the camera and to make Denver JD shoot himself.

When she was cumming he spread her ass cheeks wide as fuck and purred like a cat in her ass. She felt the vibrations and squirted fast as she felt compelled. It was too late for compassion now, it was the final stages and for her grand finale.

He leaned back on his sweaty shirt and wiped his beady forehead, trying to catch his breath in his expanded chest. He felt like his old ass was about to have an asthma attack! His Chi-PYT was too much for one day. He would kick her out the room once she came back out of the bathroom. If he had a heart attack or needed any medical assistance, she was sure to run for it and save herself. Besides, he noticed how she frowned seeing his gray hairs down there.

Teasing Tasha came back out then, ready for the finale, to a snoring old man with his mouth open. Well hell, he made it that much easier.

See, Tasha's plans were premeditated. She didn't use the bathroom for 2 whole days to make sure she could perform at this moment. She pulled back out her phone and did a Snapchat video specific for Denver JD. Payback and get back was a bitch called karma!

"Hey JD! I love and miss you, baby. Guess what? Yup—I got ya Daddy, ya faggot messy-mouth nigga…and don't you ever fuck with a bitch from the Chi like dat! This a Mob City, fool—notorious mobsters. So, for you running ya shit box, I'ma shit in ya Daddy box for you to watch. I bet you won't share this Snapchat wit da world and put all on the Gram. So, check ya self and get silly if you want after this and I'll put this Snapchat of your Daddy and shittin' on him on blast! Believe dat, Jo!" Tasha said, slick and devious, then sent it to Denver JD.

She got on the bed and stood over his Daddy, knocked out. She squatted down naked and used her abdominal muscles to push her lower intestines to make a bowel movement. She did the unthinkable and shit all over his chest. Shit splattered and stunk from her holding it for 2 whole days and nights. Even Tasha had to admit and wanted to hold her breath. She paused, then backed up and scooted in the right angle for the camera and to shit in his mouth. She missed and it ran all down his face as she took a fat man hog shit. She wiped her ass all on his lips so shit could get into his mouth, too. She wanted Denver JD to taste her shit every time his Daddy kissed him. She was ill and vicious like that, both her Puerto Rican and Jamaican side were flaring at its best, nasty like two girls in one cup!

She sent Denver JD the nasty shitty Snapchat video immediately and went to the bathroom, cleaned up and took a long hot steaming shower while his Pops still snored in a drunken slumber. All he did was roll over on his side. The shit didn't seem to bother or wake him. And his mouth was shut full of fecal matter. She snatched her keys up and got on her phone as she exited the suite, sent the DMs screenshots to JD with poop emojis.

"Girl, you won't believe this shit. OMG! Shame the devil. He a lie! I swear SMH—I can't believe what I jus actually did fa-real. Some treachery. I'll tell you all about it…" Teasing Tasha said, talking on the phone to her cousin, waiting on the elevator, embarrassed to tell her shameless heinous acts.

* * *

Pandora wasn't a box. It was a thot rendezvous spot, AKA a thot den. The Bible says, "Don't go down into her chambers. You may not return." They would jump it off wherever cars, parks, motels, theaters, hallways, elevators, bandos, and wherever else was convenient to them and for you to have full access. Don't be the explorer to Pandora. It was raunchiness at its best. Anything goes when it comes to thot hos.

Back in Atlanta, GA, NaeNae was off work and finally caught up on much-needed rest from going too hard on work nights. Plus, yesterday after work, she went to the clinic to get her asshole bleached, which she did every six months like an HIV test. She told Sirachi she did it to have the prettiest ass and pussy in the A. It was just the same concept as having matching bra and panty sets.

She pulled out the garage and hit her opener back

shut. She was in her other Classic. She had two, not just the pussy-pink Chevy two-door box. She had a Georgia peach '79 Malibu with Prada pink bucket seats with a Georgia peach on the rear corner panels by the gas tank, looking oh so lovely. This Classic she had on some shiny chrome 24 inches. She had swag and ATL had its own culture within itself. You had to be there to grasp it. A redbone with her devil red hair. Even the rappers and ballplayers couldn't help but want to fuck with her. She was hood but had sex appeal and they knew she swung both ways, too. They were curious and wanted to explore her to see if all them rumors were true. Most of them were tired of the same ol' routine sex life with their wives. Nobody's wifey was down to share. Some celebs had hall passes, but never would the Misses join into the twisted ménage triangle.

She had to meet Sirachi at Pappadeaux and order while waiting on Big Tricky and his BM ratchet Rika, a.k.a. Paprika, which was her real name. NaeNae swore ATL was home of some of the most ratchet names. She was crazy but cool. Her gut stuck out more than her big butt. She was chocolate and country as hell from East Point with bad table manners. Well, really, she didn't have none, or home training. That's why NaeNae couldn't stand to be around her too long and hated every time Sirachi and Big Tricky's tired ass tried to go on couple missions. Rika would hashtag "Pop gums and flip weaves" typical thot sayings and hashtags around the A, thot pop gum so ratchet.

When NaeNae pulled up, Sirachi was already eating fried gator, his favorite. She ordered the shrimp, then checked him because he was too busy thot texting and didn't even notice her coming in. She looked too cute today and smelled like platinum Chanel. almost every female hated and felt jealous and insecure when a man was texting a thot while on the phone with his main thang. Besides it being rude, it was another bitch! She was used to it over the years and still wouldn't let Sirachi go. Shit, he was her main thang, too.

NaeNae was happy that Big Tricky and his BM ratchet Rika hadn't pulled up yet and she could eat in peace without Rika doing all that begging for this or that. And all those "Owww…gurrl, where did you get dis?" and "Damn, Nae, you look good! Who did your hair, bitch? I need mine done like that fly shit, too."

As NaeNae was fucking her fried shrimp up and admiring her man, horny shaking one of her legs, Sirachi glanced up and saw a rental car driving super slow, and then hit the brakes on his Hawks dunk, jacked up on them 6's. His antennas went up—Jack Boys!

"Nae—Fuck, I—Damn it, baby! You got ya gun on you, shawty?" Sirachi whispered.

"Yup—ya know it! Here, Daddy, dats dem Decatur niggahs, too," NaeNae replied as she slid him her Louis V bag under the table. Sirachi grabbed it and snatched the Glock 9 mm.

"I left Yappa in the car."

NaeNae leaned back and watched as Sirachi stood up like he was yawning. He acted like there wasn't about to be a problem, but his long stretch revealed the Glock in his waistline. He knew those cats were looking inside. He mean-mugged them like—You try—You die! They smirked and peeled out the parking lot burning rubber.

Just as Big Tricky was pulling into the lot, he got burnt tire smoke in his windshield. He was in his ashy-black Hawks dunk and hopped out with Ratchet Rika with her famous thot flops, the flip-flops with that black G-string plastic between her big toes with them flat dirty-ass bottoms. Sirachi always clowned Rika's thot flops so hard that NaeNae felt bad and had to get Sirachi up off that poor girl. She got on his pimp flops! Them same raggedy-ass New Balance beach sandals with that faded-ass N on the side of them looking ashy. So, he needed to shut up before he clowned her or throw them pimp flops. She called them pimp flops because he was always trying to pimp in them over the phone, asking thots if they were DTH.

NaeNae just took a sip of her sweet tea. She knew it was a wrap and officially lost her appetite. She told Sirachi slide her bag back so she could get her phone to ignore annoying Rika ass. It was too late. Rika ran up to NaeNae running her mouth, and hugged her hard. Sirachi and Big Tricky did their little Atlanta hood handshake and started chop-n-it-up, clowning and laughing.

Sirachi got straight on Rika raggedy-ass thin dreads. He told her, "Damn it, Rika. Give them poor lil things a drink! They look really thirsty—like they starving? Errbody eats B! I think u jus need to cut—cut ittt…Nae, tell ya gurl to cut it."

NaeNae busted out laughing. She tried to hold it in but Sirachi was acting up tough and wasn't lying. Her dreads were dying.

"Shut up, Sirachi. Forget you. That's why you ain't shit, Big Tricky either," Rika said. Big Tricky and she hadn't been together in years now. She'd had two more kids since then.

Then Sirachi busted out, "OK—Lazarus? C'mon now, Lazarus…Don't start dat, shawty, cuz. I'll shut cha down. Alright, Tricky, get her cuz, I'm telling you."

NaeNae intervened, "OK, let's go. C'mon now."

She knew all about them Lazarus jokes. Really it was an inside joke that most Atlanta knew about already. Rika contracted trichinosis after she stopped messing around with Big Tricky and they said her cat stunk like someone died and caught a body. It smelled like death, Lazarus that Jesus awoke from death, telling him to come forth. NaeNae shook her head and Rika sucked her teeth, knowing she had a funky trout smelly cat as she itched her thin hanging dreads. *Maybe she did need to cut them*, NaeNae thought. If you ever seen a chicken head with dreads, that was Rika, baldheaded with dreads. NaeNae figured it was from too many perms damaging her hair her whole life before trying to grow them little thin locks.

They all headed to the grocery store. This was the sole purpose of their meeting up, which they did once every month. Sirachi would purchase $200 in food stamps from Rika. Rika would pay with EBT, and NaeNae and he would fill up the shopping cart. NaeNae would buy all Whole Foods and steaks to cook with. Sirachi, on the other hand, would throw all the junk—Capri Suns, cereal, Hot Pockets, chips, and sweets.

In the car, Rika talked over NaeNae's music about both her ex's tatts she wanted to get covered up. She had one dude name on her thigh and the other on her back. NaeNae told her that's why she just didn't tatt any nigga impulsively after a few weeks. That was a thot move and she needed to slow down. She would never get Sirachi's name removed or covered up EVER! Rika showed NaeNae pictures in her phone of their daughter.

NaeNae couldn't see how Rika and Big Tricky's ugly ass had such a cute baby girl with dimples. Down South they say two ugly people make a cute baby, though.

In the store, Nae and Sirachi filled their cart with their favorites right behind Big Tricky and Ratchet Rika. Rika would buy Tricky groceries for free of charge because selling stamps was part of her hustle ripping and robbing the state. Rumor had it she got close to damn near $600 a month. Plus, Big Tricky was her baby daddy who gave her a ride to Sirachi and NaeNae to shop from East Point.

Sirachi whispered, "Nae, look at Rika's thot flops and the dirty bottoms of her feet. Whoever sucking that ho's toes—God bless em!"

NaeNae hit him and started laughing.

At the end of the EBT shopping spree, Sirachi started walking towards the exit as usual on the phone while they bagged up all the groceries. NaeNae yelled at him, saying "Sirachi!" loud as hell to come help with the groceries. He always pulled this stunt and tried to get back out in traffic and leave her to take home all the groceries, unload them, and put them away, too. She was sick of his shit and always leaving her. Plus, she had been horny all day. She woke up super soaked, wet as fuck! After Sirachi helped her to the car, once they parted ways his little slick ass pulled off.

She texted: Oh, no u didn't? Daddy I'm wet and horny…come home get dis pussy.

He texted her back saying he'd meet her there and needed to go get this money to make up for the hundred he spent with Rika. She was pissed off. He was only good for buying groceries. She pressed the gas on the Malibu, swerving in-and-out of traffic. ATL was humid and sticky hot in the summer. She needed another shower and was annoyed even more from the heat.

NaeNae got caught up by a red light and bit down on her lip in frustration. She saw a dude at the light that looked familiar. He told her he missed her banana with his lips in silence without speaking literally as his face lit up. Damn it! It was Lil Carlos! He was out of jail, all grown up, looking extra sexy with his wife beater and tatts. She mouthed him back she missed him too and blew him a kiss. Lil Carlos wasn't so little no more. He was one of her old boyfriends from high school.

She signaled for him to come here with her sexy seductive face and index finger with her stiletto nails. The light started to change. She signaled with both hands for him to hurry-hurry. He ran over as she paused her music.

"I need help with my groceries. You down to show me how much you missed me? Huh? I'm all woman now and got way better—Carlos…C'mon, jump in, niggah!" NaeNae said sweetly with her horny voice that he knew still till this day.

He hopped up in the dunk and told her he saw she riding and flying high. She said a little something. Then he asked if she was still with Sirachi from Bankhead? He already knew the answer. She said of course they lived together but he been acting up lately being the king M-thot of the A! Then asked when did he get out? And did he still live out in College Park? He replied last week and of course, born and bred! She didn't pass him the kush because she didn't want Carlos pissing dirty. However, she gave him 2 perks and told him pop those and let's go to Riverdale! Today was his lucky day, plus she hadn't had none of that fresh out good "D" in a minute, all push-ups, sit-ups, and pull-ups. Nice good energy and stamina to tear a bitch insides up! She cut the music back up and put the videos on with music as her 4 screens lit up.

NaeNae didn't even have the groceries put up yet and they were going at it. After he helped bring them in, he started kissing all on her sides, neck, and licking on her earlobe as he threw her up on the countertops. They started knocking all types of shit down as he was stroking her in and out with a nice penetrating rhythm like he was dancing, hitting the Quan.

NaeNae kept saying, "Oh shit, oh shit! Yesss—Oh shit!" in pure relief. She was wetter than the sea. After she buckled and crossed her legs tight, clutching his ass in with her feet, she had a collapsing orgasm.

He saw her squirt down all on his pelvis with his dick still hard inside of her. He picked her up off the countertop slowly as he carried her up the steps to her master bedroom. He kicked the door open more to enter as NaeNae clung to him like a baby with her arms gripped tightly around his muscular sweaty neck.

He dropped her on the bed while still inside her and fell with her. She screamed how it felt and he began going hard, flipping her, spanking her, pulling and yanking her. He tried to make her touch everything in that room. He saw her freaky sex swing but didn't know how to use it. He was fucking her like he was fresh out, good long and hard while talking shit. He asked can he take the rubber off and bust a nut all over her chest? She shook her head no in between moans. She knew what he wanted to do and skeet all over, which caused his crazy ass to turn up.

He flipped NaeNae on the bed from the back and stood off the bed to pivot and put his pound game down with hard sideways thrusts. NaeNae screamed as he went super deep and dug her out without letting up or pulling out. He was hitting the bottom of that pussy, swelling it up! She felt it in her cervices like someone was knocking on it. He began to go into his raging rants with his deep voice echoing off the walls.

"NaeNae—who pussy is dis, huh? Smack! Huh—who pussy is this, huh? Smack!" Carlos shouted like he was in the military while smacking her ass, then rubbing it down and smacking it again!

"It's urs, Daddy—UR PUSSYYY—Ohh O-O-Urs, Carlos...Ya pussyyy...Oh shit!" NaeNae screamed.

"Now, bitch, can I nut, huh? Say fuck dat nigga. Let me hear, bitch. I'ma keep punishing you. I know you love it, but can't take it too long...Bitch, I'll have you squirting piss, and nut all ova ya self! Smack!"

"Oh-Oh-Yesss...I'm 'bout to nut. Yesss...Daddy, fuck Sirachi! Oh, dis ya pussy, Carlos..." NaeNae screamed into a phat ass nut! She squirted hard all over her bed like she was really peeing. He questioned himself, did he really make her piss on herself? She felt like she was cumming back-to-back intensely for a minute straight.

Carlos pulled out, peeled the rubber off and flipped her around and skeeted a load of hot nut all over her chest and Sirachi tattoo. Nae knew that's what he wanted to do in the first place. She just made him work for it, with his kinky, jealous ass. She grabbed his dick and rubbed it all over the nut into her chest, then lifted it up and put it in her mouth. He had something else coming if he really thought he'd show her up? She sucked slowly and flicked her tongue rings all around the tip of his head, then made smacking and popping noises as she got in her zone and a sucking frenzy.

* * *

Sirachi pulled up front and parked. He opened the front door and heard NaeNae moaning and smacking like she was giving someone head in his bed. Shit, his head and in his bed? He wasn't going and grew super-hot! His eyes glowed dark red. He pulled out his Sig .40 and crept up the stairs slow. A nigga was about to die tonight, on the Hood. Sirachi vowed vengeance, and he was going to fuck her up!

Sirachi just heard his Big Cuzzo Chop-Chop's words echoing off his ears…

"A duck ho—is a no-no, Cuzzo! You mess wit a duck you gonna get plucked! She'll leave you stuck and fucked!" He also would say he was a finesser and pimpin' was a game of finesse, not a gorilla pimpin' mess. He called all white girls snow bunnies and all black girls ducks because they quack-quacked with flack, slack, and talk back. Now here he was about to catch a body and possibly bury the nigga in his bed in the woods and fuck NaeNae disrespectful ass up, too.

He sighed deeply and pushed the cracked door open

slowly with his Sig .40 pointed at shoulder length. His nose hairs got an aroused strong pussy scent. It smelt like the room was sprayed with potpourri pussy freshener. He heard NaeNae slurping hard like sweet milk out of a cereal bowl. Then a loud scream as NaeNae jumped like she saw a ghost. The scream scratched on Sirachi's eardrums like death.

"D-Daddy, I'm sorry—put the gun down, please, Daddy! Sirachi, you trippin, Pa! Here, give me the gun, Daddy. You off them pills. I don't want you to do nothing dumb. We was jus—"

"Nae—Shut up! Michelle? WTF! Damn, you into girls? I didn't know you bumped pussy? Ya husband gonna kill you! And Nae, I ain't putting this thumper down until I finish checking this whole room and bathroom! When my suspicion go down—so will the gun!" Sirachi said in a low tone as he cut NaeNae off and scanned the room in disbelief.

He couldn't believe it. Michelle? Damn, Nae was cold at pulling, turning and flipping hos. She had that down pat. Michelle was straight and married. Her husband graduated from Clark Atlanta University with a Bachelor's in Engineering Science. She was NaeNae's hair stylist for the past three years that lived in Riverdale with her husband and two kids. Everyone, including her friends, called her Michelle because she had a real K. Michelle booty. No ass shots or implants, all natural shape and shake! Sirachi was jealous as she sat there, eyes wide, shaking, scared and embarrassed with the cover over her mid-section.

When Sirachi was done shaking down the room, he snatched the covers from Michelle and told her to get out his bed! She jumped up and shot downstairs naked. He watched her cakes sway side to side with a bounce, which made his dick jump. So, he grabbed it and told NaeNae to get to talking. Then, they both heard the door slam shut hard. Sirachi yelled out, "Ya punk-bitch!" as he noticed Nae's hair was halfway done for the night.

NaeNae went on to explain how they were watching Netflix's "Orange is the New Black" and how Michelle would comment on the gay characters and how some lesbians were cute, knowing that NaeNae was really into girls and did her thing openly. Then NaeNae turned around and asked Michelle what she thought about her to see if she was curious. And she told NaeNae of course she cute, too.

Then NaeNae fast ass busted a move and stood up on her knees and kissed Michelle slowly with passion, kisses on the lips, neck, and with the tongue. She said they went at it for a few minutes till Nae got her comfortable and wet enough to go. Knowing a lot of girls were curious and would kiss a girl but wouldn't go all the way and cross that bridge to the next level, NaeNae didn't give her time to punk out or change her mind. She grabbed her by the hand and took Michelle up the stairs to her bedroom. She had been sucking on her pussy and flicking her tongue all around on her ass with them gold tongue rings, making her cum like crazy. She had her screaming in orgasms. NaeNae admitted she was trying to turn Michelle with her K. Michelle booty out. It was free hair-dos and pussy sucking and bumping hot sex sessions.

Michelle used to charge NaeNae 350 per visit for whatever hairstyle she wanted, including washed shampoo and condition treatments. That was Michelle's occupation. Three years later, she was only charging NaeNae 100 dollars. They had become cool and friends, plus NaeNae would smoke with her and give her gifts like perfume and outfits Sirachi's little boosting thots would bring.

Sirachi shook his head as he listened and broke down a blunt. He was pissed and threw it, still jealous. He told Nae go get the wax and his hookah. He felt like doing a few dabs. Sneezing, choking, ears ringing, and dabbing all off the wax.

Then he'd follow it up with a perk 30 mg.

NaeNae went to get the hookah, smiling from a devilish smirk. She had dodged a bullet, literally. Sirachi would've shot both Carlos and her . Carlos just left before Michelle pulled up. She even forgot all about the hair appointment she had scheduled on her day off. Damn, Carlos fucked her so good. She paid for him to take an Uber to College Park. She wasn't driving after that or going back out in that Georgia summer heat. Plus, he had her pussy swollen. She hoped Sirachi horny ass didn't ask for no ass right now. She saw how he was gawking at Michelle's naked ass all the way down the stairs, grabbing his dick all slick. She handed him the hookah and told him she was going to finish her hair and take a shower. She really went to put an ice pack down on her kitty kat, thinking how Michelle would double back and want to play again another day maybe at her house or a telly.

After her shower, NaeNae fell asleep with the ice pack on her pussy. When she woke up it had melted and her pussy wasn't as swollen or sore. It was already night and that meant it was party and play time. In ATL, all the freaks came out at night and she wanted to catch one of those freaks for her and her Daddy Sirachi. She knew he was still mad.

To her surprise, Sirachi was still home, passed out on the couch with his hands in his pants. The pills had him snoring as usual. NaeNae knew it was too hot for him to go anywhere or he was just playing guard dog, watching her to see if Michelle big booty came back to finish her hair or play.

She got down on her knees and began sucking Sirachi's dick like she was making love to it. He started making manly moans and woke up petting the back of her head gently like a puppy dog. NaeNae teased him and stopped, telling him to save some for later and she was going to pull the baddest bitch in the A today and bring her home to play. He could have it his way with both of them, sex swing and all. He hurried and went to get washed up and dressed.

They went to Magic City first and met up with his partner, Big Tricky. NaeNae had on a tiny red mini-skirt with a flirting slit in the front side. You could see her ass cheeks and of course she wasn't wearing any panties. She needed that hot twat to breathe. ATL was big on strip clubs and Sirachi and Big Tricky stayed at them all!

They were all drinking, throwing bands off pills. Big Tricky was the main one throwing all the big bands. NaeNae was throwing her 200 in ones and Sirachi was throwing dubs.

Suddenly the D.J. made a special announcement, "Ladies and Gentlemen, welcome to Magic City, ATL. This next song is dedicated to NaeNae from Sirachi, my own partner from the notorious Bankhead…This a banger Sirachi remember who stamped it first! Aye-let's go-let's go! Y'all turn up and throw them bands like no limit!" the D.J. said, turnt up and nodding his head as Sirachi's song faded in.

"My Bitch Tropicana—Aye, I said My Bitch Tropicana…My Bitch Tropicana…Pussy strawberry…juices taste cherry…my diamond's canary…Chevy outside jelly…choking on blueberry…In Omaha like belly…Aye—I just shot 100 to Melly…He gonna bust em down in da telly…Ridin' wit my dirty Harry! Aye…My Bitch Tropicana—I said My Bitch Tropicana…pussy strawberry…" Sirachi spit on the track that had the whole Magic City twerking and jumping.

Ballers were throwing bands, making it rain and storm. NaeNae was happy but not impressed. She knew Sirachi paid that D.J. off to play his track. She couldn't lie, it was a strip club banger with an ATL beat to it, but he still couldn't rap.

"You betta had made a song about me in this strawberry fire pussy—I know my juices taste cherry, Daddy!

And you still can't rap like you trap! We celebrating tonight, Daddy. Let's go to the Palace next so I can pull us a bad bitch and spoil you…OK, Daddy?…Aye, My Bitch Tropicana!" NaeNae said, happy, and then sang along with Sirachi.

What NaeNae didn't know was Sirachi already had his single track in Strokers, Teasers, and all the main strip clubs in ATL. He even had the D.J. from KOD in Miami spinning his track and he had it on Soundcloud to download. He would make Sirachi's Entertainment cards from Kinkos and hand them out to thots and at the Underground.

Sirachi and Big Tricky thought they were Future fishtailing getting sideways, leaving Magic with their supercharged engines. NaeNae was rolling the blunt and Sirachi told her to switch with him and drive his Hawks dunk. NaeNae was driving down Camelton and looked over at Sirachi.

"Damn, Daddy, you got ya dream car and dream bitch! Ya bad Tropicana banana redbone, feel how wet you got dis sweet pussy! And you know I don't got on no panties…" NaeNae said, bubbly off them shots of Patron and Don Julio.

Sirachi fingered her like he was gangbanging, throwing up different hand signs. He was trying to pull her towards him by that phat monkey to rub all on her g-spot. He knew where it was at and how to hit it thoroughly. She moaned and opened her legs as she let her foot off the gas, then asked him if he was sure he didn't want to go home and call it an early night for them only? He said nope! Then passed her the laced blunt.

NaeNae hit it and had to question Sirachi what type of pill was it? He told her a Molly because one time his ignorant ass gave her a blue half of a Viagra pill just to see what it did. He figured if it stimulated his libido system, it would stimulate hers, too. Really, he just wanted to give a bitch a Blue Boy, as they called them in Atlanta. NaeNae was hot and couldn't blink for 2 whole hours. She had to keep putting teardrops and water in when her eyes dried out. Plus, her clit was swollen for an hour after sex hard as hell. He was the reason she was a pill head, too! She always popped Mollies and E, but he introduced her to the prescription pills known as scripts. They mainly were painkillers, but some were for manic depression and anti-depression pills. Them perks made her horny and pussy wetter during sex. So, she really loved them.

Right now, they both were riding around looking for a bitch ass to eat, then pulled up at the Palace. NaeNae hoped they let her in, especially with her ass cheeks showing when she walked. She kept pulling it down and she knew the bouncer and blew past security.

The Palace was jumping and full of redbones, lesbos, and thots. NaeNae and Sirachi went their separate ways to do their usual routine and met back up in between. They had a simple system in play. Sirachi would pull girls and chop-n-pop at them to join the threesome. Then NaeNae would spit her G at females trying to turn and flip them, too.

The hard part was getting the girl to go. She wasn't down to do both of them. Then you had the hot ratchet ATL thots that were definitely DTF, but too ratchet, ugly, or carrying a burning STD. NaeNae and Sirachi had bad bitch standards and were in the top-notch mile high club.

Then NaeNae spotted this tropical-looking Miami bitch bad as fuck. She was trying to make her way thru the thick crowd and saw Sirachi all up on her and trying to spit at her vicious. She knew he was about to get rejected before she dismissed his already bubbly ass.

She told these ratchet hos dancing all wild that cut her off—MOVE! And within that brief time, that tropical breed was gone. NaeNae spotted Sirachi again, this time dancing. He was poppin his collar doing the new running man dance, looking like a straight jerk, like a damn fool. She knew he was really rolling hard now and all she could see was his teeth glowing and sparkling in the dark. She needed to hurry up and pull a bitch or go get her man before some hot thot snatched him up because he had priors of leaving her ass at the club, too.

NaeNae was the type of dancing thot that would dance on the spot, making her neck and booty roll as she snapped her fingers. No matter where she was at, the mall, food store, restaurant, car wash, it didn't matter.

And that's exactly what she was doing when she eased up on the bad tropical bitch. Sirachi saw NaeNae at work and eased up behind the Tropicana, as he called them. She looked ahead at NaeNae and smiled as she was dancing, feeling good to be in Atlanta finally and get out the city for a change.

"Hey, Miss Tropical...Ur bad. Damn, baby, you know what they say? Don't nobody know what a bitch wants or needs and likes better than a bitch. Can't nobody eat pussy better than a bitch, ya know," NaeNae said in a sexy luring tone as she clicked her tongue ring, rolling hard off the Molly, too. Damn, that pill crept up and smacked her, she thought, clicking her tongue rings.

"I'm sorry, sweety. Ur very beautiful, too, but I'm not into no girls. Strickly-dickly, baby girl. Ya feel me? We can kick it tonight, tho, and you can sit at my table," she replied with a thick East Coast accent.

"Damn, where you from? And I am NaeNae, by the way..." NaeNae shouted over the loud music. It was Drake with a slow tempo off his *Views* album, "Controller."

"I'm from New York City and they call me Miss Exotic cuz I'm an exotic rare mixed breed. Nice to meet you, NaeNae. Where's all the ballers at? I don't see me one, yo!" Miss Exotic replied.

"Well, Miss Exotic, today is a special day for me and my man…so I told him I was down for a ménage and you only live once—YOLO, right! What happens in ATL stays in Atlanta. We take sex serious here! Today is my 23rd B-day and my dude released his album. He a local artist who got signed. We live in Riverdale and we got all the best weed and pills in Atlanta. So, you down to play for the day and let me eat everything up? I'll make you cum just with my long tongue. You don't gotta do nothing but lean back and watch, nut or let my man cut. It's on you. Now, let's go get that table and kick it, girl. I'll show you some Southern hospitality. You ever heard of Pandora? C'mon!" NaeNae vic'd her with a befriended approach to let her guard down and extended her hand, reaching out for Miss Exotic.

Miss Exotic gave NaeNae her hand and they disappeared thru the heavy crowd. Sirachi couldn't believe NaeNae yanked that bad bitch from New York. She bit! And she used that "I can eat pussy better than a bitch" line. Damn it! He instantly popped a whole Blue Boy Viagra pill and another Molly!

The Palace was jumping but also getting tired and funky. Sirachi went over to join them at the table despite how NaeNae kept shaking her head secretly—No! thinking it was too premature and he'd ruin it and blow their chances. NaeNae wanted to bag her all the way first. He went thru the ropes of V.I.P. and flopped down, fatigued.

WTF? Who is he stalking? I told him no, already! Miss Exotic thought to herself while looking at Sirachi like he was lost.

"Oh, dis my man—da rapper I was telling you about—Sirachi!" NaeNae yelled over the music.

"Yes, we met already," Miss Exotic replied slick with her thick New York accent.

Sirachi asked them if they were ready to go get

something to eat and blow this joint.

NaeNae said, "Hell, yeah." Then she turned to Miss Exotic, "You ready to bounce? We can eat somethin' at the Waffle House."

When Exotic shrugged her shoulders, NaeNae grabbed her by the hand and the followed Sirachi as he pushed thru the crowd towards the exit. The whole Palace was hating and mad, knowing how Sirachi and Nae played.

Exotic looked at Sirachi's Atlanta Hawks dunk with pretty paint and hot wheels big as hell. In New York, she didn't know anybody who owned a car. It was all Metro trans subway, train, cab or walk. They all hopped in the front seat of the Cutlass. Exotic was sandwiched between the two of them.

Sirachi turned his system up, showing off. He played Kevin Gates' "Really-Really" song. He asked her nationality? She replied Brazilian and Haitian. He and NaeNae said "Damn!" at the same damn time.

NaeNae knew she wasn't from the A and had a Miami Mami look to her.

"I model for DJ Kay Slay and been in two issues of his *Straight Stuntin'* magazine in 2014 and 2016," Miss Exotic said as she showed them photos of her issues and some more poses in her Galaxy phone.

NaeNae and Sirachi said "Damn!" again at the same time.

This bitch was bad and, even though NaeNae had a tad bit more ass than her and they were the same size and weight, she had NaeNae beat with a smaller waist and Latina curves that were sexy as hell. Sirachi switched songs.

"My Bitch Tropicana! Pussy strawberry. Juices taste cherry!" NaeNae and Sirachi sang out Sirachi's hook.

Miss Exotic liked the Atlanta beat and vibe. It sounded a bit like T.I., though. She asked, "Who is that?" NaeNae said, "Sirachi! My Papi!" All proud and went back to rapping the verse, then told her how Sirachi made this song about her and she would see how sweet NaeNae's juices were if she was about that life right now, like Jeremiah sing about.

Sirachi's country ass was floating down I-20 as his 6's were hitting air pockets which had the front end dipping up and down. Exotic had never rode in a dunk toy on hot wheels. They went to the Waffle House westbound off I-20.

They pulled up front and it was packed trump tight. Sirachi said he wasn't even hungry no more and asked about them. They shook their heads nope. Then Miss Exotic said she was horny, not hungry…and NaeNae set it off! She kissed her long and passionately, feeling all on her breast and kissing her neck softly. Sirachi started fingering her, too. They were tag-teaming Exotic viciously. Sirachi reversed, still fingering her with his right hand as he pushed off with his left hand. He paused and gave her a perk 30 and asked if she ever fucked with a Mac Dre from the Bay. She shrugged her shoulders. He gave her a red triple stack and NaeNae two because she was a vet pill-poppin junkie like him, a straight E-head. They lit the blunt back up and flew to Riverdale. They were about to turn up and go stupid.

Sirachi pulled up in the driveway and hit the garage opener. He parked in the driveway and they all went thru the garage and up the stairs to the crib. Miss Exotic noticed two more old classics with pretty hot pink paint and spring colors, assuming one was NaeNae's. The condo was plush with cold central air, just how NaeNae liked it. She admitted NaeNae had flavor, and this condo in New York City would have run three grand a month easy. They gave her some orange juice, which boosted her high. She began to float a little and felt heavy vaginal secretions. Owwee…she was so wet and felt super good and was ready for her first ménage. And maybe taste NaeNae if she got horny enough or really fucked up.

The trio went to the bedroom and Sirachi poured them a drink of apple Cîroc. Next thing you knew NaeNae was stripping her clothes and Miss Exotic's, too. They began kissing each other and Nae busted Exotic's legs open like she was giving her a vaginal exam! She began swirling her tongue in small circles, dancing around her tingling clitoris. She went nuts when NaeNae put the tongue rings on the rim of her asshole. That shit had turned her on.. Sirachi played his position and stood watch as NaeNae went to work showing off to heat Exotic up. They had another victim to their crazy sex crave, which was never satisfied even though they had the best of both worlds.

After Exotic came, Nae started scissor-kicking as they bumped pussies while NaeNae had Exotic's feet in her mouth and sucking all between her toes. Exotic was in ecstasy and rolling hard on Ecstasy. She was ready to get nasty and freaky. She was down to eat NaeNae's pussy if Nae ever slowed down. She was so aggressive like she had a craving appetite for pussy—a pussy monster like she was really into girls, too. NaeNae had her crème all over the place again.

Sirachi intervened and broke them two up by pushing them apart. NaeNae told him to get the magnums. She started sucking on his dick first and motioned for Exotic to come join her and they teased Sirachi, took turns sharing his love stick and swapping spit, tongue-kissing each other, then the dick. NaeNae licked on his balls with her tongue rings as Exotic blew his mind. It was enough of foreplay. He put the rubber on and bent Exotic over first.

She had a pretty pussy, too. He told her to eat Nae's pussy out while he hit her from the back. NaeNae laid down and spread her legs and tucked them behind her head to make her pussy pop out so Exotic could lick everything, booty and all.

NaeNae kept telling her, "Yeah, like that," and to swirl her tongue faster and press down harder until she got it down pat. Nae could turn and teach any bitch how to eat pussy quick. She the one that turned Sirachi into a pussy-eating vet. He was going around the A saying niggas better get their tongue game up. He got that from NaeNae herself, too.

Sirachi worked his thumb in her ass as he slobbered all over it as he hit her from the back. Then he began to fuck her fast, then put it in her ass in-and-out slow. She was going berserk, moaning and cumming. He was smacking her ass with 2 hands still stroking it sideways, this way-that way.

He looked down at NaeNae as they both looked at each other like they weren't shit and cheaters. Nae had two fists full of Exotic's hair wrapped up knuckle deep into her scalp as she pushed her head all into her pussy and down on her ass with her legs still bent behind her head.

She and Sirachi started saying how much they loved each other, getting very vocal and ready to cum together. He told Exotic keep eating Nae's pussy just like that as he pulled out her ass and put it right in Nae's mouth, skeeting all down her throat as she choked!

Miss Exotic was thru—Done! All she wanted was a drink of water afterwards but couldn't move. Sirachi had her in stuck mode. She watched Sirachi put this vibrating ring around his dick and fuck NaeNae like a wild stallion every which way and all on the sex swing. They were like real porno stars. OMG! All night long. They weren't worried about her no longer—she felt used. Then she passed out.

Chapter 7
"Back Stage"

Nasty Neesha had been laying low back in LA. She was still working the backs and catfishing who she could but was no longer at her favorite hotel she called the million-dollar spot next to LAX. She didn't have the room in her actual government name. She wasn't stupid. However, she ran game on Trinidad Slauson for beating that Rancho Cucamonga trick silly, robbing him and blowing up her spot, that she probably had a warrant out for her arrest for robbery. He broke her off most the money and split the rest with her sister Sugar Baby. Plus, he shot her another couple hundred on her rent. Neesha was homeless and lived out of LA weekly motels all over. That's why she had suitcases and bags full of shit at her actual real motel room under her government. She used aliases and fake IDs for the rooms she turnt tricks from Craigslist in.

Today was her shopping day in LA. Neesha was, Beverly Hills bound, Rodeo Drive style. She had this thing for designer bags and loved clutch bags. She was already plus-sized and didn't need a plus-sized purse like the fat lady with the fat bag with fat kids.

She was listening to Beyoncé's *Lemonade* and singing "She ain't sorry! I ain't sorry—Hell nawh." She was loyal to Beyoncé, her idol, and pledged allegiance to the Beehive tribe. She loved the Sorry song.

However, today she was feeling like a plus-size Barbie and wanted to get her Nicki Minaj on. So, she put her pink wig on, fixed the bobby pins, and then patted the loose Indian synthetic hair in place. She adjusted it to the left a little in the motel mirror, then sucked in her gut and poked out her butt.

She was so indecisive over her heels versus flats. She had some hot-pink flats but a matching Barbie pink Prada heels. She knew flats made you look fatter, though. She decided on the heels and put on her Oprah Spanx with her Kim K. V-shaped girdle, too. She was tired of hiding behind her make-up and motels. She wanted to get out more. There would be no more online shopping. She was sick of filling her shopping cart up on Amazon.

Snapchat had some of the best filters, especially if you were a real-life walking catfish like her who'd mask her God-given identity for her insecurities. She worked wonders with them snap filters.

She would rent a drop-top Benz to cruise thru Hollywood and the LA strips, especially Sunset, to feel better than them street walkers because she felt like they were the real prostitutes. Neesha was just a smart businesswoman.

Sometimes she would drive all the way past the Hills to Calabasas just to shop at the Whole Foods store; really, with hopes of meeting a BBW millionaire trick! Wishful thinking. She checked her phone for LA weather. It read 89 degrees currently and an expected high of 95 degrees, which was beautiful breezy drop-top LA weather.

She pushed the Benz to Hollywood with the top down and pink wig blowing in the wind like it was real. She adjusted her Chanel frames off the brim of her nose like she was a rich prissy bitch.

Rodeo Drive was beautiful and full of skinny Hollywood bitches and very thin model-looking white girls.

And the paparazzi was out thick in full force trying to stalk their prey. The Drive had all designer stores and brand names. Neesha planned to go down to Melrose next. She went into the Louis Vuitton store first. She was inside for 10 minutes without no assistance. She even said, "Excuse me" a few times to get some help, but nothing.

"She knew I was calling her...old snoozy dried-up bitch!" Neesha said to herself. There were even a few couples that walked in after her that were helped right away. What, her money wasn't good enough? Or she wasn't white enough? Neesha couldn't bite her tongue anymore.

"Ummh—EXCUSE ME? I said EXCUSE ME!" Nasty Neesha shouted rudely as the two clerks and all the store patrons looked at her like she was the loud fat black girl being disruptive as usual.

"Oh, I'm sorry, but oh my God—for Christ's sake, don't give me a heart attack, young lady! Or scare off my customers. Anyways, are you lost? What can I do for you today? You know a lot of stuff in here is clearly over your limit. Unless you're carrying around a few grand in hard cash? But you're a long way from Compton...Now, I'm going to have to ask you to leave—please," the skinny old white lady said.

Nasty Neesha flipped out and went off. She started cursing the lady out, calling her a retired old prune volunteer worker, which got Neesha escorted to her car by security and banned her from the store. She flipped the officer and clerk off as she sped off.

Neesha was beyond heated. She sparked up some loud in the rental with no worries like Weezy. She couldn't believe that racist bitch told her to go back to Compton in so many words. She tried to stay out of Compton ever since she got shot in the leg on the Shaw. It happened when she was out being a little hot thot with her two older sisters. Some rival gangbangers shot up the car in front of them and hit her sister's car up in the crossfire. Bullets really didn't have no names. Sugar Baby even got grazed in the hand holding onto the steering wheel. Neesha told herself never would she cruise up and down Crenshaw again. Foothill Blvd—Hell no!

Her phone went off and she answered as she let the roof of the Benz pull back up from the trunk.

"Hello?" Neesha answered, a thot with an attitude.

"Damn, bitch—excuse da fuck out of me, shit! Ummh, anyways, fuck wit cha goin' thru, sis, but social media is going nuts! You didn't get my Snapchat? Well, they did a big concert announcement for the 23rd of July dis month, girl. Guess who, too? My boo! Fetty Wap! They gonna be all performing at Coachella. Him, 2-Chainz, Kevin Gates, and Future!" Sugar Baby said, turnt up as she was braiding her son's hair, knowing it was going to be lit as fuck!

"What? Fuck Fetty Wap! He ain't got shit on my baby daddy—Future! I'ma tell him I suck dick better than a skinny bitch! If he let me backstage I'll change ya life with a Beyoncé plus-size BBW. Heyyy! Sis, I'm gonna get us some backstage passes, watch, and some come-fuck-me outfits, too! It's going down in Coachella Valley—Cali, baby!" Nasty Neesha replied in a bragging tone, now with her mind on the prize and hopes of seducing Future, maybe to be his trophy like he sing about.

* * *

Back in sleepless Seattle, Slutty Shelly was doing her usual phone sex operator job and bossing Jax around when she heard the news over MTV Bottom Line News about the Coachella concert on the 23rd with Future, 2-Chainz, Kevin Gates, and Fetty Wap exclusively.

She needed a young rich black guy and she figured Fetty Wap was her guy with his one eye. He had one eye and she had one leg. Plus, she knew she was older in her thirties but still hot as fuck just with a wicked-looking scar on her neck. All the brothers from the Seattle Seahawks wanted her and would always throw money and numbers at her. She, too, wanted to seduce Fetty Wap with her vicious head game, some straight thot top. She would make him move to Seattle if she had her way with him. She would be his down white wife for life.

She even had some callbacks from her old boss, Steve, to come back and work the strip joint as a bartender. She gladly declined and screened his calls. She knew it would be too much temptation to drink and she took an oath after her incident to never become an alcoholic or work in another strip club again! Besides, Steve old ass just wanted to get some head and hit her with her one leg. Then she had to worry about all the perverts that wanted to see her pussy and long legs. They would pay to sneak a peek and have her crotch in their faces to get a quick whiff, mainly to put that leg on the bar.

It was time for her to save up and make that most needed trip to California. She really was looking for a mate and to mate. She felt she was too cute and hot to let her handicap hold her back or down.

The problem was her long, slender, sexy frame with them long legs everyone wanted to see and some skin. She could never find regular pants to fit too tight to show off her slender frame because the strap-on leg would pop out of place, scaring people when she walked. It was aluminum but she decorated it with pink Hello Kitty stickers on it. She even worked on her walk to where you could barely tell she had a limp. You had to study it. Before, she would hobble like a dwarf.

She also had to find someone to take care of Jax for the weekend or possibly whole week. She started becoming more attached to her K-9 since every guy would hit and run, checking her off on their bucket list.

Slutty Shelly decided to just call her Mom and ask her for a 5-grand loan since her Dad couldn't really talk or argue about it. Maybe she could even get a grand out of Steve? But he would want a sexual retainer, she was sure of that. Right now, she just needed to find the perfect jeans online.

* * *

In the Windy City of the Chi, Teasing Tasha kept getting Snaps left and right. And the Gram was going ham into a frenzy with thot thoughts and comments. She even seen all her BFF Tina's Snaps and comments showing out and displaying outfits at her pop's house on the South Side. She shook her head, jealous and hating on Tina and how much her dad spoiled that girl.

Tasha wasn't trippin and knew she had Tina beat with an exotic, more tropical-island look. She was the Bad in their Triple B's Club. This sent Teasing Tasha into a competitive mode. She knew how to get it how she lived, too.

Being lazy tired, Tasha overslept until 3 p.m. from smoking and club-hopping all night in the summertime breezy Chi. She missed the social media bombshell they were broadcasting special concert announcements in Coachella, CA: Future, 2-Chainz, Fetty Wap and her baby Kevin Gates! It was going to get lit!

If it wasn't for Kevin Gates, she wouldn't even be trying to get a flight at the O'Hare Airport. Kevin Gates was sexy with his grill and face tatts. Hood and gutta as hell! He talking about doing all the etc....to a female, too? She had a thing for niggas with face tatts, too. It read bold and that thug Tupac my attitude is fuck it mentality! She loved it and she loved her a nigga from the South with a Southern accent and a diamond grill.

She wouldn't let Tina or no other bitch show her up! She was the undiscovered dime of this lifetime! So, she got all washed up and dressed up with no make-up and started sending Snaps back, too, and getting ratchet as she turnt up!

"See, I'm here. Hashtag Snapchat no-filter, bitches! What y'all know about that! Top-notch bitches at Coachella only! Y'all broke bitches, hot thots, and baby mamas stay at home! And please, y'all groupies, don't none of them rappers want y'all love—at all! This ya girl from the Triple B's in the Windy Go—Tasha signing off...Deuces!" Tasha snapped as she did a Snap and sent it. Then heated up Instagram looking oh so naturally beautiful, showing off her curvy hips and exotic face. It was going down in the DMs as usual. And it was going down across the nation, too. Lit!

* * *

Thot Flocks! thots flock from across the nation with plans to go to Coachella concerts. Groupies, too, by the herds. All thot flocks are a group of thots, females, birds and chickens. Birds of a feather flock together. This concert of the summer turnt up and would be a high sold-out turnout lit of thots, hot wives, groupies, ratchets, and of course them weasel hos, too. They would come by buses, plane, or train, however, by any means necessary. You had to really be on your A+ game! It was cute and bad bitches but they were broke or just bums. Then it was mediocre hos that stay high and fly from boosting designer high-end apparel and credit card schemes that would fool the average but didn't fit the bill for an actual rap star.

* * *

Back in the ATL, shawty NaeNae was heading back to the Up Top barber shop to pick Sirachi up. He had better be done because they were already late and woke up late with a late start. Today he had an interview at Atlanta's V 103 FM hot hip-hop radio station. His single had been heating up thru the city, and they wanted to interview this independent rapper and for the people to hear from him and know all about Sirachi. And all future projects, too, with The Ryan Report.

NaeNae was behind Sirachi her man, but he had been feeling his lil nuts too much lately with a swelt-up fat big head like them posters. She walked in the barber shop showing all skin while fanning herself and sipping on her favorite Arizona sweet tea.

"Hey, now, watch me whip-whip, watch me, NaeNae." The song played thru the barber shop as NaeNae did her dance, saying, "Aye!" Suddenly Sirachi heard his song and jumped up, causing the barber to nick his hair, taking a straight patch out his naps.

"Aye—my bitch Tropicana! Aye dat's me, cuh, straight up! Big Oomp did that beat for me! I cashed him out and freestyled! Ugghh…Nae, we on V 103 FM da radio, baby. Yesss!" Sirachi rejoiced still with his black barber tarp on, with no regards for his patch out the top of his head.

Then the radio personnel cut right in, saying that was ATL's own Sirachi from Bankhead and he would be there today for a guest appearance for the drive at five rush hour. So please call in to the studios if any questions for him.

Next, they followed up with a turn-up tour and concert special announcement of ATL's 2Chainz and Future! Along with Kevin Gates and Fetty Wap, too, at Coachella on July 23rd summer heat! The male disc jockey clowned, saying if you musty or funky, don't go down there ratchet while rep'n the A-Town on your back. They all laughed, then announced they were giving away Coachella tickets free every hour until they ran out! The phone lines were ringing—ringing off the hook—as they went into commercial. It was a beautiful thing. They had a switchboard. They haven't seen it lit up like that and so rapidly in a long time.

Sirachi tipped his barber and had NaeNae drive as he rolled and smoked the loud and sipped some Henny to relax his nerves as they went to V 103 radio station. He knew he had the interview 3 days ago. Big Tricky peeps plugged him and got him a spin at V 103 for new late night underground artist. His 404 number and 770 number had both been blowing up lately. He was beginning to get fans, groupies, and stalkers around the A, but mainly building a fan base, which was important for his marketing strategies.

As Sirachi passed the blunt to NaeNae, all she could do is think about how she never fucked 2-Chainz or fucked Kevin Gates, but if she did she'd do a ménage with them and make them eat her ass like a cupcake! Just like Nicki Minaj say about Weezy and Drake. She heard 2-Chainz was strapped like them NBA players.

NaeNae had a thing for 2-Chainz and would never catch him solo in the A. She saw him twice but he never saw or noticed her with her devil-red thot hair. He was so hard to catch, unlike most rappers in ATL she bumped into. And Sirachi would kill her if he knew she slept with his childhood idol from the West Side. If she did, she'd take it to the grave..

She had a thing for Kevin Gates, too. She wanted to see if he was really about all that freaky shit he rapped about. Sirachi was thinking success—she was thinking SEX! His Big Cuzzo Chop-Chop told him in the Feds over the phone,

"Bitches chase dick! —We chase money! So why not make her chase ya money while chasing her dick? Else she was a flat-backing hood rat! With a hot twat and no spot!"

NaeNae plotted how to get to Coachella. She had to sneak without Sirachi knowing or following behind her. She sighed harshly and told Sirachi let her hit that bottle of Yac really quick! He looked at her like, Bitch, what you on this early? Then passed it to her as he went back to texting on his Note 4.

They pulled into the back of the radio station. Sirachi instructed Nae to park where he could see his whip in clear view during the interview and told her to tuck his pistol, too. Sirachi French-inhaled the thick kush smoke thru his nostrils and held it into the entrance, coughing and slobbering going into the building.

They told NaeNae to sit in the waiting room and she could listen to the interview from there. Only Sirachi was allowed in the studio. Then they went live on the air introducing Sirachi to ATL. They told him to intro his Tropicana track first and they'll be back with him live and more. He complied, nervous with the first-time jitters, and it felt like he needed to take a shit. He popped a perk lil right in front of them. They were staring at him like *I know he didn't pop a pill right in front of us in the studio?*

"And we're back, V 103 FM, with Sirachi in the studios! Speak to Atlanta traffic and listeners, Sirachi," the woman DJ stated, turnt-up.

"Aye…Sup, Atlanta, dis ya boy Sirachi—Sirachi live! Shoutout to the West Side Bankhead, Zone 4, Zone 2, East Side, Decatur, Macon, Savannah, Stone Mountain, South Side, the whole A-Town. Stand up, we in the building. Shoutout my Tropicana Strawberry, NaeNae! And Big Oomp for dis killa beat that got me a big buzz and strip club anthem from the A to Miami! I'm still unsigned and pushing independent, so any sponsors get at me. My Twitter, IG, FB, and Snap is all Sirachi...S-I-R-A-C-H-I! Aye...Turn up!" Sirachi said, pumped up like he was the most famous rapper up out of Atlanta. NaeNae was texting and smirking as she shook her head. She was telling her white sister all about Sirachi and his interview while she was working at the famous East Atlanta Wal-Mart where all the thots and ratchets shopped. She listened as a bunch of callers, mainly females, flirted with her man like he had fame already instead of a city strip club buzz. Her heart began to race with anxiety at the thought of losing Sirachi to one of them rich R&B hos once he blew all the way up. And he would probably kick her out the condo and tell his Aunt to break her lease, terminating both her and the lease. NaeNae began to get paranoid and nervous as her insecurities kicked in. It wasn't guilt. NaeNae really loved Sirachi and remembered the words of the Song of Solomon .

Set me as a seal upon your heart, as a seal upon your arm; For love is as strong as death; Jealousy as cruel as the grave; Its flames are flames of fire, a most vehement flame! Many waters cannot quench love, nor can the floods drown it. If a man would give for love all the wealth of his house, it will be utterly despised.

She used the words as strength, knowing love was crazy without no limits and worse than a drug, because a withdrawal from a drug is treatable; however, withdrawal from love is dangerous and deadly. There was no real known cure for it. She just loved Sirachi beyond words and didn't want to lose her Boo.

She wiped her eyes dry as she cried, just as she heard them saying thanks for stopping by and their goodbyes to Sirachi. She was so emotional lately. Was it all the different pills she was popping? Or just PMS? It couldn't be another cycle coming on because Sirachi fucked her so hard and long from their ménage night with Miss Exotic that she went straight on her period!

Then she hoped and prayed she wasn't pregnant. She only had unprotected sex with Cheesy besides Sirachi. And Sirachi couldn't have no more kids from his incident with his BM crazy Cuban ass. She needed to get a First Response EPT pregnancy test, then call Cheesy for abortion money before Sirachi found out or noticed and killed her! And she wasn't about to pay for it, either. She told him to put on a damn condom. But could it really be possible it was Sirachi's baby, too? Her head began to hurt and throb as Sirachi came out cheesing hard like a superstar already. She threw him the keys and told him to drive because she drove there and needed to relax under the A/C.

* * *

The weeks were flying by and Coachella was just days away. Some thots were already out in LA and the Bay. They had their fits ready, rental cars, and hotel reservations. They came out to play.

Teasing Tasha and Tina caught the same flight out to LA unintentionally and saw each other, but didn't speak. They would steady tweet.

When Tasha got outside LAX, she was right next to Slutty Shelly. Both had been waiting on an Uber, but they were now banned from LAX. They stood with their arms folded, pissed off, and their luggage waist-side. Tasha had designer Gucci luggage.

Shelly started talking to Tasha, saying she flew out from Seattle and it was her first time in LA. She came out for the concert at Coachella and wondered if Tasha knew any decent inexpensive hotels .

"Girl, I'm from Chicago! I don't know LA either. My first time, too. But we 'bout to turn up in this bitch! Heyyy!" Tasha replied as she bust a move snapped her fingers like a hot thot just as her BFF Tina finally got her luggage and came out to catch a cab, too. LAX was super packed with people coming and going, double parking and getting dropped off left and right. Tina killed her vibe and she wanted to curse her ass out and tell her to go back to the Go and quit following her.

Then, Tasha looked back at Shelly and told her she going to the Ritz Carlton and had already called two weeks prior for her reservations of her double suite. Tina knew she was being loud trying to get her point across. She wanted to tell Tasha to shut up, bitch! Plus, her Daddy got her a room two weeks ago, too, at the Hampton Inn.

They all got into separate cabs and parted ways in beautiful sunny Los Angeles, sightseeing and snapping their phone cams.

Sirachi had just flown back from New York City solo. He had finished doing another radio interview at The Breakfast Club talking about his ATL strip club and radio smash hit "Tropicana." He told them how he had Money Mayweather pipe dreams of making 100 million an hour just like Mayweather did after 12 rounds, paid in full, even though it was wishful thinking he could ever get Mayweather money team-type money.

He was stacking his peanuts and all strip clubs that paid him for appearances and to perform that song, and from the radio interviews, too. He had reached out to the Twins, who were the concert promoters for Coachella. The Twins' Daddy went to the Feds for money laundering and put them up on G since they were only 15 years old, renting out and selling out venues. Now the Twins were still teens, only 19 years old with a household name and pulling household-name hot artists to LA. They were responsible for 2-Chainz, Future, Kevin Gates, and Fetty Wap. Big-big names.

So Sirachi reached out to the Twins with an offer of 20 bands to let him perform as the 1st opening act for his one-hit ATL strip club banger. They gladly accepted and pocketed that extra 20k. Besides, they only had 2 opening acts anyways, a rapper and R&B girl group out of the Bay.

Sirachi wanted to tell NaeNae they were going to LA for him to perform at Coachella and open for 2-Chainz and them. Of course, he was seeking her validation only and even though he was faking it 'til he made it, he wouldn't dare tell Nae he spent 20 whole bands to perform instead of receiving that to perform like the rest of the real rappers.

He pulled up to CNN and NaeNae was sitting outside with her legs crossed and phone in her hand. She jumped in and asked, "So what's her surprise?"

"Damn—No 'I miss you, Sirachi'? 'I love you, Papi,' or nothing, huh? Whoa—what a way to spoil it. Love, we going to Coachella! I'm taking you backstage with all the rappers, baby. I got a gig to perform there to open up to set it off! Damn, imagine that, love. Ya niggah, Sirachi, dat couldn't rap, getting on the map! Uggh…with Atlanta on my back! So, get ya shit ready. We leaving tomorrow. And have you been being a good girl while Daddy was gone in NYC getting doe?" Sirachi said in a slick tone, puffing on the blunt.

"Boy, please, have you? Dis pussy is super tight and right! And ya not going with Big Tricky being a M-thot around the A tonight! Ya staying at home with me tonight and helping me pack all our stuff, Daddy. Plus, we got an appointment with Mr. Sex Swing tonight cuz I'm horny as hell as always. This pussy stay wet—wet for you!" NaeNae replied, trying to hide her overwhelming excitement. She was on her way to LA to play and have sex with a rapper backstage after or before the show! She didn't care and was 'bout that life. She wasn't worried about King M-thot Sirachi himself, because she was sure he'd be doing his usual creeping and sneaking, too. She was happy her pregnancy test all came back negative. She figured it was just stress from all the pressure of losing her heart, Sirachi. She loved the shit out of him.

She told Sirachi no bringing his ATL entourage to LA and she wasn't sharing no rooms with no damn Big Tricky fat ass. He told her she knew he didn't have an entourage or fuck with hating-ass Atlanta niggas and Big Tricky black ass was the only nigga he fucked with. Then right there he caught on to her joke and being funny, calling Big Tricky his whole entourage.

The next day they arrived in LA at the last minute a day before the big concert. They still had to drive up to Coachella and do a sound check and meet up with the DJ the Twins had for Sirachi. He was behind schedule with no manager and self-promo. He didn't even have sense enough to put NaeNae to work, which she knew he was still playing and not too serious. He just wanted the groupie love and thots attention. He didn't have that go-getter natural drive mentality. He had a go-party and play-natural mentality.

They told the cab driver to take them to the nearest hotel. And, of course, a few ways from LAX, he took them to an old vintage-looking hotel next to LAX. He wasn't sure if he was in Inglewood or what. His GPS was off. And they had to get a rental ASAP after they checked into the hotel next to the McDonald's. He'd make NaeNae drive because he heard about LA's wild 24/7-type rush hour bumper-to-bumper traffic. He knew he had to get on the 105 to get to Coachella. Or was it the 110? He already was lost and confused. He loved LA already because every other car had a bad bitch in it. All nice cars, too. The women all looked independent, too.

They weren't in the hotel for 10 minutes and they

heard someone next door getting their back blown out and screaming! Then once again within the hour before they left the room. NaeNae said all that moaning had her horny and she wanted some "D" and for them to please bless the room before they drove up to Coachella to do his mic check. He told her they'd play later and he promised, but needed to save some energy for the concert tomorrow. He didn't want to be burnt out. Sirachi also told her it was his turn to knock a bad bitch for them to eat and beat up. Nae liked that idea even better. She had to get out of the hotel room before the neighbors made her start playing with herself.

As they walked down the hall, they saw a construction worker come out the neighbor's room and a big girl with clown-type drawn-on make-up escorting him. NaeNae giggled at the fact big girl was getting hers, too. They needed love, too.

Sirachi did two rehearsals and met up with the Twins and their young LA DJ. They went over the track and he told them exactly how he wanted it laced. When to pause, speed up tempo and let that Choppa spray at the end like a Desiigner-Panda track.

NaeNae was backstage snooping around, peeping the scene. She saw the crew setting up the backstage lounge and then setting out all the outside chairs and perimeters. Then she saw a trailer that had 2-Chainz on the door. She wanted to sneak in right away and hide in the bathroom 'til the concert started tomorrow evening, if she could shake Sirachi. She prayed they didn't move his outside trailer. Sirachi came back looking for her to bounce. It was showtime. They needed to get back and rest for his big cameo.

* * *

Teasing Tasha was pissed off from the heavy LA traffic and dirty smog. She could see the pollution. It was messing with her damn allergies because she knew she wasn't allergic to Cali. She was already late for the backstage access passes. She saw online who to look for. Everyone with neon green wristbands had backstage passes for sale at 300 apiece. In Cali everything was a hustle, being from Land of the Superstars.

She sighed and sat back talking slick to the taxi driver. He barely spoke English and kept smiling, saying, "Yes-Yes...Coachella yes-yes..." which even made her more pissed off because the air in that taxi sucked. Plus, she was being a little ho today wearing no panties. Men would flock around her more when she didn't have on any panties in the club for some reason, like their antennas and endorphins went up.

She had on some $2,500 red bottoms and a Fendi red miniskirt. She was trying to kill all hos and groupies backstage. K.O.S. Chicago-style. She did light make-up on her face and flat-ironed her hair out, dropping it to the middle of her back. She was trying to make Kevin Gates forget a line or two.

* * *

Nasty Neesha and her older sister, Sugar Baby, already had been backstage for 30 minutes at the lounge, sipping and laughing. Sugar Baby was flamed up in a cherry red catsuit gripping her thighs and hips, which had her pussy print in a fist grip, along with some throwback '80s hoop gold earrings.

Nasty Neesha big ass had the nerve to squeeze into a platinum sparkling one-piece skirt, the same one in Beyoncé's

"Put a Ring on It" video, with a Marc Jacobs clutch bag. The make-up looked Photoshopped and the Snap dog-puppy filter looked like she was a dead puppy dog in the casket with a horrible mortician. It was hideous and the awful thing was she was two-tones. Her neck and legs were two different colors than her face. The make-up made her look like she had dried-up sunscreen on. Neesha was a hot mess, but Sugar Baby had her back and loved her no matter what. Neesha had gotten free backstage passes from Trinidad Slauson from his guilt of smashing and stomping out that Rancho Cucamonga trick that night. Plus, he had the hook-up like Master P.

* * *

Slutty Shelly paid a whole thousand dollars for her backstage pass. Knowing she was a white girl green as a thumb from Seattle, they fished her in and busted her head open to the white meat. Of course, that cat left the whole parking lot after his swindle.

Shelly found her some nice Latina stretchy blue pants that looked like actual jeans but was more elastic, so her fake leg could retract quick and she could still look sexy, with a white halter top revealing her nipple ring bars perking out. She stood still up against the stage's first passageway as she used the wall to catch her pivot. She had on red-hot fire dick-sucking lipstick with her platinum hair blowing in the wind. Her intention was to catch a rapper, mainly Fetty Wap.

* * *

As dusk settled over Coachella Valley, it was going down. They were finally all backstage. The bouncers and security kept chasing groupies down and kicking them out the lounge. It was hard, sweaty work because the girls outnumbered security 50 to 1. And to make matters worse, Big Boy radio station in LA was giving out free backstage passes, too. The security knew the difference between the fictitious ones. The real ones had holograms. Some ratchets didn't even have bogus ones or passes at all, they would just sneak past security and break for the back. It was a crazy estrogen frenzy! It was booty-booty everywhere! Ass cheeks hung out of cut-off booty shorts and skimpy tennis skirts. Cleavage and titties bounced all over the place and implants both on their breasts and butts. Then, of course, you had your bitches with gold teeth and high craft and stitched hairdos like they were at the hair show. Teasing Tasha wasn't the only girl that wasn't wearing any panties; half the place didn't. Nor did the ladies have time to pull thongs out their ass all night long. They came to get down and loose as a tooth.

Sirachi had on all Gucci everything. A Gucci bucket hat like Schoolboy Q's. Gucci belt with the gold G's on it. Some Gucci brown and gold loafs and all gold Gucci frames. NaeNae stared over at him, shaking her head. She kept telling him to slow down.

He had been going too hard way too early, like he finally made it and found a billion-dollar way like Dr. Dre. He already popped two Xanny bars, them yellow buses and a perk 30 mg, but that wasn't NaeNae's concern. He also had been drinking a few Heineken beers, sipping pineapple Cîroc, and taking shots of Patron, too. Then smoking blunt after blunt of that Cali Kurupt, the rapper kush, like he was Snoop Dogg and the main headliner of the night, but really an opening act.

NaeNae just click-clacked her tongue rings, horny, rolling herself off them white Molly capsules. Her red-laced thong was already sticky wet, too. She wanted to take them off and rub them in 2-Chainz's face or smear it all in Kevin Gates' nose like a dog. Let them get a dose of that good-good really quick so it could stay on their minds all performance long.

NaeNae plotted, conniving on her devious plans of entrapment of some rapper's dick. She was going to be one of the sure chosen ones tonight by the rapper's security guards to come back to the trailer or hotel to party and play. So, it was a good thing Sirachi was acting a donkey, showing his bare-naked ass. She just didn't want him scummy drunk and done because she wasn't about to babysit his grown-ass all the way out in Cali or the A. If he got jacked by one of them groupies that was on him and what he got for slipping off his square and celebrating like it's New Year's in Times Square.

NaeNae felt like a goddess and the Queen Bee of the A. She had her hair freshly dipped an auburn electric red that Michelle did back home with a swoop and baby hairs gelled down in swirls. She had on a Michael Kors white mini-dress on with a V-shape cut out on the front and back with a sexy side split, and matching Michael Kors red heels and red tote bag. She was glowing and knew she was the shit and they couldn't outdo a real Atlanta bitch.

The DJ played all types of West Coast new shit nobody heard yet in ATL. He was spinning and scratching, mixing it up on the ones and twos, getting the crowd pumped.

He shouted into the mic, "Are you ready to turn up? Who they came to see?"

The crowd erupted with screams.

He wound the crowd up more and then he shouted, "Welcome Sirachi from ATL with his hit single 'Tropicana,' the first opening act to warm it up in 10 minutes."

* * *

Tasha's BFF Tina heard the DJ screaming thru the parking lot. Of course, she had found some San Bernardino ballers to trick off and ride shotgun with all the way up to Coachella and had brought her backstage passes, too.

They were sitting in the baller's teal Lexus truck on 24-inch rims, drinking, smoking, and touching. Tina got very loose off that Goose with her drunk pussy. She already got flipped once at her hotel by an LA young team, and had a few cats in and out as if she was really getting paid. And all times she was very bubbly and belligerent. She'd been sucking on a bottle every day since she had arrived in LA.

Tina got out in a pink slutty skirt that really looked like a shirt, like she had on a small pink wife-beater that she kept pulling down every few steps she walked. She had started off with a G-string but it got lost somewhere in the teal Lexus truck. She had on some ho 8-inch black gladiator heels with pussy pink bottoms. She had helluva guys doing catcalls her way. She smirked devilishly and waved them off, bubbly as her ass switched and hips twisted left to right.

Teasing Tasha couldn't believe her BFF Tina came up in here with an entourage or squad, whatever the fuck she thought it was, but Tina was trippin' and drunk already, and probably got run thru like a track meet. And WTF was she wearing, OMG! Does she have a pimp? Was she really selling pussy now and turned up and out? Tasha felt helpless and wanted to help her BFF out, even though they had fallen out on non-talking terms. And Tina couldn't have that swap-meet slutty skirt picked out weeks ago from Chicago, especially with all them pretty outfits on her Snaps. Even though Tina's drunk ass was giving Tasha the stink face emoji stare, she didn't care and knew she was bubbly. She wanted to go grab her by the hand and tell her, bitch, come on—you trippin' and slippin'.

* * *

NaeNae pushed Sirachi towards the stage passageway after dusting him off and fixing his clothes and wiping his sweaty forehead with a few baby wipes.

"Sirachi, focus and go kill 'em, Daddy—ATL style," she said as she pecked his lips.

Sirachi took a deep breath and beat on his chest like King Kong and did the Lebron James ritual, pushing both hands down towards the ground with knee raises, just like he won his third championship ring and brought the title back to the A instead of Cleveland. He was bubbly, too, really faded but still could walk and talk.

"Aye-Aye!! Turn up-up! Y'all lit? Let's go! Sirachi A-Town in dis bitch, shawty—Aye…Turn my shit up, DJ. Coachella—LA—The Bay! Y'all ready? C'mon!" Sirachi said, bouncing on his tippy-toes, straining his voice hard, pumped up.

Everyone was looking at him like, who is this country Atlanta light-skinned nigga?

"Aye…Aye…My Bitch Tropicana! I said My Bitch Tropicana…pussy strawberry…juices taste cherry…My diamonds Canary…Chevy outside jelly…" Sirachi spit his verse, pausing briefly in-between bars with a slurred tempo. The crowd just thought it was his country Southern accent. NaeNae knew better, though.

Sirachi could see Atlanta was in the house, probably from all the free V 103 FM ticket winners. They were singing along, turnt up. And even though the crowd didn't know his song or lyrics, ATL ratchets made him feel the love and support to boost his confidence. They were lit to the max.

The rest of the crowd was bopping their heads to the hot beat but was ready for the real concert to start. Some were even on their phones. Sirachi didn't need them to respect or honor his song. They thought he was just another typical rapper out of Atlanta, but just with a T.I. sound like he grew up listening to TIP.

Sirachi finished his performance, the last man standing, no back-up singers, dancers or pyrotechnics, just some sound effects from the DJ. As his song was fading out, he started doing that new running man dance, popping his collar again, sticking out his tongue like a dog. Then busted out in the whip and NaeNae! The crowd was cheering him on, saying, Go head! NaeNae just busted out laughing as she recorded her Daddy Sirachi's whole performance on her phone.

The music stopped and Sirachi started talking, doing shout-outs, and suddenly Nae heard someone singing a cappella with a Drake tone and turned straight around. It was Sirachi. He really had the crowd's attention now. And after the Twins heard he really had vocals, they leaned back and let him finish to kill some time. None of the rappers performing tonight were ready and Future hadn't even shown up yet. He was stuck in traffic, he claimed, for the past two hours now. And the place was lit!

Sirachi's vocals silenced the whole crowd as they were all recording on their phones and e-devices.

"I'm in love wit a thot…and I know dat she hot…She twerking it slow…and she twerking it soft…and she twerking on the pole…and she ready to go…Girl, you know I'm trying to go!" Sirachi mastered a Drake tone as he repeated the hook twice, melting them hot panties and splashing the girls' honeypot that didn't have any on. Then he did a mic drop and a church-style two-step off stage like if he was stepping side to side up to the pulpit to get baptized. NaeNae met his drunk ass with towels and bottled water because she knew them pills would dehydrate you quick in that Cali heat.

* * *

Next opening act was Denver JD! Teasing Tasha heard that and almost choked on her drink! OMG! Bloodshot redness to her eyes as she despised. She ran up to see if it was really him and of course she saw that same ugly butchy nose as his Dad's. Ugh, her vibe was killed!

Denver JD had on Versace-Versace-Versace! He had his Versace silk shirt open, showing off his tatted chest and stomach and his Medusa head belt. He looked like a Migos reject. He knew he was supposed to be the opening act for the concert, but they put some local joker from ATL named Sirachi. Denver JD had radio spins all thru the West Coast, so most of the crowd knew his singles.

Teasing Tasha sat there still in disgust. She said he sounded like a fake O.T. Genasis and bit his style. She was hating. Denver JD swore he saw that bitch from Snapchat, that rat who shit all over his Pop's chest. He was trippin as he did a double-take. Lost in the sea of women, she was gone. He performed his two hit songs and was gone, too. The crowd was moved more by him than Sirachi strip club banger.

After the trio girl group from the Bay finished, Kevin Gates was first up for bat. NaeNae made sure she found a way to throw herself in his way soon as he was going to the stage.

"Damn, excuse me, baby girl. I see you looking righteous in dat red hair and matching skirt. I'm 'bout to go perform and get dis whole place lit, ya heard?" Kevin Gates said, high as hell and smelt like kush and cologne. NaeNae was flattered as he went to grab the mic.

"I got two phones! One for the plug, one for the hos—I got two phones!" Kevin Gates sang and the thots went berserk and flashing him or snapping pics and recording live.

* * *

Slutty Shelly posted up by the bar area as Denver JD sat on the stool next to her. He spoke to her and they made small talk, that was until he saw Teasing Tasha come walking up.

"Hey there, Mr. JD, Jr. himself. What's really, really good, nigga? I say we stop all the beefing and fuck and get it over with, huh?" Tasha said as she heard the crowd lit from Kevin Gates' next single, "Really, Really."

"Hell, yeah, I was thinking the same thing and we just started off on the wrong foot. You look way better in person anyways, I must say. Damn. Besides, I ain't mad, cuz I put you on blast first. But damn, you stoop too low on that one, tho...shit?" Denver JD snapped back, trying to hide his ulterior motive of wanting to take her to the hotel and fuck her off, too.

Tasha already saw him coming into the lounge and went deeper backstage, checking around and all the bathrooms until she found exactly what she needed, and would use it when the time was right. Little did Denver JD know he may not make it back to the hotel.

* * *

Nasty Neesha knew where Future was posted because of his entourage crowding outside his door and running in and out. She may have been big, but she was swift on her toes. She busted the ultimate move and strode right into his backstage trailer.

It got quiet as everyone turned and stared at Neesha. She saw Future look dead at her and frown awkwardly.

Really? WTF? he was saying in his head as he looked at her bright-lime green Kylie Jenner lipstick. She looked like a pig in a wig for real.

Neesha froze and couldn't utter a single sound from the lump in her throat. That was obvious. Feeling like the elephant, she put her head down, chin resting on her chest. She was crushed, heartbroken. Maybe she was living a lie and would never be as beautiful and curvy as Beyoncé after all. She felt very low and ugly. She retreated from the room and darted out the door and down hallway.

Future's entourage said, "WTF was that?" as they all started passing blunts and continuing their session before his performance.

* * *

NaeNae heard everyone turnt up and lit to Future onstage performing his Dirty Sprite 2 tracks, and saw Sirachi occupied bouncing and spitting the lyrics with Future backstage behind the lines where the crowd couldn't see him. So, she busted her move and dashed off to 2-Chainz's trailer. She was about to try and get some sausage quick.

Nae eased the door open slowly and snuck in. She was relieved she was in, and finally shook Sirachi faded ass! She was ready to bust it wide open.

She was inside for a few minutes unnoticed. Then, 2-Chainz was the first to notice her. He started asking his partners if that was their thot.

"Who thot is dis? Dis y'all thot? Umh—turn around… now walk out dat door!" 2Chainz said quick and slick as he made her about-face military style.

NaeNae was happy 2-Chainz noticed her and spoke to her directly and didn't even mind being called a thot. But soon as he told her to turn around, she thought he wanted to check her ass out until he kicked her out and made her bounce like "bye Felicia." She was pissed and slammed the door on her way out.

* * *

Sirachi was taking pics with Fetty Wap before he went on live. Slutty Shelly seized the opportunity to make a helluva first impression as she warmed her leg up, then walked over there to get a selfie. She waited for him in that same spot until he finished his stage set. However, he never came back that way. She was pissed and went back towards the lounge.

Teasing Tasha finally caught Denver JD slipping and spiked his drink with Benzene, a clear flammable poisonous liquid used as a solvent in plastic, etc. She found it backstage in a chemical closet, then poured it in his drink like it was straight alcohol. She was swift, then dipped to the opposite side of the room.

Slutty Shelly came right back next to Denver JD as he killed the rest of his drink, which burnt extra harsh and felt queasy. All the thots were in one room: Teasing Tasha, Nasty Neesha, Slutty Shelly, and the Notorious NaeNae. All of them were at work on the prowl, but all so far had failed and were all treated like hot thots!

There was a commotion by the ladies' room by the lounge. The line was held up and girls were talking smack, getting real greasy because they had to pee and fix their make-up and weave! Then NaeNae saw two guys come out the ladies' room, zipping and adjusting their pants. She looked around for Sirachi but didn't see him, then jumped up and headed towards the ladies' room.

"Oh, hell nawh! Some bitch getting flipped or turnt-out? Either way, Sirachi better not be his ass in there in line, disrespecting me like dat! Especially after the humiliation 2-Chainz put a bitch thru and his lil partner recording clown!" NaeNae said, lit as she stormed to the bathroom, pushing bitches out the way rude, saying, move! Like she was back in Atlanta!

Teasing Tasha was ear-hustling and overheard NaeNae's tipsy rants. She wanted to be nosy, too. She got up and walked past the bathroom and saw a group of 5-6 guys and some with their meat all jacked up in their hands and a caramel pair of legs sprawled out. Once she sat back down, she said, Umh…and shook her head. Then it dawned on her as she scanned the damn lounge, Where the F is Tina? Oh Lord, she thought and ran towards the bathroom, right past NaeNae. Sirachi was coming from another area.

"Oh, fuck nawh, Jo! Dats my sis and y'all taking advantage of her in the ladies' room. She obviously drunk as fuck! Move, nigga! Watch out, dude! I swear I'll mace all y'all muthafuckas! Tina bitch, look at you! And they recording ya drunk ass sucking dick and getting flip like a bust-down ho? Let's go, bitch!" Tasha spit with venom, glowing from light bright to dark red.

"Fuck dat—she grown as hell and ain't nobody rapist here. She going! Ain't dat right, Tina? Huh? Tell who you came with and leaving with, huh? Matter of fact, come on, bitch, get ya shit. Let's go back to San Bernardino, ho? C'mon!" the pudgy baller snapped back viciously.

"S-Sorry, Tasha, but I'm out here kicking it with them, and it's coo, I ain't drunk, just tipsy a bit. They my Cali boys," Tina said bubbly, bashfully looking down at the ground and for her skimpy miniskirt, butt naked in her 8-inch ho heels. Cats were exiting the bathroom as NaeNae and Sirachi walked in.

"Sup, is you good, girl? Or what! I got cha back faded how we do in the A!" NaeNae told Tasha.

"Nawh, I'm good, girl, just trying to get my dumb drunk BFF from ruining her career! And out of here!" Tasha yelled back but directing it towards Tina.

"What's happening, partner? Dis Sirachi Bankhead. I'm from them Holmes, known as dem Jetz and Bricks homeboy! So, we got a problem, huh? We could fade, shoot it out, or walk it out? On da projetz, homeboy, however you want it, you can get it, cuz I'ma bring it, partner! Dis shit rape! Y'all wouldn't make it in da Feds or Penn period, punk!" Sirachi said, turnt-up, bubbly, stepping into every dude's face in that semi-circle left. They threw their hands up and smirked, nodding their heads, telling him fuck that thot anyway!

Tasha thanked them and ran over to take Tina water and pink wet-up mini-skirt that was skeeted on all over. Tasha wanted to put her in an Uber and make sure she got straight to her hotel room safe.

NaeNae began to hit on Tasha fine sexy ass just to try her luck. Nae knew she was out there and backstage being a groupie or hot thot like her, too, and most likely straight and not down for a ménage or to suck pussy. She gave towels to Tasha and wiped her forehead and patted her side with one towel.

"Girl, you sweating like crazy all turnt-up! You very pretty, all y'all LA girls is. What's good for tonight, tho?" Nae said as she wiped her soft sexually with a sinister look in her face.

"I'm the one and only from Triple B's in Chicago, Tasha! But I don't know nothing bout LA either or where the afterparty. I heard a club on Sunset, then Future's afterparty in Calabasas?" Tasha replied, not getting NaeNae's hint. She was too busy staring at Denver JD to see if the poison reaction took effect in his bloodstream yet?

"And I'm NaeNae from the A! It's nice to meet you…Tasha, if you don't mind you can come kick it with us tonight, too. I could tell you ain't into girls, but you ever been with a girl before? Like got down or been curious—ever? Cuz me and my man trying to experience and have some fun. I told him I'm down so I guess I got to own it now, and you're very bad and sexy as fuck. I'll lick all dat pussy and ass right if you 'bout dat life right now—cuz I am," NaeNae seduced Tasha with her lesbo web of game.

"Damn, to be honest I don't even like dick like that, I mean I do but it's complicated…like I can't take too much of it, unlike most girls that can't get enuff! But yeah, I've been curious and wanted to let her, my BFF, get down on me. They say she eat pussy good as fuck! But only when I'm super high and horny. I guess I can be open maybe. It depends on the night how it play out. But if so I'm coo on ya dude, Jo! And I ain't tasting no kitty kat but you can eat mines for the first time, we'll see my mood," Tasha said in a devious tone.

"Well, shit, girl, I'm wit dat straight-up. And I respect that. Ur super bad, girl. Of course, we can get it poppin, no doubt! And my niggah da one that opened up doing that singing at the end of his 'Tropicana' single. He cool, tho. But c'mon! Let's blow dis joint. It's hot and stuffy and I'm tired of lookin' at all these hot thots and funny-looking squirrel groupies—Sirachi, you ready, Daddy? Tasha from Chicago gonna ride wit us for da night, OK? So, Tasha, wassup, girl?" NaeNae said slick, trying to close the deal and snatch Tasha up and run off.

Teasing Tasha saw Denver JD's eyes started twitching and rolling in the back of his head as his body began to seize.

She turned back over to NaeNae and said, "C'mon— I'm ready! But we gotta take my BFF Tina with us and drop her off at my hotel so she can rest and sober all the way up.

I can't let her go back to her hotel cuz them low-life niggas know where her room is and may double-back and having her doing Lord knows what."

"OK, c'mon, y'all, let's go…Uhh, Tina girl, you wake-up, Miss Blame-it-on-the-alcohol! Daddy, c'mon!" NaeNae replied right as Denver JD busted his head on the floor. It was a big thud. Slutty Shelly screamed, then quickly lifted his head and rolled him sideways. He started to foam. It wasn't an ordinary seizure.

Hitachi Choparazzi

Chapter 8
"Hot Thots"

Denver JD sat in ICU in a coma. They were still flushing his system out, but he was alive. Slutty Shelly stood by his side from calling 911 and security to riding in the ambulance with him. Besides Denver JD's manager and 2 cousins that flew out to Coachella with him, everyone thought she was his date and didn't bother the white girl. It was 3 a.m. and she sat weary at his bedside with red eyes. She still couldn't believe someone would poison him. Who could be that evil? She was done with Cali after this episode. At least in Seattle she didn't have to put up with treachery like that. She passed out around 4 a.m.

* * *

Meanwhile, NaeNae, Sirachi, Tasha, and Tina were all still together. They had been partying thru LA and left Tina passed out in the rental backseat. She threw up twice all over herself. They pulled up at Tasha's hotel to drop them both off. She had Sirachi carry Tina's stinking drunk ass to her suite, then rode out with him and NaeNae to their telly. She was with it. And she did take a liking to Sirachi, too. He had a face tatt and a gold grill with sexy chocolate diamonds in them. She may let him play with the pussy, too. Besides, she was feeling good off the two pills NaeNae slid her. NaeNae claimed they were both some perks but she thought at least one was X because she was super wet and even started being attracted to NaeNae more. NaeNae started kissing all on her lips. First, it started with a peck on her lips. Then Nae would kiss all in her ears and on her neck, and slid her fingers in between her legs, then pulled them out and sucked on them. Tasha was mainly surprised how freaky NaeNae turned her out, too. NaeNae played with herself, then put her fingers in Tasha's mouth. And she started sucking Nae's fingers back, too, tasting pussy for the first time herself, and she liked it.

The good part about it was the fact Sirachi didn't intervene or throw himself all at her or on her like a horny dog, like some of them Chicago hounds, which really made her more comfortable and with it. She trusted Sirachi wouldn't take advantage of her and forcing all that "D" in her.

NaeNae had Sirachi break down the blunt as she broke down the buds and laced it with sprinkles of Molly. She wanted to get this bad bitch Tasha loose. She felt Tasha's wet, warm, tight pussy. Then Tasha told them she was a mixed breed of Puerto Rican and Jamaican. Nae was just like a nigga when it came down to hos. She had to have them under her belt. She was about to catch a body tonight, like Dreezy say, because Tasha was going to get wet up. Nae couldn't wait to rub her swelt-up clit against Tasha's and grind her phat pussy all up and down Tasha's hot wet twat. That shit turned her on so damn much she couldn't explain it. She would just tell Sirachi it was way better than any pill and just enhanced her sex drive and made sex fun. Sex wasn't meant to be the same, she'd always say to Sirachi, who didn't dare to disagree with her being bisexual. He agreed long as she shared with him. She couldn't agree more. And they wore that title around Atlanta, the ménage king and queen.

Teasing Tasha hit the laced Molly blunt twice and was

zooted for five minutes straight. She was stuck high all the way up like Fat Joe and Remy Ma! After she began to gain control back of her senses, the blunt was gone and NaeNae and Sirachi was already going at it. She wanted to play, too, but couldn't move, glued to the hotel chair.

NaeNae's pussy fluttered and asshole twitched at the same time, yearning for Sirachi and the anticipation. She loved when he got this bubbly and freaky as he tongue-kissed her nasty and sloppy. She couldn't go without "P" or "D," period. She was really bi and needed both daily. A fine balance but a double daily dose.

Sirachi knew with NaeNae what he was getting—wet, wild, freaky, and kinky hot sex, especially off a Blue Boy and perk 30. So, he'd say fuck a new bitch if he didn't know what she was working with. He wasn't paying Teasing Tasha no attention and was too busy with Nae.

When Nae and Sirachi did their drunken love, it was like 2 famous porn stars, the elite THOT King and Queen. They got super nasty and triple X-rated, too much!

Teasing Tasha was turned on and wet as fuck listening to NaeNae's sexy ass moan as Sirachi put his tongue game down. He had his face buried all in her ass like an ostrich. Then Sirachi told her to come lay down so Nae could eat her pussy out softly, which his demand and words turned her on. She believed she was ready to experience and cum on another girl's tongue.

Tasha laid on the bed and straddled Nae's face, then began sucking her teeth as if she was sliding into a cold swimming pool. She inhaled shallowly and let out a faint moan at first until she couldn't hold back despite how much she tried to hide it. NaeNae ate pussy better than any nigga ever! Then NaeNae would work her fingers on her clit and flicking her tongue rings around the rim of her booty, which made Tasha creme and scream Yasss! Tasha called them buttgasms, making her cum by manipulating her nerve endings in her butt. She was such a raunchy little slut. She caressed Nae's good grade of silky soft baby hairs on the nape of her neck.

NaeNae started moaning and breathing hard on her pussy. Sirachi started working her asshole with his thumb. He loved how pretty Nae's asshole was bleached and how wet it got like the pussy. NaeNae believed getting banged in her back door was all part of sex and getting dicked down good. However, she would only let Sirachi go anal on her because that was her way of having some type of morality. She had to set some type of standards to shield her cheating guilt. So, her ass was sacred and off limits to the passing public.

Sirachi would ease in slowly and out with a fast stroking pace while reaching around, rubbing the mess out of Nae's clit. NaeNae came and caused Tasha to crème and Sirachi, too. It was a chain knee-jerk reaction. They all fell like some dominos. Sirachi flowed all in her butt as she collapsed from her convulsion spaghetti legs. She felt like that Drake song "Controller."

Sirachi's dick was Arm-and-Hammer strong and long from that Blue Boy pill. He felt like the damn Energizer bunny, but NaeNae was panting like a bulldog and he knew every time he went anal how she would tap out and either run to the bathroom and sit on the toilet, or lay on the bed rocking back-and-forth holding her stomach, just like she was doing now.

"Oh shittt…Daddy…I'm gonna need a break for a few and I'm rolling too hard, super hard. My head spinning, get me some water, Pa, please…Daddy, go play with Tasha. That big thang still swollen. Damn!" NaeNae said, overwhelmed, out of breath.

Tasha looked at Sirachi and told him she couldn't

handle all that and would wake the hotel up, and Hell no! She said she would suck it, though. Sirachi told her don't trip. He'd be easy and was a vet. She just looked at NaeNae like she really was cool with her getting down with her man right in front of her. But for some strange reason this twisted behavior turned her on more. It was foreign to her, but made her compete, to try to show NaeNae up and teach her a lesson about sharing her man. In Chicago, they old heads say don't share your man. He may like it. Meaning ménage à trois were a dangerous game that could end in shame. However, Nae wasn't worried or insecure. She didn't see Tasha's hidden competitive agenda.

Teasing Tasha sat back as Sirachi ate her pussy and ass thoroughly like a vet and had her squirming and her toes curled. She nutted all over his gold teeth as he sucked them all over her pretty pussy.

Then he opened her legs into a banana split. He saw quick off the bat how she flinched and kept scooting back. She couldn't take no real dick! So, he would just only work his head in and out slowly until her screams idled into moans. It was just like tuning up a car. Sirachi was such an M-thot. He had run across a handful of bitches in ATL that couldn't take no real "D" either, and this was his way of breaking them in. But Tasha's pussy was really the truth and that thing felt like it was sucking on his dick from its pulling suction grips. And it was slippery wet and warm. She had that black gold between her legs.

Sirachi wanted to let out a manly moan, but knew Nae was watching. Or so he thought. NaeNae was curled up snoring. Even Tasha didn't know she passed out. Sirachi let out a few moans and skeeted super hard and fell onto Tasha. Tasha started kissing him and holding him like he was all hers, then asked him did he want to do it again, and was he ready? This time Sirachi needed a drink of water.

He hit it sideways and from the back. They went at it for an hour after Nae passed out. He was still slow-stroking with his head but had her cumming out of this world, scratching his back up, biting on his ears and down on his broad shoulders. A man never made her come with his "D," only his tongue. They went on a mini sex-a-thon.

Sirachi was woken up by getting his dick sucked. He looked up. It was Tasha. She signaled for him to hush.

"Shhh…sheesh! Don't kiss and tell… It's all good, I just wanted to thank you for doing me right and my body never felt like that. Them pills and dat stroke—OMG! You got the magic touch, Sirachi. No doubt. Now come on, get on the floor with me and get up in this wet pussy. I'ma show you how wet-wet Tasha-Fierce get in the morning and give you something to think about on ya flight to Atlanta…" Tasha said in a soft, slick, devious tone, cautious of NaeNae. What Tasha wants, Tasha gets. She always spoiled herself and Sirachi was her sweet treat. Now she really was about to fuck NaeNae's man and get her a last-minute taste before she flew back to Chicago. She made the duck face, puckering her lips, kissing on his dick while giving him direct eye contact.

Sirachi pushed her on the floor and they went at it for another whole hour all over the room and they ended up in the bathroom tub somehow.

Tasha started moaning loud, disrespecting NaeNae. She didn't care if she awoke or caught them. The dick made her switch that quick! She was gone…Sirachi had her dick dizzy for sure.

When they were thru they cut on the shower and washed up together. Nae could sleep thru a hurricane if Tasha's high moans and screaming orgasms didn't awake her. But then Tasha did forget the Ecstasy had the best of NaeNae, though. She was snoring hard like a drunk rock star.

As Teasing Tasha was getting dressed to leave, she

looked over at NaeNae knocked out, jealous. She got very envious over Sirachi. She wanted him to herself and knew Sirachi had the best of both worlds with Nae and wouldn't just leave Nae to be with one girl, especially one that couldn't take all the "D." And she knew they did this ménage game often, that Nae ran game on her and was more gay than bi.

Then she told him a guy never made her cum with his dick before, or took the time to learn and work her body. Never time out to just slow down and figure how her body works and how much "D" she could take. They were too busy trying to jam, stuff, and drill it in her because she was a bad bitch that won multiple twerk team awards online and at clubs. She always shut down amateur nights at strip clubs thru the Chi and Lake County, Indiana, too.

Then she handed Sirachi her phone and told him to put his number in there. And if he ever did a show in Chicago, he didn't have to worry about getting a room, but don't bring her, as she rolled her eyes at NaeNae sprawled out naked, slobbering all over the sheets.

Sirachi put his 770 number in there and his Snap and IG handles, too. He kissed her and smacked her on her ass as she walked to the door. She slammed the door behind her and NaeNae jumped up, eyes wide, looking around, startled. She was oblivious to what took place over the last 6 hours since she been knocked out. She told Sirachi to come back to bed and lay down with her then they'll go get something to eat at the McDonald's.

* * *

Teasing Tasha went into her hotel suite. It stank bad like foul throw-up and alcohol. She kicked Tina on the floor and told her BFF, "Get up—bitch!"

"Nooo—Damn…Tasha, WTF, Jo! I got a headache," Tina said as she sat up, groggy.

"Bitch, you banned from drinking, period! Them niggas was recording ya nasty drunk ass, too!" Tasha snapped, shaking her head.

"What? —What happened? I don't remember nothing last night. I didn't even see Future's performance or come out backstage," Tina replied, lost.

"Bitch, you got flipped in the ladies' room! Damn, you better get checked, too, cuz none of them had rubbers on. And get a Plan B pill," Tasha snapped again.

"Oh, hell nawh—I must have been drugged again in my drink—"

"Please, bitch, dat gets old. You need to own it. And lucky I was there to save you, cuz it was a football line in there, bitch!" Tasha cut Tina off.

"Oh, hold up, bitch…Hell nawh, Jo! Bitch—you been fucking, too, huh? I see the look on ya face. You got dat glow from the dick! That's dick intoxication from multiple nutting. OMG! Tasha, go look at ya face in the mirror. Look how low ya eyes is? Damn, bitch, don't tell me you got a rapper? Aw, who was it, Tash?" Tina said in awe as she stood up.

Teasing Tasha went to the bathroom and looked at her sex face and dreamy eyes and knew that her BFF was right, and was Sirachi's doing. He was the sex culprit behind her eyes. He all she could see and really had her world spinning dick dizzy. She told her BFF, "Yeah, it was a rapper from Atlanta," and Tina started screaming, going nuts, jumping on the bed, and started guessing who it was with that good dick.

"Future?!" Tina said, puzzled.

"Nope!" Tasha replied.

"2-Chainz?" Tina asked, curious.

"No, girl!" Tasha answered.

"What? Who then, bitch? You lying now!" Tina yelled.

"Sirachi! The nigga with the Gucci fisherman hat wit da grill and first opening act. And I did my first ménage, too! With dat bitch backstage with that dyed red-hot hair!" Tasha proclaimed with no shame in her game, her thoterism she gloated in.

"What! Dammmn—Bitch, you nasty! Tell me err thang, bitch...And did you eat her pussy, too? SMH! My BFF!" Tina said, ecstatic, and just like that they were back talking and attached at the hips. They never said sorry to each other or brought up the past. Typical Chicago hos. Tasha sparked the blunt and gave her BFF the whole rundown, even from Nae being asleep and eating her ass out swell.

* * *

NaeNae rolled over, trying to play. Sirachi had gone back to sleep. He was drained from Tasha's clingy horny ass. He tried to blow NaeNae right off. She told him that's the first as she took his dick out her mouth. He told her after he got some food and his system because the concert had him burnt. She told him, well, to get up and come on because she was wet as a puddle splash. They got dressed and went to the McDonald's.

NaeNae was mainly horny because their neighbor was having hot screaming sex again. Then right before they got dressed, big girl was getting hers. NaeNae could have sworn she saw her backstage last night, too. She couldn't hate on the big girl because she was getting hers more than NaeNae herself.

When they were walking down the hallway, their neighbor popped out, escorting some older white man.

Sirachi looked at Nae and told her, "That bitch selling pussy! She out of bounds, too. Straight up renegade!" NaeNae told him, please! knowing he wasn't a pimp.

Once Nasty Neesha escorted the trick to the elevator and he boarded it, she walked back to her room. Sirachi snapped his fingers like he was doing poetry downtown Atlanta at the coffee store. NaeNae told him about finger-snapping at thots. She shook her head and pulled Sirachi's arm down, praying he didn't ask her if she was DTH! He had been talking to Chop-Chop too damn much and really thought he had some pimp bones in his body, especially after he managed to get a few stacks out of hot thots successfully in the past by asking if they were DTH. Sirachi went straight into character, too…

"Say, bitch! You selling pussy without no pimp? You renegade ho! Put it in my hand or socket it to my pocket—like a rocket! God damn me," Sirachi demanded as he snatched off Nasty Neesha's blonde Beyoncé short bob wig and snatched her nappy new growth up by the roots.

"Ouch-ouch…Damn, fool, let go—let go of my hair, muthafucka! I don't pay no pimps! I'm I-N-D-E-P-E-N-D-E-N-T. Do you know what that means?" Neesha yelled.

"Shut up and break ya self, you renegade, and choose up! I'll take you back to Atlanta and really get us paid! Not ducking off in hotels all day!" Sirachi said slick and quick.

"Man, let me go! Get off me, dude! I ain't paying you shit—Fool! Let me go!" Neesha screamed, swinging at Sirachi.

"Sirachi, let her go before they call the police and have ya dumb ass in jail! Daddy, let her go and come on!" NaeNae intervened as she pulled Sirachi's hand off her back arms. She spit at Sirachi and he kicked her dead square in her ass as she tried to run. NaeNae was hot and left his dumb ass. He really was getting on her last nerves and being way disrespectful, trying to break a fat ho O.T. just acting up in LA. She was ready to go back to the A—ASAP, like Rocky.

Nasty Neesha stood her ground and went back into her room to get her gun. It was a 9mm she had registered. She never shot nobody, but if Sirachi tried to break her or break in her room, he was a dead dog! And she banged that on Blood.

* * *

Back at the hospital, Denver JD was out of ICU and they had successfully flushed the poison out of his system. He was now in the recovery and rehabilitation ward on the 5th floor, still comatose in a vegetable state.

Slutty Shelly still been at his bedside for the past 3 days now, alongside his Dad. His mama was there for one whole day and couldn't stand the sight of a lot of machine tubes down his throat and needles in his arms and hands. She kept saying that wasn't her baby! From his puffy face from the poison, under his eyes were purple like he got into a ring with Tyson.

Both his baby mamas showed up to check on him, just being nosy. And once they saw an older white girl by his bedside, they were hating in disgust. She looked like her peoples were rich and came from a long line of family-owned businesses and inheritance. He hadn't been with either one of his BMs sexually since he had been on traveling state-to-state, doing shows and making big doe. He would never know they had flown all the way out to Cali to check on him with hopes of being that first and only bitch at his bedside ride or die. They hated all the girls and groupies thoting around on his Instagram. And he had helluva Snapchat views, mainly females, too. They hated it.

Shelly kept making phone calls, checking on Jax and

making sure he didn't run out of food and water. She paid her 12-year-old neighbor to dog-sit for her. The only problem is she was supposed to be back home 3 whole days ago. Pre-teens get weary and restless, even though Jax wasn't a real burden and a trained dog. He wouldn't be in anybody's way, period.

On day five, Denver JD finally awoke in a groggy state. He was trying to pull the tubes out his mouth and arms. His Pops told him to relax and restrained him. Shelly ran to get the nurse. Denver JD didn't recognize his Pops because his vision was blurry, but knew his voice.

The nurse checked his vitals and then began taking the tube out of his mouth and the needles out of his arms, too. He took a long sip of the ice water, then talked in a raspy voice. He vaguely remembered anything. He definitely didn't know who the hell Shelly was. His Pops said she was his hero and the only reason he was alive, because she could have left him backstage to die. Especially after everyone broke once they called the police and security. Even the authorities questioned Shelly multiple times to see if she saw or heard anything, arguments or stalkers swapping drinks.

Shelly told him he was hospitalized at Cedars Sinai for the past 72 hours, and she was by his side the whole time, sleeping on the chair next to him and praying for him 24/7. She lied, saying they were kicking it backstage and had made after-party plans for the night.

Then it hit him—Tasha from Chicago! He just saw a picture of her face and that damn hot red hair! His blood pressure began to go back up. He couldn't believe she spiked his drink with a lethal dose! She really had fucked up! He was playing for keeps and put out a 30-rack bounty on her head for any of them young Chi-Raq wolves to trunk that bitch.

His Pops hugged him and told him he's got to be

more careful! He wanted to leave him and his acquaintance for some alone time. He called her JD, Jr.'s guardian angel.

There was an awkward silence between the two. Even though Denver JD didn't remember her and couldn't recall their initial encounter, he still wasn't trippin. He was enjoying her company. His BMs or no other bitches were there, especially when he felt that could have been him laying on his deathbed.

He made small talk and asked her name again. She told him Shelly from Seattle. Soon the nurse did her second rounds to check his vitals and told him they needed to keep him for observation for another 48 hours to make sure none of his organs failed. He felt fatigued but ready to go. He wanted to seek some vengeance on this Snapchat hood rat named Tasha. That's all he could think about.

Shelly asked him, "What's the matter?" And she saw the look written all over his face. He wasn't about to pillow talk with some snow bunny that saved his life.

Slutty Shelly started off getting him fresh water, then rubbing his feet and massaging his legs. He didn't mind at all and saw she was really digging him so he told her don't be shy. And that was all she needed to hear. She got the green light and unzipped his pants and started massaging his swollen manhood, then engulfing him all into her mouth.

Damn, slow down! This snow bunny vicious with good head! Denver JD said to himself. She was using both hands, one on the shaft and the other on his nuts, jerking, rubbing, and sucking with plenty of spit. He was fingering her from the front. She started talking on the dick, asking if he wanted to get nasty? And did he want to behave naughty in the hospital room? He whimpered um-hmm like a puppy as he nodded his head up and down. He couldn't talk. That's how good and vicious her head game really was.

She stood up and went to go secure the hospital room

door. She pulled her pants down below her ass cheeks and bent over, holding the chair next to the bed.

Denver JD rolled over on his side and had to twist his hips just for penetration. He was stroking her in an awkward position. He didn't feel comfortable and told her to just get into the bed and let him dig it out from the back. She was hesitant. He told her don't be shy and he wouldn't dog her. He was just hooked up to those monitors. He began to stroke it slowly, then picked up his pace. Only thing was her pants kept getting in the way. He snatched her hand out the way and yanked them down further. Suddenly, her leg popped out. *WTF?* He jumped worse than when he saw a rat. *This bitch really got one leg, and catfished me!* he thought.

Chapter 9
"Thievery"

Thievery was an art form. Some people felt like peeling isn't stealing if the other person is willing? However, the rare art form craft came in the mastery of conniving.

Teasing Tasha had been doing just that since Coachella. Back in Chicago, she had Sirachi on all social media platforms and would receive notifications whenever he logged on, Tweeted, posted, and Snapped.

She would mainly bust it open and send him her Snap videos. She would send him different Twerk Team videos of herself killing the real Twerk Team ladies. Sirachi even got off to a few of her explicit videos. Somehow, she even got his other 404 Atlanta number, too. She was trying to seduce him to her likeness in the Chi, but would he really bite the bait? And could she really compete with bi-sexual NaeNae? She wasn't 'bout that open relationship life. She wasn't down to share, even though she loved how NaeNae tasted her ass like ice cream and stuck her long flicking tongue in there, too.

Since Coachella Sirachi had 100,000 YouTube hits from his a cappella thot anthem he sung after his performance, which boosted his IG to over 100,000 followers. All straight Thots! He was heating up! You couldn't tell him nothing, especially NaeNae. He had been caught sending DMs to Panda Supreme, a super bad Instagram sensation whose body was on fleek! NaeNae scared her away quick with threatening messages warning her to stay away from her husband! Panda Supreme ignored Sirachi's DMs ever since. No reply!

Sirachi came back home and put a lump sum cash down payment to lease a fire red Ferrari for 36 months. He put $7,500 down and had monthly payments of $2,500 not including full-coverage insurance.

NaeNae was hot because she felt it was a backwards ass move, and a big waste of money, because he was only leasing it and would have to give it back. The only good thing was that he was building his credit.

She hated how now he was in quote-unquote Grind Mode. "You trap-trappin' script pills just to cover that damn Ferrari note trying to keep up with Kanye!" Sirachi was stunting and frontin around the A and pulling up in valet parking, he didn't care flat out about Nae bickering. It was his time to shine. And he been getting his Cali plug to ship that loud pack out there for the lo-low.

He had been playing along into Teasing Tasha's game, too. He slipped up off them pills and told her he loved her just like he did out of habit to NaeNae. She believed him and felt loved, especially not having love from a man after the loss of her father.

He didn't know he was leading Tasha on. He already told her it was just a lust thing and she was stuck, infatuated with him and his "D." She said so what and that's not it! Then she asked could she be his other bitch until he and NaeNae split? He told her hell yeah, she could be his social media sidepiece. She had NaeNae beat! She was a Tropicana for real. Nae was more a domestic Atlanta Tropicana redbone.

What he didn't know or see was Tasha's possessive Puerto Rican side and her crazy cut-throat Jamaican side. She smirked, knowing she had that nigga in her clutch and once he came to the Chi, he wouldn't be going back to the A or NaeNae. She was going to cook, trick on him some shoes and fits, and hook his ass quick! She would even get down with her nasty-ass BFF Tina and put on a helluva show if she had to, just to blow his mind and steal him from NaeNae at whatever price. Sirachi just looked at her as sweet eye candy and a bad bitch to creep with if she came to visit Atlanta.

NaeNae got the Hot Thot of the Year award and made a slot topic on TMZ! One of 2-Chainz's entourage released it online clowning and TMZ had their way with it. She got called a THOT and told to turn around and walk straight back out the way she came in.

After NaeNae's page on the Gram crashed that day and half ATL clowning her, she filed a petition against 2-Chainz to sue for defamation of character and asking for a settlement of $2.6 million after attorney fees.

This had made TMZ's Top 10 storylines and they wanted NaeNae to guest on their midday TMZ live show via Skype. She agreed to clear the air and defend her honor and reputation, too, which was shot.

Sirachi was trying to get the black guy, Van, to promote his Sirachi shirt with a hot sauce bottle and green lid. Sirachi even offered to pay him. Van declined him and his generous wages.

They went in live. NaeNae was down in her living room, showing off her Afrocentric elephants and black background. Harvey showed her video and then stated her allegations for viewers. He asked her don't she think $2.6 million is a bit much? She lied and told him it was because she lost her job.

Then Raquel jumped in, saying $2.6 million is far-fetched. And Van put his 2 cents in, asking her where did she work? NaeNae told them CNN. They all said Oh...Oh...in shock. Harvey sucked on his straw, looking down towards the ground.

NaeNae told them because of this, she couldn't get a

job nowhere around Atlanta and had to move to Minnesota, and told them if so, he would pay for all her expenses, too. Then said "Tru," mimicking 2-Chainz's ad-lib. They looked at NaeNae like she was another hot mess gold-digging groupie. All 2-Chainz did was call her a thot, which she was for sneaking in people's trailer. If NaeNae was lucky, she could get a small settlement to stop at the Gucci or jewelry store like 2-Chainz said he wanted to be buried in. That concluded their interview. She had her 15 seconds of fame and TMZ would mail her a small check.

That night NaeNae was annoyed once again by all the ugly social media haters. She was hot at her sister da white girl because she told her to be outside of Wal-Mart on time. She hated this East Point ratchet Wal-Mart, and told her sister stop having kids and get a damn car or a ride from one of them sorry-ass baby daddies.

She noticed an all-black late-model Impala creeping and peeping very slowly. She didn't even grab her gun, so thrown off balance with that TMZ scandal and social media. She hit Sirachi.

"Hello!" Sirachi answered, blown.

"Daddy—Sup? Where you at? Cuz I think some nigga's trying to liq me at the Wal-Mart on the East Side, waiting on da white girl. I'm 'bout to leave her ass, too. Oh, here she come now. OK, Daddy, come this way just in case they try to follow me, K? I love ya, Pa!" Nae said in a rush.

"I'm on my way, NaeNae. Don't trip. The Ferrari won't take long. I'll be there in 10! Luv ya, too, babe." *Click!* Sirachi replied as he passed the blunt to Big Tricky, his dogg. He told Big Tricky they had to go pull up on Nae because someone was trying to jack her for her 4's on the peach Malibu! Sirachi burnt rubber as he shifted gears all the way into 3rd gear darting down 285.

The Impala circled the lot and turned right back

around, unnoticed by NaeNae. She was too busy looking down at her phone in her lap, reading comments and shit people were posting about her.

Da white girl came out and jumped shotgun. She apologized to her sister and thanked her at the same time. She told NaeNae to blaze that weed up! Nae threw her the sack of loud and told her to roll up, still looking down, manipulating her screen for a second. NaeNae looked up, asked her sister if she was ready to go, and pulled the wood-grain knob shifter into drive. She turned her system up and, all of a sudden, her head smacked dead on the windshield and busted her lip on the Grant wood-grain steering wheel as she got rear-ended. She spit out blood from her bottom lip and said, "SHIT—WTF!" Da white girl was shaken up, but alright.

NaeNae went to open her Malibu Classic door and was snatched out by two guys wearing ski masks and dressed in all black. She saw death and had a terrified look in her eyes as she cried, looking back at her sister.

They dragged NaeNae to the Impala as she resisted and screaming for help! They told her to shut up and get into the trunk before they came down on her chin with the butt of the .357 Taurus, splitting her chin and sliding her unconscious. They trunked her and sped off, peeling out like it was stolen.

The white girl picked up Nae's phone and called Sirachi, then 911! Sirachi flipped out! It wasn't a jack boy. Nope! Someone jacked his bitch! He knew it was from a prior liq, too. He told NaeNae about robbing all these different ballers around ATL. Not all of them were suckas and tricks. Some would kill a bitch quick! He prayed that wasn't the case because couldn't no bitch alive take NaeNae place! Sheesh!

Sirachi pulled up and jumped out the Ferrari with his Sig .40 drawn. He didn't give a fuck! He rushed over to the white girl and asked, "Who was it? Did you see how many niggas it was? Which way they went?"

She told Sirachi they beat Nae with the gun and stuffed her in their trunk as she cried an Amazon river. Sirachi told Big Tricky get back in the whip and let's go get them choppas from ya crib! He wanted to smash out before the Atlanta PD nosey ass showed up asking a million questions and investigating everything and everybody else besides who they supposed to be and doing their damn job! Plus, he was riding dirty for real, pills, guns, and more drugs.

They rode around Atlanta till 4 a.m. looking for NaeNae and any all-black late model Impala. That night they didn't see one. They drank bottle after bottle of Henny. Sirachi felt no peace—no sleep! He didn't realize how much he loved that girl until she was gone.

Teasing Tasha been blowing both his phones up. She sent the eyes emoji, the zucchini emoji, then the 100 emoji. She really thought he was dissing her and said fuck her finally. She wasn't going and in one last desperate attempt, she recorded the nastiest freaky dancehall Caribbean-style twerking naked as she could, then sent it with all sad face and crying emojis, challenging him.

Sirachi finally texted her back, saying he couldn't talk and was going thru some real-life shit, and to please leave him alone until his mind was back right. However, he did comment on the nasty nude twerk Snap video. He told her she needed to be in LA—Hollywood Ace of Diamond and getting really paid instead of snowy Chicago! Of course, being a typical nosey female, Tasha tried to pry for what was going on with him down in ATL, but he never replied.

* * *

NaeNae's heart was beating super hard and was going stupid, full of distress and anxiety. She kept sliding from side-to-side from the crazy driver bending corners, then gas and hitting brakes. That lasted all of a rough 10 minutes, then the Impala came to a halting stop and then the trunk opened. She screamed again as the stock of the SKS hit her in the back of her head. NaeNae sighed out "Weezy" as she blacked out, again.

She woke up with a throbbing headache and she couldn't feel her legs. She looked around. It was pitch dark and cold from an outside breeze. She felt the duct tape over her mouth so she could not scream for help or talk. And she noticed she was laid flat on her stomach, hogtied with plastic sturdy zip ties. Fuck! This is the end...was all she thought. Then she smelt the strong urine odor, ugh! And realized it was her own piss. Oh, God please don't let me die like this, she prayed. She wasn't a spiritual person but that time she felt only God could take her out of these evil men's hands. She prayed for deliverance and mercy non-stop around the clock!

"Damn, big homie! Where you been at? It's been two hours since we snatched that bitch up for you! So, what's da bizz?" Lil Dirty asked, annoyed.

"Man, lil nigga, dis my spot and don't I let y'all clock out this bando? Huh? My million-dollar money make! Y'all could take y'all bad broke ass back down Lake? So, lean back. All y'all gotta do is dig the ditch in the woods first, then pop da bitch in the head and before y'all bury da bitch—let me piss on the lil thieving bitch! Bet dat? It's about time I caught this ho! It's been damn near two years now...but I got y'all as promised. Here is a quarter chicken. And y'all could continue to trap out dis bando. Luv y'all lil niggas... and Lil Dirty, buy you some shoes, boy, and fix dem damn dreads up, boy!" Ant-Loc said in a demanding vicious tone, scaring NaeNae to pee on herself again, this time while she was awake. She jumped when he slammed the door and left.

Damn it! She couldn't believe it, it was a certain death sentence! Unavoidable, too. She knew both of them from Decatur. It was Lil Dirty who was a jack boy and would do a few liqz for her, too, back then. Then his big homie from the projects, Ant-Loc black ass. She fucked AntLoc and robbed his ass for 27 bands and some powder and zips of hard. She didn't know nothing about dope and she hit him for 54 ounces total, liq'd him for a birdie and a half.

She gave the dope to Sirachi and even paid for him to get his grill and chocolate diamond slugged up! Now look. Sirachi wasn't nowhere in sight to save his bitch, who was about to get shot in her head and buried in the damn woods in a shallow ditch with leaves covered all over it. She knew a damn dog would probably find her body in the late fall, but she knew Sirachi would tear ATL up for her and looking for her, too. It was just too late. And she blamed herself for not bringing her gun, too. She would've let that thang go off! And murked Lil Dirty soon as he ran up, especially as high as she was, sitting very tall in the BU on 4's.

She knew she was in a bando trap spot from all the smokers and traffic coming in-and-out non-stop. Plus, she heard Ant-Loc saying it was a million-dollar spot. They had her in the cold attic. Her whole body felt numb and feet and legs were tingling. Her body started shaking, then she fell unconscious again. NaeNae was done with money and a sitting dead duck in water. Time wasn't on her side at all.

The sun came up in the A, and Sirachi sat up and watched it as tears flowed down his cheeks. He wasn't scared to cry around his dogg Big Tricky. Besides, it looked like Big Tricky teddy bear ass had watery red eyes himself. They both were drunk anyway.

Sirachi just knew she was gone! If he could've been

there a few minutes earlier when she first hit him, he would let that Sig bark and spark up the parking lot and Wal-Mart! *Why she didn't have her pistol? But always getting on him for not having his, skating around the A all day.* He shook his head. He knew in Atlanta if they could pay a quarter brick of hard to get you murked, then a whole brick would get you chopped up and buried! He didn't know what liq it was from or who she liq'd lately. NaeNae was so damn sneaky he had to watch her and check her ass being slick and shit. He sighed and told Big Tricky let's go get another bottle cuz the liquor store's back open. He was so sick he couldn't even go up in NaeNae's room or be in their condo solo. Big Tricky kept him company.

The DEA was in full force this Tuesday morning. You know how the Hot Boys song goes—on Tuesday and Thursday you better watch for the sweep! Today they were hitting 4 different areas, all raids, warrants, and indictments, all Federal from their C.I.'s and snitches behind bars that couldn't do the time without bitches and blunts.

They hit an abandoned trap spot and discovered NaeNae's body. They didn't have no suspects responsible or at the spot at the time of the raid. Lil Dirty and his homeboy lucked up! They were busy in the woods digging ditches. The first one was too muddy, and a lot of tree roots. Plus, they were texting hos and smoking blunt after blunt till the sun came up on them slow playing.

When the firefighters arrived first on the scene, they told the DEA NaeNae had a faint pulse and was indeed alive. They cut her zip ties and put the oxygen mask on her and ran an IV thru her arms. The DEA thought she was D.O.A. Her body looked lifeless, plus all her blood was rushed down to her pinned-up body and slow in her head. Her face was all pale, too.

They rushed NaeNae to Grady Hospital, the same

one she was born at by downtown. Sirachi was riding slow in his cherry Ferrari when he got that call from da white girl saying they found Nae and she was at Grady.

Sirachi came back to life and sat up and flipped a bitch in the middle of a two-way intersection recklessly. He didn't give a fuck. He smashed to Grady and at some points hitting a buck in the Ferrari flying.

NaeNae was up but fatigued and drugged when Sirachi came in the room. He saw her all fucked up and asked who did this? Who? However, NaeNae just shook her head. She didn't tell the detectives or Sirachi shit either. She wanted to give Ant-Loc a pass in hopes he would just squash it, but she was going to Virginia to buy an AR-15 to keep in her trunk. She'd be damned if she got kidnapped or thrown in a trunk again! Her thievery days were done.

Chapter 10
"Thot Fights"

"Damn, bitch, you ain't been out nowhere since Mr. Sirachi and ya wild ménage! And look at you getting fat, bitch. Damn, go walk. Get some fresh air and some exercise, Jo! I swear, ugh…you dick dizzy! I don't see none of ya post, comments, or Snaps—no more! My BFF dick dizzy by a nigga all the way in Atlanta. Wow! SMH! I want my BFF back…And Tasha, you coming with me to the 95th block party, too. It's the last one of the summer. And you need to clean up, too. Tasha, WTF? What's da matter, geesh, with you, Jo? OMG!" Tina snapped, all bug-eyed wide, talking to a half-sleep Tasha in her stuffy hot apartment.

"Please, bitch, I'm just tired, and ain't nobody fat. I'm just thick, and you know where all my weight goes—to my ass, hips, and thighs, bitch! Like I said—thick! And you need to cut it—cut it, bitch! Ain't nobody sprung ova dat boy Sirachi, please," Tasha replied, wiping the sleep from her eyes and thinking about Sirachi, lying.

"What the fuck ever. C'mon, Tasha, get up and roll one, shit. I'm ready to smoke. I didn't get dropped off over here for this bullshit. I could've stayed laid up too, Jo," Tina said, annoyed as she frowned at her BFF Tasha.

Two months had flown by since the Coachella concert and Teasing Tasha was finally out and about with Tina around the Go once again. Tasha still had and got just a little thick in the ass, thighs, and hips. She still had thousands of views every Snap she took. Tina stopped on Peoria to get some money from a nigga, then on Wentworth, too. She was getting cashed out hustling cats. They went to the Mini-Mall on 63rd and Halsted, then to their favorite Evergreen Plaza shopping center. They were getting their outfits for the block party tonight. Plus, Chicago was getting a little bit nippy in September, all the wind coming off Lake Erie and down from Canada. Tasha already felt sick. She really wasn't feeling it, or no crowds and cats trying to fuck all on her. She was sick of Chicago and going to New York every summer just for the Puerto Rican Day Parade. Maybe ATL wasn't a bad move after all? And she would be closer to her fuck buddy Sirachi. They went to Tina's Pop's house to get dressed.

The 95th block party was deep as fuck, shoulder-to-shoulder packed. Bitches were already hating and staring hard at the Triple B's. They danced for a few songs and kept moving around thru the crowds.

Tasha's feet were already swollen from standing and dancing. Plus, the walking had her exhausted, she was tired of walking, too. Then the worst part was all the niggas in the crowd playing grab-and-go would grab their ass and take off. They basically were getting free feels. She wasn't feeling that at all. Tina kept telling her, "OK, two more songs and we can be gone, girl!"

Then Tasha and Tina ran across Pham, the girl from the hookah lounge who got her face slashed up by Tasha crazy ass. Tasha told Tina, there goes them Westside bitches again. Tasha wasn't in no damn fighting mode but she had her same exact wooden ratchet she cut their asses up with before. The rival girls stared hard like they had the sun in their eyes at night, but kept it pushing with smirks planted on their faces.

Tasha told Tina they better had kept it moving, and

they went back to walking thru the crowd and dancing to Chicago DJ's hottest mixtape bangers.

Pham, Shamika, and her cousin Fatima all circled back around the area where Tasha and Tina was dancing in.

"Tima, you still got ur gun, girl?" Pham asked with a stank face.

"You betta believe it, cuzzin," Fatima replied slick.

"Girl, let me see it? I'm 'bout to shoot this bitch right in her face for fucking mines up with all these ugly scars and shit...fo real, Jo," Pham said with vengeance.

"Here," Fatima said and handed her the .380 Beretta with a carbon pink handle.

Pham racked the slide of the gun as the hammer went back and crept unnoticed thru the swaying crowd with the gun waist-side. Fatima and her homegirl, Shamika, were right behind her. They wanted to see and be nosey. Plus, Shamika was the one stomping out Tina that night at the new hookah lounge off Lake Shore Drive. Tasha cut her up, too. Her scars weren't like Pham's, though. Pham looked like she had a Y-shape zipper on her face, ugly. She'd never be a wife.

Teasing Tasha couldn't understand why she was so damn cold and nipples been fully erect for the past 3 days and sore, too. She knew it was probably her period coming on. A juke song came on, "Watch my Feet," and cats started juking all crazy. She backed up. Tina drunk ass started trying to juke, too. Tasha shook her head.

" Tina, last song and I'm gone!"

Pham had the gun drawn high as hell as she got a few feet behind Tasha. Then she pointed at the back of Tasha's head and yanked.

Tasha turned around, ready to go—*Pow!* A single shot went off, missing Tasha by milliseconds and millimeters.

Tasha stood there in shock as the girl let off one more shot, pointing directly at her head—*POW!* Tasha flinched and saw Pham turn around and run. Tasha threw her hands up to her face with her jaw jacked wide open. She felt around for blood and a wound. Nothing! Her heart jumped out of her chest and adrenaline raced. The crowd scattered into a frenzy after that second shot. The first one wasn't really a scare over the loud music.

Tasha didn't want to turn around for the life of her. It took every ounce of energy in her body to turn around. She heard a body thump hard like a bowling ball on the street. She was praying it wasn't her BFF, Tina. However, she knew Tina was too quiet, and prayed she scrambled, too.

Tasha saw Tina's lifeless body sprawled out face first. She knew Tina was gone by how her body was folded into a scrunched-up position on her face and chin with her ass up a little as she was propped on her knees like she tried to catch herself and buckled as she dropped on her knees before dying.

Tasha turned Tina around and saw her looking directly at her with her eyes fully dilated. She saw the bullet exit wound out the brim part of her nose as blood leaked out and trickled out her nose and the back of her head.

Tasha closed Tina's eyes and cried her lungs out, holding her. Tina died on her feet, dancing to the beat. She never heard or saw the shot coming. It ripped thru her head viciously, striking her cerebral cortex, her circuit board of all her senses and operations, then bounced off her frontal lobe skull and exited thru her nose region.

Tasha just wanted to get the hell out of there. She was done with Chicago for real this time. She heard the police sirens in the distance and didn't have time for no Chicago first-48-type shit. She knew Tina's Dad would blame her for his daughter's death and demand answers or have her pushing up daisies, too. This was too much. Tasha tried to stand up and threw up twice.

"Damn it!" she said and shuffled to her feet and fled the scene, crying like a baby.

* * *

Sirachi had been just at home with NaeNae more for the past month, caring for and catering to her in a major way. She really hadn't been out the house too much since she got trunked up. He brought her a short-style AR-15 military edition that she rode around with it in her trunk or sometimes the backseat. She wasn't ever going again, and wouldn't even roll her neck or snap her fingers to the beat in her classics. She felt different, more real, more ready, and more jittery. If you thought she would shoot before, it was morphed times ten! It was the prime example of the victimizer becomes the vic and the prowler gets preyed on!

Sirachi's phone was going off—911 and ASAP text messages and voicemails. It was Tasha. He ignored her until NaeNae fell asleep.

"Hello, sup, Tasha? You Gucci, lil mah—"

"Hell–hell nawh! It's crazy. A bitch tried to kill me at the block party and missed me twice! I saw my life flash before my eyes! OMG—I'm scared, Sirachi! I need to come out there. I only got $640 dollars to my name…Could you help me out or what?" Teasing Tasha panicked and cut Sirachi off.

"Girl, you know dat's Chi-Raq where you live at! But I got you, tho. I'll find you a spot and will pay for a nice hotel—"

"Sirachi, remember my girl, Tina, the drunk one that got flipped? She got killed cuz of me. Now her family after me, too. I'm about to jump on the Greyhound, not a plane. I need to leave tonight!" Tasha panicked, again cutting him off.

"Damn, slo–slow down, Tash…" Sirachi said.

"Sirachi, shut up. Don't tell ME to slow down! You have no idea…And what took you so damn long to call me back, too, nigga? Oh, let me guess, NaeNae? And I've something to tell you too," Tasha said and paused.

"What?" Sirachi asked.

"You know ur the only nigga I been with since the concert, right?" Tasha replied.

"Yeah, OK—And?" Sirachi said, not believing a word or the drag she was putting in his ear.

"Well, when I was waiting for you to call me back and packing up all my good shit, I ran across a pregnancy test in my closet and decided to try it. I peed on both them sticks to double-check…and two lines popped up! I'm pregnant! And yes, I swear, it's yours, two months now. I've not had my period since. I'll give you a DNA test with no problems—and I'm having my baby no matter what! It's too much killing, dying, and not enough living," Tasha said in a sterner tone.

Sirachi was speechless. He didn't really believe this bitch, but what if it was really his? Was it possible? He was damaged and ruined by his crazy, local Cuban BM! And he would've had a sea of kids around Atlanta right now. He had strong doubts.

"H-Hello? Hello…Damn, Sirachi, like that, cat got your tongue PIMPIN'! Huh? Whatever, nigga, now I'll be to Atlanta in two days if I catch this 5 a.m. bus. You know the bus stop in every lil town on the map. So, you gonna pick me and ur child up on time, or what? Do you know where it is?" Tasha snapped.

"Yeah, I got cha; no, my mind was just wondering cuz I can't have kids from my accident, so I thought. But yeah, the bus terminal by the Fed building downtown. I know where it is. I try to stay away from both of 'em places, ya know. I got ya and hopefully will have a condo for you by then to stay in, K? Don't trip or stress, lil mah, I got cha. C'mon to the A, and make it safe. Kisses," Sirachi replied in a soft tone, still messed up in the head with reasonable doubt like the Jay-Z CD.

"OK, bye, I love you, Sirachi, and thanks for helping me out and starting over in a new city. Please, Sirachi, keep your phone on and don't put my text messages on red either, fool!" Tasha snapped back.

"OK, I got cha, baby. Be safe!" Sirachi clicked.

* * *

Pham couldn't believe she missed that bitch! But when she found out she killed another girl, she was shocked. Once they showed Tina's face all over the news, she knew it was Tasha's BFF, so she didn't feel too bad and remorse. She tried to hand her cousin Fatima back her gun. Fatima told her hell nawh! They threw it in Lake Michigan and took Pham to hide out in Indiana 'til the heat died down. They thought for sure Tasha would snitch because she was a bitch, traumatized.

Teasing Tasha made it safely to Atlanta, but waited at the downtown bus terminal for 2 hours. Sirachi was super late and she didn't have nobody else to call or place to go. She didn't even know her way around town yet. Sirachi had the nerve to pull up in a Ferrari! At least her baby daddy was a rapper with money. Sirachi was feeling all on her, talking about how thick she had gotten!

They had sex every day and she didn't realize how much she needed it and how better it felt now that she was pregnant and got that much wetter. Sirachi would rub her little knot forming in her womb. She kept telling him she going to name this baby Miracle because he really got her pregnant and she dodged 2 bullets zipping past her head. The baby was probably meant to change the world or be President or something.

Sirachi had been chauffeuring Tasha around in his foreign for the past few days, cup caking like a mug. He took her sightseeing, shopping, and buying stuff for their new spot. She knew he was staying with NaeNae still, but things would change once the baby came. And she kept asking Sirachi did he break the news to his wifey Nae about her being pregnant and bearing his child, with emphasis. He kept telling her of course and yeah, baby, but she knew his high-yellow freckle-face ass was lying thru them damn gold teeth.

Right now, they were coming from meeting his beautiful Aunt Cheryl. She had another condo over in College Park for $1,100 a month, but since Tasha claimed to be pregnant with his seed, they agreed on $900 a month. No deposit needed or a credit check. Sirachi had his Aunt waive the first month fee, but told Tasha he cashed her out the first $900. Next month was on her and she should be working by then. Tasha just looked at him like *Whatever, and she not working!*

NaeNae was rushing back to Riverdale to meet up with Michelle for her hair appointment. It had been a minute since Michelle did her hair over at her house since they got busted playing around by Sirachi.

NaeNae was in her same peach of the freak Malibu on 24's, the one she got abducted from. She had been very agile and vigilant lately. That's when she spotted Sirachi's Ferrari.

At first, she just looked over there and hit the blunt of loud, knowing he was out trappin' a thousand pills by the boat straight pushing, until she saw a bitch ducked off all low, leaning all up on Sirachi's side. He could barely shift how she was all up on him, and it looked like she was either rubbing his legs or jacking his dick. She knew he was always doing wrong when he didn't even notice her at the same light in the opposite direction corner.

When her light turned green, she hit the gas and got a closer look. It was Tasha from Chicago! That's why his ass been acting super paranoid and funny lately, hiding both his phones, which was real weird. That bitch Tasha was in town creeping with her hubby. She knew that bitch plotted once she fell asleep that night. Ugh! And she caught that nasty-ass Snap video with all them emojis of rain and waterfalls caption as she played with it, squirting all over her bedsheets. She just never told Sirachi she was snooping thru his phone and caught them because Tasha was all the way out in Chicago and no factor or real threat. Now she was in NaeNae's backyard with her man.

NaeNae and Tasha were two alpha females that wouldn't ever get along and be under one roof, because both their personalities were too strong.

NaeNae said, "Fuck this!"

She was about to scare that bitch off for good and didn't care about Sirachi dumb ass well-being or Ferrari at the moment. She stuck her wrist out the window and gathered her grip and let her Glock rip as she squeezed endlessly.

Bloch! B-Bloch! Bloch-Bloch-Bloch! Bloch-Bloch!

Teasing Tasha flinched while Sirachi froze up like a little bitch. She watched him damn near dive under the steering wheel of the foreign, trying to get low. It wasn't much of space to take refuge in. They felt the slugs cutting thru the Ferrari and shattering glass. They came so fast and rapid. It was over in a flash.

Teasing Tasha was shaking her head at Sirachi scary ass, and he had a gun on him and didn't even shoot back! In Chicago, 15 people on average a day were getting shot, every weekend over 60 people. She was living in a rival war zone Iraq-style at home, but she would be damned if she came to Atlanta for the same thing. This was the second time she got shot at in the past five days now.

"Dodging bullets, this baby must be very special or a damn angel," Tasha told Sirachi.

Sirachi got out and looked at his riddled Swiss Cheese Ferrari and shook his head. He wanted to shed a thug tear. He placed his hand on his head and yelled out "Fuck!" and told Tasha welcome to hating-ass ATL!

"It was a light-skinned nigga in a pink old-school 2-door with big wheels—," she started.

"What? Wait—was it pussy hot pink? Like a Pepto Bismol color?" Sirachi snapped.

"Yep-Yup!! You know him?" Tasha replied.

"Him—Dat was nobody but NaeNae! Dat bitch busted at me before! I'm 'bout to go choke dat ignorant bitch out. And she ate up my foreign whip and shit," Sirachi said in a menacing tone as he popped the clutch and hit the gas, fleeing the scene.

"Nigga, fuck this car, Jo! Your child, Sirachi? You still don't believe me, huh? I am pregnant and it's ya baby… You—are da father, fool! She could've killed us and ya baby and all you worrying about is an imported Italian car in Atlanta instead of ya baby! OMG! Sirachi, you got issues, ugh," Tasha snapped with flaring emotions.

Sirachi just sucked his teeth and blew her off. He was too busy speeding thru traffic and cutting thru neighborhoods.

* * *

Michelle parked idled in front of their condo when NaeNae pulled up. She noticed NaeNae had a guiltless look planted on her face and was fidgety. Suddenly, Sirachi came screeching around the corner and punching down Woodlake Drive.

NaeNae tried to run up the stairs into the house. Sirachi jumped out on her bumper and snatched her up quick-fast.

"Bitch—You got me fucked up! And you know Tasha pregnant and you wet up the whip! You know how much dem payments be, bitch! Ya ass gonna learn about pulling guns and shooting at people. Nae, today ya ass gonna learn, bitch!" Sirachi yelled, choking Nae's ass out.

"Daddy, she ain't pregnant. Dat bitch playing you, and tryna break us up! I can't breathe. Put me down, niggah…" NaeNae screamed as she choked and coughed on her words while kicking her dangling legs.

Michelle ran over to aid her girl Nae. "Sirachi, put her down—Dude! Nope! You ain't 'bout to do her like dis out here…" Michelle said, failing to pull them apart. Then she started taking off on him like Mayweather and beating on the back of his head like a drum until he dropped Nae.

NaeNae started swinging on him, too. Teasing Tasha couldn't believe these punk bitches were jumping her baby daddy? She had enough of Miss NaeNae and stepped out of the Ferrari with her dress on and kicked her heels off in the grass. She went directly for NaeNae. NaeNae was lucky she didn't have her wooden ratchet. She swung at NaeNae and missed.

"Oh, hell nawh, bitch! You tried to sneak me? Wassup, bitch? I'm bout to whoop ya ass all the way back to Chicago! And you better not ever bring ya fat ass back to ATL round my dude…Bitch, ya not prego—ya FAT! C'mon, run up…I wish you would, ho!" NaeNae yelled, dancing around like the great Ali, trying to shake and intimidate Tasha.

Tasha told her, "We'll see if you can fight better than

you can shoot," with a thick Jamaican accent and squared up. Sirachi threw Michelle thick ass up against the house and told her to bounce.

Tasha was whooping Nae ass all out her shirt and had her nose leaking and busted her lip, too. Sirachi didn't even help. NaeNae was fighting back, but too slowly for Tasha's wild ass. She punched Tasha in her stomach twice and kicked her once when she was on the ground, which had Tasha going even harder on her ass.

Sirachi knew Nae didn't have hands like she had a loud mouth. Michelle kept cheering Nae on, saying beat that bitch-ass girl. Sirachi wasn't shit and never intervened. They fought all over the yard and out in the street. Neighbors were coming outside with their phones held high.

NaeNae got frustrated and walked away, knowing Tasha kept getting the best of her. Sirachi told Tasha to run to the car now, and then told Michelle to grab NaeNae's keys.

"Shut up, nigga, and you not going nowhere but in the house! Straight up! And I wish you would leave wit dat thot fat ass bitch! Ugh, look at my nose bleeding and lip busted. Move—SIRACHI! Let me pop this trunk real quick..." NaeNae screamed, tussling with Sirachi.

Sirachi wasn't going to let Nae pop that trunk to get that AR-15. This time she might not miss. He snatched the keys and chucked them on the roof and ran to the Ferrari before she grabbed her other clip out of the glove box. She was too emotional; her mental wasn't there. All she saw was blood and rage.

He darted out in the Ferrari for fear it would get shot up even more. He was looking back in his rearview, paranoid. He was listening to Jay-Z and Future "I Got the Keys" song. Tasha turned that shit off. She told him he better get rid of that lunatic bitch and she wasn't allowed around her baby either. Then she noticed another dancing pregnant girl popping with a pot pregnant belly out all in the street. ATL was also home of the prego dancing thots. She saw them twerkin' and poppin' on porches, streets, stores, yards and even like Too Short said with a baby in their arms, too. Where the hell did she move to? Chicago was faster than ATL, but ATL was more ratchet and country black folks.

"Hello? Big Cuzzo, sup? Man, shit been crazy round here…Nae wet up my foreign and shit. I got a top-notch Chi-Town broad prego. Cuh, shit. Jus cray-cray," Sirachi vented after he accepted the call.

"Damn, cuzzo! I told u keep it pimpin'! I heard Nae got snatched up, too. Man, you know me, pushin' a hard line, checkin' cats' paperwork, and smashin' rats off da yard. I jus got a new neckpiece…Eccles 4:14, 'He gets out of prison to be KING! Even tho he was born poor'…Feel me? And I told ya since that ho burnt you in ya throat, eating dat dirty pussy, you caught strep and still ain't learnt after getting' burnt? Damn, it's poppin off! Gotta go, Cuzzo—Teflon!" *Click!* Chop-Chop rushed.

Chapter 11
"Thot Top"

Nasty Neesha was up to her usual catfishing tricks and reeling them in from the Backpages. Today her 7 p.m. appointment texted her on his way. She fixed her Beyoncé-style mini performance skirt and adjusted that same dingy blonde wig some called a thot top. thot top wasn't just good top! It was also that same old tired raggedy daily hairpiece thots wore. All of them were in denial, though, which made it worse. You couldn't tell them nothing because they felt like everybody else was throwing shade their way. Usually thot tops would range from hair weaves to wigs, all tacky and ratchet in an assortment of colors.

Neesha had been binging on drugs and alcohol lately after her Coachella incident where Future made her feel like the big elephant in the room. She didn't do well with rejection or denial. He had broken her spirit.

She heard a light knock at the hotel door. She answered it to see a Hindu man with a long handlebar mustache that curled up and carrying a black military-style duffle bag, but it was square-shaped, like he had a giant cube hiding or just a shitload of cash? Maybe even a safe.

Neesha looked the frail Hindu up and down. Nawh, he couldn't be the police and he was harmless, she told herself. Then she began to run her scripted game to lure them in the room and not let her looks scare them off or her weight turn them around.

The Hindu man cut her off in the middle of her blah-blah and told her she fine and fit perfect for his special service fetish! Long as he could bring his bag of tricks? With a strong India accent. Neesha thought that was easy and the first; usually they'd break their damn ankles trying to make it to the elevator. Shit, some would even take the steps and haul ass down to the lobby away from a big ugly catfish. Neesha looked at his cube-shaped duffle bag and shook her head as she closed the door behind them. She could tell things were about to get kinky and foreign. Just when she thought in these five years she had seen it all.

She asked the Hindu, "OK, so what is your special fetish request?" and to lay it on her. He unzipped the duffle bag and revealed a green box with 2 side holes in it. He told her, head in a box. She shook her head hell no! and told him her big ass ain't getting in no damn box, period! Then told him for the right price, she would knock a hole in the bathroom door or wall with the chair? She'd seen online before how some people's fetishes were sticking their dicks inside holes in the wall or bathroom stalls. The only problem was that everyone that she saw participate in that behavior were homosexuals, none of her Johns, though.

Then he told her, "OK, one thousand dollars. I make you offer you can't refuse!" He pulled out the 10 hundred-dollar bills. Neesha had to think first, though; not about the helluva offer, but how the hell was she going to squeeze her plus-size ass in 4x8? She didn't know the actual damn treasure chest box size, she just estimated. She was in between a box and a hard place. She snatched the stack and put it in her sports bra, then told him to help her in and don't shut it all the way to squish her, either! She took a drink of her Remy liquor and was ready as he helped lure her in to the box. It took Nasty Neesha five cuts before she squeezed down into the box. It was a helluva tight fit. He had to adjust her, flip, and twist her this way-that way.

Finally, she got into position and he pulled out and stuck his limp dick in the hole. Neesha frowned inside the box because his penis stank like eggplant and old cottage cheese, but she began to proceed sucking viciously, giving him true thot top! He came within seconds. Neesha said, what a sicko, as he made the most obscene grunts and noises. And he kept saying, "Oh Yes—Oh Yes!" Sounding like the store clerk on the Simpsons who says thank you, come again!

After he got up he went directly to the bathroom to clean up, so Neesha thought. She didn't even know he slipped right out the door. And she failed to realize the box had a lock on it and he locked it on her ass. This was the bizarre part of his fetish he always forgot to mention first offhand. It was getting head in a box and locking a bitch in the box.

Neesha realized fast that he was gone and she was stuck, locked in! She tried to peek out the hole but it was too uncomfortable. She began to hyperventilate as she screamed for help but they all fell on deaf ears. He closed the door plus her screams from the box were muffled. Then panic set in as she realized she was in dire trouble. She was suffocating at her darkest hour. Tears flowed down her squinched-up cheeks like the West Nile.

Forty-eight hours later, Neesha was discovered unconscious but alive by a thieving room service lady who would knock-knock first, then enter with her access card, announcing room services, then jacking all your prized possessions. A thief! This time she stumbled across a safe, so she thought, and wanted to lift the whole damn thing out of her greed, but it was just too damn big! Neesha scared the mess out of her and damn near gave her old ass a heart attack! She put her hands on her pounding chest and called 911. They had to cut Neesha out of the box, how much her whole body swelt. She looked like a stuffed turkey in an old crock pot all big and raw. A thief in the night saved her life.

She was hospitalized for a week. She wouldn't cooperate with authorities and kept acting like she didn't know or couldn't remember. She was no help so they never had any descriptions or suspects. But she did remember that raggedy-ass stack sweaty in her bra that she couldn't do shit with besides die with it. She thought she was gone. This was a big wake-up call to her this go-around. She hadn't EVER experienced anything near-death like this.

When she woke up, her big sister Sugar Baby and the kids was there bedside. She was devastated by the horrible news of her toes being amputated. They had to cut off her left pinky toe and her 3rd and 4th right toes, too, from no circulation and was dead already, worse than frostbite. She was crying aloud and cursing all in front of the kids. But she looked like the biggest kid of them all with all that snot running down both nostrils.

Her sister Sugar Baby said it's all good, she was going to be alright, that she had Trinidad Slauson on stand-by to handle it. She was just happy her little sis was alive. She told Neesha to look at the bright side: better to be missing toes and alive than having all toes and dead! Neesha shook her head, sobbing.

* * *

Slutty Shelly had been waiting over two months for Denver JD's call, but nothing! She was so embarrassed when her leg detached like that during sex on the hospital bed. She lied and told him she was an amputee from the Boston bombings. They exchanged numbers. She even hit him up on social media with no reply. Oh well, it was back to the basics of her boring life. Being a phone sex operator and baking her cookies were the top highlight of her day.

Denver JD had put some bands on Teasing Tasha's head for her last stunt she pulled and for shitting all on his Pop's chest and wiping her filthy ass on his drunken lips. Nobody around the Chi saw her. At least none of his hitters he knew that would really trunk and ice that bitch could find her.

Today he had a show to do in Sea-Town. It had been two months now and he remembered that white girl who saved his life. She had hit his DMs a few times, too. He had her number saved under Sloppy Thot Top. He would roll thru after the show and see if he could pull up on her whatever side of town she in, and take her out to eat, then get some thot top. He still couldn't believe that cute snow bunny had a fake leg, but some really good head! She had the type of head game a nigga would kill for and over. Like her jaw detached like her leg did. thot top wasn't just good head from a thot, you could have a female give you nasty sloppy head like a hot thot, too.

Slutty Shelly was shocked when Denver JD called, but was even more surprised he wanted to stop by. Then she was pissed because she had just started her period and by the fact he had been in town all day and did a show without contacting her to attend.

She hopped around on that one good leg, which was something she had gotten used to. Sometimes she didn't have time to put her fake leg on, or feel like it. She rushed to wash up, change her Tampax, and do her make-up. He was talking about a dinner date to thank her and show his appreciation for being his hero. She got dressed. She wore the same jeans from that day at the hospital. She figured they were her lucky jeans and had high hopes of keeping him in town and around until she got off her bloody rag. She hadn't had any dick in 40 days.

Denver JD took her out to Five Guys, because he was high off that Seattle strain of cookie dough kush. It was fire. They went to the new Five Guys on the Northeast side and he was fucking up some plates like he never ate. Shelly just watched and was afraid to indulge because she was already bloated from her cycle. White girls had a phobia of getting fat and eating too much. She was one of them that ate very little like a bird to stay lean.

Denver JD couldn't even tell her mood wasn't the same, he was too busy on his phone checking his DMs.

"Shelly, you don't want nothing else?" Denver JD asked, puzzled.

"No—Thanks," Shelly replied in an undertone.

"OK, I was jus checkin' on you, beautiful. Sorry, I just have a lot of bizz and traffic on this phone. I need to hire a PR agent... But you ready to go? I know I gotta drop you back off," Denver JD said, giving her direct eye contact for the first time since they sat down at the Five Guys.

"Umh...Well, JD, I was hoping that you can come in for a while since you're in town, ya know?" Shelly said.

"I really don't have time, seriously, but for you, Shelly, my hero, I will, beautiful," he replied with a compliment. She lit up like the Fourth of July inside.

Back at her house she didn't waste no time throwing her dog Jax out back and giving Denver JD some mouth and lip service like she wasn't nervous.

Denver JD's eyes were rolling in the back of his head with his toes curled like he was the girl. Now he knew why snow bunnies were worth a lot of money because their head game wasn't funny! And saw why they called it a blowjob. The audio was vicious from her slurping and gagging, but it sounded like a microphone being breathed and blown into.

"Mmhhm...Mmhhmm...Ur not going nowhere, JD—Ur staying with ME tonight! Mmhhhmm...Right? Mmhm..." Shelly said as she moaned on his stiff dick as she tasted his sweet pre-cum.

"O-o-ooh...y-yeah...oh yeah, bitch, yeah, I'm staying right here. Damn oh...shit, don't stop...I'm bout to bust!" Denver JD said as he panted like a wild dog and squirmed like a fish caught in the net. In his mind, he thought soon as he done—he was ghost!

Shelly had him talking to himself. She kept saying, what? He was mumbling some inaudible stuff and body seizing up like he got poisoned all over again.

Denver JD came so fast, hard, and long that he farted and overwhelming tears fell from his eyes. She didn't stop and sucked him dry and right to sleep. He didn't even realize he was nodding like a dope fiend. She swallowed all his babies and milked him like a cow.

Denver JD woke up the next morning at 9:40 a.m. to a damn golden retriever licking his face. Ugh, he jumped! The dog breath smelt like ass! Real life shit! He for a moment forgot where he was at until he smelt bacon and cookies. Then Shelly came hopping in on one leg. They both scared each other. He wasn't used to that one leg shit yet.

"Oh—that's my training dog, Jax. The state gave him to help aid me in my disability. But I'm sorry to startle you and I see my leg makes you uncomfortable because you keep staring at it, obviously. But JD, I cooked you breakfast. I'll go put my leg on and some pants if that makes you more comfortable, then bring you breakfast in bed. And some more head since I'm on my monthly, OK?" Shelly pleaded.

"Oh—nawh...Umh, it's all good! I'll come out there and join you. And your leg don't bother me, beautiful," Denver JD played it off, ready to go.

"Really?" Shelly replied, astonished.

"For really-really," Denver JD lied thru the gap between his teeth. He checked his pocket for his bread and jewelry, then thought about his great escape. Her top had a spell on him.

* * *

Tina laid stiff and stretched out in a grayish casket. They did an excellent job on her make-up, not too much, not too little. Her hair was done up professional in style. Her Pops paid $800 out of his pocket to make sure of that. She had on her all-white Vera Wang prom dress. Her Pops chose it because that's when she was the happiest and innocent before Tasha had influenced her and turned her out to partying and the life of alcohol and drugs.

Her services were held at Mount Zion Baptist Church on the low-ends. She had a pretty decent turnout and a lot of Italians from her Mom's side that she never even met when she was alive. A bunch of square pointy noses all in the place.

Her long-lost brother sat in the back aisle, crushed. Word had spread Tasha was responsible and left Tina for dead. His Pops didn't claim him, but later in life finally acknowledged him as his son and told his son it was never him, it was his mama snitching on him after the shootings that landed him in Joliet back then.

Tina's brother's name was Ronnie but everyone on the Southside called him Ratchet Folks. His Mama was originally from the C. Greens before they got torn down. And her family was all from Mississippi. They were country and wild as they come.

Tina had always stayed in touch with Ratchet Folks and acknowledged him as her brother even when her Pops was in denial and in jail, because he looked just like her Dad, but shorter and a darker version. Ratchet Folks always had that special bond connection with his older sister even though she was out there. It still was love and blood.

When it was time for a final good-bye and to view the body, Ratchet Folks walked up front, stepped out of line, hugged his Pops tight and hard, then paused at his sister's casket, holding up the line. He saw the plug they put in her nose to try and cover it up to the public. His eyes were glowing a steamy red but he didn't cry, just burnt up inside. Ratchet Folks was known for knocking cats off the map with that Mac. He wasn't part of the solution in Chicago. He was part of the problem and vowed vengeance.

* * *

Sirachi got his Ferrari repo and they kept his deposit and took a mark on his credit report, all for getting it shot-up. They blamed him and would not ever lease to another rapper again. They would have to purchase it flat out.

Sirachi blamed NaeNae for the repo games. He was back in the chicken coop dunk. This also brought him back down off his high horse, faking it till he made it. However, he had a lot of thots and ballers around the A fooled.

He crept into the condo and saw NaeNae sleeping half-naked on the couch watching Netflix. He had been staying with Tasha lately since NaeNae shot at him for the second time. He was there to get some more of his clothes and stuff. He slid past her and tippy-toed up the steps to the master bedroom.

NaeNae awoke, startled to some rummage upstairs. She scrambled to get her gun as she wiped the drool from her mouth. She peeked out the window and saw Sirachi's chicken coop and sighed out in relief.

"Sirachi!" NaeNae yelled out as she went up the stairs.

"Y-Yeah! Sup, love? I'm in the room...I didn't want to bother you. I wanted you to get rest. I know you gotta work tomorrow, babe..." Sirachi yelled back.

"Hey, Daddy! I love you, Sirachi, and don't want to argue or lose you. I know you gonna go wit dat fat punk bitch regardless...I just don't want to lose my husband to no other bitch! And once that baby is born, you'll see it's not yours...and y'all done, Daddy! Dat's it. I can't take no more...Now—nope...I need some, please, Daddy. It's been ten days now, ugh! I hate when you play games and leave this pussy horny wet on stuck!" NaeNae said in a seductive voice, clicking her tongue ring across the back of her teeth.

Sirachi didn't reply, he just nodded his head as he packed some of his shit. NaeNae felt she was fighting for Sirachi's love and attention. She wasn't getting no affection and felt rejection. So, she went for hers, telling him to come here while she tussled with his Gucci belt. He pushed her back, then sucked his teeth like he sat in a cold tub. Damn it! He bit his lip, knowing Nae got him as she began to give him sloppy thot toppy! He leaned his head back as Nae pushed his chest back down on the king-size bed, then told him he wasn't going nowhere for the night and not leaving her home alone.

She snatched off his Yeezys as she kept sucking him off with no hands! Had Sirachi like Damn! Nae always gave sloppy slobbering blowjobs and massaging his nuts fast.

"Yeah, Daddy, the world is yours...You know dat? Yours, Daddy...so is this...pussy...throat...and ass...all these three holes is all yours...and nobody else's," NaeNae said as she smacked, popped, and slurped in between words.

"Aww...Aww...Y-Yeah. Da world is mines...so is these hos—I mean holes," Sirachi moaned as he fingered both her holes like a bowling ball with two in the pussy and a thumb in her butt! Then he smacked her hard on her ass…

Ppatt-Pat! Ppatt-Pat!

"Oh…Yasss, Daddy! Smack dat ass!" Nae screamed in ecstasy.

He started telling NaeNae, "Bitch, suck it like a real THOT and give me dat top! Suck it like you want this dick, and like you need dis dick, then like you scandalous nasty! Now, like you love dis hard phat dick, bitch!"

NaeNae loved when he fucked her and called her a bitch during sex, because it made her feel like one and very slutty. They both were very kinky and freaky in a weird bizarre way.

Nae flicked her gold tongue rings around his head, then in reverse. Next, she jammed her tongue ring into his damaged pee hole! Deep down his shaft. Sirachi didn't flinch or freeze up. Nope—he loved it and was used to it, and even encouraged Nae by telling her to go ahead and do it again.

NaeNae felt his dick swell even more, getting turned on as his dick throbbed and leaked pre-cum. She got to sucking vicious, trying to take him down her throat deep as she could, as she stroked his shaft with her left and rubbed his balls with the right, gagging.

Sirachi's body did the jerk dance as he felt a jolt electrify from between his ass and nuts to explode like thunder and lightning! NaeNae always made him cum super hard. And this was part of the reason why he couldn't ever let her go! She knew too many freaky tricks and they never had routine sex. Always spontaneous and adventurous. Hot and raw with no limits. It was hard to choose a thot at the club that was brand new because her sex game could've been lame compared to NaeNae's.

"Aww…Awwhh…Shit, Nae, good girl, oh…aww… H-Here it comes…Shit!" Sirachi shouted, out of breath, as his heart skipped a beat from when he skeet-skeet.

NaeNae swallowed his load and sounded like she sneezed in one motion. Sirachi looked down to see Nae blowing cum bubbles out of her nose! He called it the spaghetti trick because he saw people put strings in their mouth and out their nose. NaeNae was the number 1 and only and had mad skills that Tasha couldn't ever compete on no real level.

She wiped his nut from her nose and started sucking on her fingers and licking the cum from her lips X-rated, then began playing with his dick, springing it back to life again.

He knew she only sucked his dick on a scale of 10 when she wanted to get fucked hard and be dominated in very suggestive submissive positions.

She was half-white, so he would call her black side his bitch Nae, and the white side his snow bunny Anne, her middle name. Then ask her who did she want him to fuck? Who wanted him the most—Nae or Anne? And regardless whoever she said…he told her who he wanted to fuck that night.

This night he chose the snow bunny Anne. And Anne would say, "Oh…Yasss, fuck yeah!" with a high-pitch Valley girl accent.

NaeNae's pussy had frequent flyer mileage on it. He called it salvaged wet pussy. He had to stroke it in a rhythm, waiting for it to bounce back like some dope.

Sirachi fucked NaeNae hard handcuffed to the refrigerator and one leg to the dishwasher until she passed out. Of course, he cheated off the Blue Boy pill and a concoction of Molly, liquor, perks, and Ecstasy. His shit was all the way up! Forget drunken love, the Viagra had them going all night! As Teasing Tasha blew up his two phones. This is why divorce rate is so high, from Becky with good hair, known as thot top!

Chapter 12
"Athotery"

Athotery is adultery from a married thot. But trife can go all ways, like you don't have to be married and still commit athotery acts, too. It was treachery, a sin committing thoterism.

ATL just didn't have housewives, they had helluva hot wives, too—athotery. They say you can't turn a thot into a housewife? Well, it's when you turn a thot into a housewife, you got athotery or athotery acts, basically a thot's scandal from being hot. Athotery was in all of thots genealogy no matter how much they tried to hide or deny it. They couldn't control it or their impulse. Them hos won't be loyal, not for anybody; they for everybody, like Juicy J say.

They committed athotery. And you knew everyone told you not to marry a thot and she was hot from the start. You suffer from a common disease called suffering sucka tacks. This is truly why the divorce rate is extremely at an all-time high since the beginning of time. It was ugly but the truth. Some cats will step their game up and switch up! But getting bad luck and fucked with another mess divorce for half your stash. You couldn't go backwards from a hot wife to another hot thot! That wouldn't truly be switching up; it's just you getting stuck.

NaeNae was up to her usual self of sex schemes since her play husband Sirachi been neglecting her, playing stepdaddy, knowing that wasn't his damn baby. And Tasha was getting bigger and bigger.

NaeNae was creeping with Michelle big ol' booty lately. They were at Michelle's spot in her room when they got busted again, this time by her husband. She was guilty as sin. NaeNae just sat there naked, looking up like she ain't sorry, like Beyoncé without no shame in her game.

Michelle's husband, the Clark, Atlanta engineering graduate, darted out the house and sped off in the car. Two days later he committed suicide. He blew his brains out by sticking a .357 revolver in his mouth and left a note in Red Kylie Jenner lipstick saying, "Fuck y'all!"

It was something about seeing a girl with a girl versus your girl cheating on you with an actual girl! He felt some type of way, something indescribable. It did something to his pride, which had a considerable influence on his decision to take his own life.

Michelle took it the hardest, popping pills, drinking, and smoking heavy kush. She had been staying with NaeNae lately. Her husband's family blamed her for his death. They wouldn't even allow her to pay her respects to her late husband and attend his funeral. She also had lost her kids for coming up dirty for drugs in her system. His family had full custody of her kids. She only had supervised visits.

NaeNae had turned Michelle all the way out—full-fledged lesbo! Michelle said she was done with men and didn't want no more dick in her life. It repulsed her now.

NaeNae would vic Michelle and douche her ass out and lube it up with light caramel so Michelle could say Nae's ass taste sweet. And she would put a dab of honey in her pussy with light spring water, too.

Nae used the same tricks on Sirachi and figured she could fool a bitch, too. They never knew, either. Sirachi crazy ass wrote a hit strip club song from it saying it was strawberry and tasted cherry! With his country ass. She had Southern tricks. You had to watch them girls down South! They were known for taking your man and keeping their man in the house. They invented the spaghetti spell concoction when they cooked, whipped, and NaeNae'd.

Sirachi said his girl had a live-in girlfriend staying in the guest room. He had been home more lately but Michelle wouldn't give him no play or time of day. NaeNae talked her into letting Sirachi watch and for her to watch them next. She agreed long as Sirachi didn't touch. Nae knew Sirachi wanted to fuck Michelle bad and desired her because he would cum prematurely after her and Nae got down for their crown.

Michelle was cashing NaeNae out with all her husband insurance policy money. Paying her rent! Buying her designer shit—Tom Ford, Marc Jacobs, Michael Kors, Jimmy Choo, Louis V red bottoms, and Birkin bags.

However, the icing on the cake was her tatts. She got NaeNae tatted on both ass cheeks. When she walked, it bounced—NaeNae. Then she tatted a cupcake on her pussy because NaeNae had a peach and said her pussy was sweet to eat like a cupcake, too.

NaeNae woke up to Michelle handing her the phone. It was Tasha on the line, crying, saying Sirachi was in Dekalb County Jail and needed NaeNae to bond him out for $1,500 cash. Then she told NaeNae it was for domestic violence, but they were just having sex, not fighting. And the nosey-ass hating neighbors called the cops! NaeNae told her, oh well, and clicked! She rolled over, sucked her teeth, and told Michelle to let her borrow a thousand dollars because she had the other 5. Michelle didn't want to do it at first for Sirachi's sorry ass, who was always hating on their relationship.

Nae got dressed quick and threw on some pajama pants and a coat, then headed out the door just as Sirachi was blowing her up collect.

"Hello—Sirachi, I need money on the phone with a credit card! If you can hear me—I'm on my way to come bond you out now and cuss ya dumb ass out, too, Daddy!" NaeNae answered, yelling thru the phone before it hung up.

They had her downtown all night waiting for Sirachi to get processed out. The damn sun was coming up, and she was tired, bored, and kept dozing off and would drive around downtown looking for Sirachi and checking her phone.

She was flicking her tongue ring when this nigga Sirachi really came out in his silk boxer shorts with them damn raggedy New Balance pimp flops! Why was he always clowning on Rika's thot flops? She was about to curse him out bad. He really was fucking that fat pregnant bitch and went down for her yelling, hollering, carrying on, and faking.

NaeNae chewed his ass out all the way back to Riverdale and he got arrested without neither one of his phones, so he was getting an earful and poking fingers upside his head.

NaeNae rolled a blunt and drank some Starbucks as she sat in the living room waiting for Sirachi to wash that county jail smell off him. She didn't want to fall asleep, afraid he was going to leave right back to the same bitch that got him thrown in jail versus the bitch that got him out of jail.

That was exactly what Sirachi did, too. As soon as he got dressed and out of the shower, he made his grand escape, or at least attempted to. Nae saw the look on his face. It was stern and he didn't even acknowledge her on the couch or look her way.

NaeNae jumped up and sprang to life as tears started to flow. She ran and beat him to the door as she blocked the entrance, using her body as a shield.

"No-no…Nope! No—Sirachi, you're not going back over there or leaving me…Please don't leave me, Daddy… OMG! Sirachi, do you love her? You got feeling for that thot fat bitch? Daddy, please don't go! I jus want my hubby back home here with me. So, what Michelle living here with me, Daddy? I need you—my dude here, too…P-please…" NaeNae cried and then slid down, defeated from her mixed emotions.

"Man—NaeNae, move! I'm telling you, Nae, move out the way, gurrl! I shouldn't have to sneak in-and-out my own crib! Move—NaeNae!" Sirachi demanded.

"Oh…Hell nawh, Nae, let him go, girl…with his sorry ass! I told you he ain't shit… Nothing but a straight LANCE! L-A-N-C-E! Lying-Ass-Nigga-Cheating-Everyday! Got a girl at home and a hundred thots in his phone! Please, ugh!" Michelle intervened, trying to pull NaeNae up off the ground and from blocking the entrance so Sirachi could just bounce!

"Bitch! Who u calling a LANCE? You lucky to be in my shit…That's why ya husband killed himself and said fuck y'all! You don't kno a ho place! I would've blew my brains out, too. He thinking he found true love with you, but you let Nae turn you out to a straight lesbo bitch!" Sirachi fired back as he gave her a venomous stare.

"Michelle, we good. Jus leave us, please…Daddy, I'm sorry…Just don't leave ya favorite redbone…or am I still, huh?" NaeNae whined, still puffy-eyed.

"Please…gurrl, dat niggah a straight M-DOT! A DOT…dat niggah out cherr!" Michelle said, turnt up with her thick ATL Southern accent. Her thots sounded like she was saying Dots. She was lit.

"Man—Didn't I tell you to shut ya ass up and get out my crib! And you way more out therr den ME, ho! Let NaeNae turn a married woman out! Please…" Sirachi snapped back, pushing her out the way while attempting to pull NaeNae out of the doorway.

"Oh, OK! I see what dis is now! Oh…I kno what dis about. It's about a dominance thang, huh? —Nae, it's a dominance thang, gurrl! Sirachi is da king of his castle and ain't got a piece of dis sweet potato pie! Huh, Sirachi—Ain't dat right? Yeah, I kno—I bet! Come one, less get dis ova with now! We all might as well go have a big ass orgy…ménage, fuck, and make-up! I see how you been gawking at my phat ass since day one…Dat's how I knew you wasn't shit and used to tell NaeNae about that shit! Don't freeze up and get quiet now—C'mon! Let's go upstairs, y'all! Nae, get up girl. I bet cha dis will keep his sorry ass at home err day and night pouncing on all dis ass, if he can even handle it!" Michelle shouted, turnt up, pulling on a quiet, shocked Sirachi. After NaeNae stopped sobbing, he was hesitant but then didn't resist Michelle and went along.

NaeNae still sat slouched over, guarding the front door while Michelle took Sirachi by the hand like a little kid. Sirachi watched her phat ass sway and bounce as she walked up the stairs provocatively. He kept resisting, slowing her up. He knew she was putting on a show and some, how it played on his psyche, that she really been wanting him and got wetter every step she took, especially from the twitch in her hip. Sirachi vowed to punish her for popping off at the lip.

She pushed him down on the bed and dropped down on her knees to please him. Then once he was right and ready with a stiff dick, she asked him to hit it doggy style off the bed, then to get the Magnums out their dresser drawer with intentions for him to hit it, and cum quick!

Sirachi told her Nawh, and to get into the sex swing. She squinched her face up with a nasty frown. She contemplated, looking a bit lost and lost for words, too. She sighed out harshly and told Sirachi she guessed…but didn't know how it worked because she never experienced it before.

Sirachi instructed her, holding his throbbing dick. He told her to place one leg in each loop slot and pulled them all the way up to her high thighs and it would fit her into a U-shape harness. Once he sat down on the other part of the sex swing, it would propel her up in the air like she was rock climbing.

Sirachi entered her from the back. She thought it wasn't nothing special about a damn sex swing and was too overrated! Until Sirachi's slow strokes increased, as he found his rhythm and balance beneath him.

She started moaning and breathing heavy. Sirachi was tossing her up and meeting her with all dick as she was forced back down by the gravitational pull. He was hitting her with deep thrusts like he was grind dancing in her. She screamed as he rubbed her clit and fucked her fast and hard, hitting the bottom of that shit. She felt his nuts touch with every pound as their bodies smacked. Her ass was giggling in waves like the sea with her NaeNae tatt. She screamed at the top of her lungs as she came fast and hard unexpectedly. She wet Sirachi's nuts and thighs up, splashing her pool of love juices. Damn, this was what she was missing and was in denial. She could definitely get down with Sirachi in a ménage every now and then. But did that really make her bi like NaeNae? She was super confused and lost in her Ecstasy, pills, and potions.

NaeNae still sat downstairs, blocking the door. She was too broken to join them. Plus, she didn't want to abandon her post. She heard them going at it for about 40 minutes until she nodded off from being up waiting on Sirachi to get released from DeKalb County all night. She never heard Michelle so damn vocal before and knew Sirachi was fucking her like a straight hot little thot, dogging her ass.

Michelle was wet, open, and ready now. She started telling Sirachi…

"Knock dis phat pussy out da box! Fuck me! Dig all in dis wet pussy. Oh, it feels sooo good—Yasss! Fuck dis pussy out dat box, Sirachi!" as her hips felt like they kept getting knocked out of place and like he was busting thru her fluttering uterus, a good discomfort pleasurable pain.

However, she wasn't screaming yet. Sirachi wasn't done and was about to finish punishing her. She was about to holler bloody murder and have NaeNae come running up the steps.

He took it out her pussy and reached on the dresser for Nae's lube. She still sat up jackknifed in the mid-air. He spread the lube all around her booty hole and around the head of his dick.

Michelle was baffled and froze up. She didn't know what to say. She never even let her husband enter her back door, all the years she was married. And here she was letting a thug-rat go anal on a sex swing. He was being gentle and easing in and out slowly while he kept encouraging her to just relax and stop flinching up. She felt heavy pressure on her rectum. That damn K-Y gel didn't make the pressure and pain easier, just helped the access. Then Sirachi started picking up the pace. She yelled out for him to slow down. But it was too late, he beat it like fight night.

Sirachi ignored her screams, pleas, and reached over into NaeNae's panties drawer. He thumbed thru it and pulled out the collar and placed it around her neck. She didn't think nothing of it, a choke collar, besides knowing how kinky Sirachi and Nae played. Until Sirachi dug back into the drawer. She kept trying to look back at him but couldn't all the way because of the collar. Migos' Fight Night still played in his head.

Sirachi put the chained nipple clamps down on full erect nipples. She moaned from the pinching pleasures. Then Sirachi took out the remote controller to the dog collar. He had tricked her and put a shocking dog collar around her neck. He knew how to work it and her and to bestow the fear of God in her ass and establish his dominance. It would exacerbate her heart rate.

He went hard as he really began punishing, smacking, and dominating her. He shocked her for the first time quick. She jumped. *WTF? This niggah really put a damn dog collar and was shocking me like a dog, and fucking me like a dog, too?* she thought as she couldn't do nothing but pray he came quick.

Sirachi grabbed NaeNae's bullet vibrator and placed on her clitoris as he turned it all the way up. She began to moan and scream in pure ecstasy like she was on E. Sirachi would take it out her ass and go back and forth between both her holes. He would finger her asshole, then put it in her mouth to suck them.

He started to bang her ass out viciously and pressed the bullet toy harder on her clit, until he felt her thighs trembling and contracting hard. It was causing him to lose his grip but not his dancing Bohemian rhythm.

"Oww…Owwee…Oh…O-o-ooo…Oh   Sirachi! SIRACHI-SIRACHI! O-o-ooo… Oweee—I'm 'bout to nut! O-o-ooo yasss…SI-SIRACHI OMG! Ahh—shit yasss—oh it feels so good. Dis dat good dick dat got Nae stuck!" Michelle yelled in a screaming, gushing orgasm while Sirachi shocked the holy mess out of her repeatedly as she came hard. Super hard and back-to-back. It was the best orgasm of a lifetime. She never knew you could take sex to the next level on some extreme dominance type shit. She saw why people of the world were into S&M dominatrix and why NaeNae was stuck at the door. Sirachi had that good dick and had gotten her on stuck. He knew it, too. He came all over her ass crack and let it drip as he got up off the swing and pulled her down to skeet all in her face nasty.

She sucked on his balls and jacked his dick off until the very last drop. He collapsed on the bed. Michelle was walking bow-legged like a cowboy getting off a horse to get him a hot towel. She cleaned him up, like her husband.

They both fell asleep, laying with each other. Sirachi conquered her body and established dominance, too. When NaeNae woke up, she ran upstairs to see if Sirachi was gone. He didn't go back to Tasha for the next couple of days.

* * *

Nasty Neesha hadn't been out of the hospital a full 24 hours and was back at it! She didn't even give time for her toes to heal or get the stitches out yet. She was now a bona fide ho with seven toes.

They even banned and barred her from her hotel she made famous. She easily disbarred that and had Sugar Baby get it in her name after paying her $300 and a promise not to be doing no more bizarre shit or turning special tricks.

Sugar Baby and Trinidad Slauson came by to bring Neesha lunch and check on her. Trinidad Slauson went to Crenshaw High School. He was one of them fly niggas on the wall and graduated despite all the heavy gang activity in and out of school back then. He felt bad for Neesha's fat and now crippled ass. And she was back at, too. He told her to just lean back and collect that disability check every month now. Especially with her seven hobbling toes, she really qualified for SSI. He offered her a job selling gold at Slauson Swap Meet helping him out. Neesha kept hitting the Snoop Dogg triple strain of concoction kush. She wasn't hungry for no food. Especially them cold-ass McDonald's fries. Shit, she could have walked to McDonald's herself, at least she thought. She sipped the Bacardi bottle heavy and craved money. That's what she was hungry for. Money! She kicked the two lovebirds out the room, lying, saying she was exhausted and needed her rest. Really, she was ready to get back online to vic and solicit tricks.

thots were abusing Snapchat and using it for their thotery and committing athotery acts. Snapchat gave you the right to Snap whenever, wherever you wanted to, which gave every thot her own instant reality show into their lifestyle like the rich and famous. They all thought they were celebrities now. They were abusing Snaps with no authority or limits.

Neesha was no exception. She went right back to her favorite game, catfish, with hopes of turning into a sea turtle, but she was more like that shark fish with them catfish whiskers.

She had vic some tricks and set up some dates. She now had to wait to see how many showed up. It was this one trick asking for a special and just simply requesting for a Beyoncé prototype.

Neesha hurried up and replied to his classified ad up. She hit him with her favorite punchline—She a little round, but look just like Beyoncé laying down.

Finally, at 8 p.m. her first trick showed up. The rest were all no call, no shows. She bait-trapped the middle-aged man. He simply wanted to get laid, but refused to pay her full price for catfishing him. Her whole profile pics were Photoshop and screenshot with filters on filters.

Neesha told him OK, and slashed the price in half like Wal-Mart. He gave her the $150 and stepped into the room. Neesha went her big ass straight to work. He noticed her feet all wrapped up and asked WTF? Was she OK, because he saw the bloodstains on the cast-like gauze wrappings. She simply replied it was an accident leaving the Baldwin Hills Mall, as she rolled the latex to practice safe sex and mounted him as she straddled on top of him.

Not even five minutes into her riding him like a pony at the State Fair all slow, she heard a bunch of rushing footsteps sounding like a damn safari stampede advancing towards her door. She briefly paused to listen as it got quiet suddenly. She thought, *no biggie* and assumed the kush had her highly paranoid, until she heard a 3-count, then "CLEAR" as the hotel door came flying in off the hinges. It was vice.

"Freeze—Freeze! Get down on the ground now! Hands up high, get on the ground now!" the Vice Squad captain shouted with his tactical weapon pointed at the duo.

Neesha was still straddling the trick with her hands held up high. He screamed, "Hands up, don't shoot!" as he pushed Neesha's big ass off him and dove to the floor. The Vice Squad roughed him up. He told him he didn't do nothing or know this girl. He said he'd just met her on Backpages, snitching directly on her.

Nasty Neesha was apprehended and booked into the LA County Jail. She was pointed out in a photo line-up by that same Rancho Cucamonga trick they had assaulted and robbed. He had fished Nasty Neesha with that Beyoncé hook and she bit like a true catfish, a straight scavenger. She never saw the set-up coming.

The Rancho Cucamonga trick had been hospitalized and his wife had divorced him when she found out he was robbed and savagely beaten by a prostitute in a hotel room, according to the police at the hospital. He had a real vendetta against Neesha and had been working with the Vice Squad ever since to catch a predator like Neesha.

Nasty Neesha was booked on a slew of charges stemming from robbery, assault, fraud, and soliciting, and was held at a half-a-million-dollar all cash bond. She was ineligible for the 10 percent or collateral to compensate.

They took her into the infirmary unit because of her freshly wrapped-up missing toes, mainly to monitor so she wouldn't catch staph infection, for which they would be liable. The LA County Jail already had a joint lawsuit on their medical personnel.

Nasty Neesha lay there crying, feeling naked and afraid. She had a headache and needed a blunt to numb her body pain,. She had called her sis Sugar Baby and she didn't accept the collect call. Neesha tried again and her sister hung up hard in her face. Right there she knew Sugar Baby was mad she got caught up in trouble under her name. Neesha didn't have nobody else to turn to.

She didn't remember any of her other sisters' numbers. They all were stored in her phone. She screamed, "Fuck!" as tears streamed down her face, knowing she was really stuck.

She had no hustle; all she knew how to do was sell her ass. It's what she was good at and had mastered. She saw *Orange is the New Black* and wasn't trying to go to prison. There was a bitch in the infirmary with no hands. What did she do? And it smelled like Skid Row!

* * *

Slutty Shelly hadn't heard anything from her favorite rapper Denver JD since that sleepover night. She had been stalking his page and blowing up his DMs so tough he blocked her and her number, too. All them damn text messages had been annoying the mess out of him. He was done with her and was only in town for one night.

Shelly was back to her boring life. She had been extra horny lately from no guys showing up to nail her. She needed to get laid bad and that phone sex operator gig made matters worse. She was so damn horny she was antsy and couldn't think. If she had money she would've found a gigolo to pay off to fuck her hard. She was tired of her plain white finger-size vibrating 3-speed dildo.

"Ugh...Fuck! Damn it! —I'm freaking too horny...

ughhh!" Shelly screamed as she pulled her hair by the blonde roots, irritated and cherry red in the face.

She jumped up and got the leash and tied Jax to the Arcadia back inside door. Jax thought he was going for a walk, all excited with a wagging high curled tail, until he saw Shelly grab the jar of creamy peanut butter. His tail instantly went down and he went from standing on all fours to sitting on his hind legs.

Slutty Shelly's sleezy ass smeared light peanut butter up the crack of her ass. She figured dogs liked sniffing ass, so they would like licking ass, too. She secured him to the door just in case his little pink thing popped out, he wouldn't try to hump her like a bitch dog in heat. It was another one of Shelly's bizarre sick episodes.

She encouraged Jax to go ahead and lick all the peanut butter while patting her ass as she spread it. Jax sniffed in the crack of her ass, then put his long snout down as he sniffed out his nose hard like a doggy sneeze, rejecting her invitation.

She called Jax back again, this time by yelling at poor Jax. "Jax—Jax! Go head, boy, Jax, c'mon, honey…come to Mommy, Jax…Good boy…Come here, Jax…There you go, eat up like a good boy, Jax!" she shouted until he licked away.

She kept spreading peanut butter all in the crack of her ass and on her vajj as fast as Jax licked it off while she held her sex toy stimulating on her clit.

Shelly's next-door neighbor's kids were playing catch football and throwing it back and forth when it flew into her backyard. One of the boys went to retrieve the football to see a dog licking a bent-over woman on a chair. He said, ewwehh…grossed out and ran to tell his parents.

The little boy's parents came running and almost threw up their lunch in disgust! They turned straight around, covering little Timmy's eyes, and quickly left to call the authorities immediately. The father took out his phone to record for evidence to give the Seattle Police Dept.

Slutty Shelly already came twice and was unaware that she had a crowd behind her in the backyard. She was stone cold busted.

She jumped hard as repeatedly pounding bangs beat down her front door. She was clueless and hopped to the door, checking the peephole to see Seattle PD. She hurried up and opened the door as they rushed and cuffed her. Then they read her Miranda rights as they seized Jax.

The police took Shelly to the county jail on animal cruelty and bestiality charges, which made national headlines and the Fox 10 o'clock News.

They took Jax to an animal shelter but couldn't adopt him to a family until his 90-day observation period was over. They wanted to monitor his behavior and interaction around people and especially kids first before he was cleared to be released or else he'd be put to sleep. They didn't know how far Shelly went with the poor dog or how much abuse he had suffered.

The secret life of pets. If Jax could talk, he'd testify on that bitch! Now if nobody wanted to adopt him, he would really get put down. Somehow that sick video got out all over the net and spread fast. Her athotery bestiality acts had her family put to shame and embarrassed once again and they disowned Shelly. She was on her own, right on house arrest, on her good leg, as animal rights activists protested outside her home.

* * *

Back in Chi-Raq, Tina's bro Ratchet Folks got word that Teasing Tasha was down in ATL hiding out. Everybody put respect on Ratchet Folks' name because his grave résumé was so treacherous. Even his Pops knew it, just like the rest of south and west sides of the Chi.

He stopped by his Pops' house to tell him the news on Tasha's status and his plans. His Pops just nodded his head in acknowledgement and didn't speak on the murderous plots. He knew Ratchet Folks had his mind made up regardless and was a straight-up killa that will kill for his family and favorite sister. His baby girl was gone so he didn't object.

Ratchet Folks had his Pops drop him off at the Chicago bus terminal. He was going to use the Amtrak at first, but figured he could plan, plot, and strategize on the Greyhound, then catch the train back to the city.

He took his favorite thumper of choice, a .44 Desert Eagle, and stashed it in his Adidas carry-on bag and placed it in the upper luggage rack two seats in front of him to keep a close eye on it just in case the Jake got on board, frisking around with that damn K-9.

He didn't have a specific location on Tasha or her whereabouts, but knowing Tasha, he didn't need it. All he had to do was go to all ATL hot spots to find a hot thot. It was that simple. Tasha's sexy ass stuck out like a sore thumb, and he could always recognize a Southside Chicago ho anywhere he went. Even if he was in the UK, he could point her out in the crowd, real shit.

He didn't know that Teasing Tasha was pregnant and due any day now. However, that didn't mean shit to Ratchet Folks nor would that stop him and alter his twisted mind that was plagued with vengeance and that tooth for tooth, eye for eye motto that they lived by in the Chi. If one of their guys died, so did one on the rival side.

Ratchet Folks rode the Greyhound just picturing how he was going to stamp a DE hole in Tasha's forehead.

* * *

5:45 p.m., Clermont Lounge, Atlanta, GA strip club. Sirachi sat at the bar taking shots of watermelon vodka as he manipulated his phone. His whole buzz and 15 seconds of rap fame was short-lived and dying down. He was a one-hit Soundcloud wonder, just another local joker. But he still had a lot of thot followers and sack chasing. As an M-thot he had benefitted swell. It wasn't totally in vain, though. It was fun while it lasted and he wasn't mad.

He got interrupted by a text message that read: Sirachi, whatz Gucci, cuzzo? Dis pimpin' and I wanted to give u my new number. Dis my phone so hit me. I'm on these minions all out of pocket. PMAO!

It was his Big Cuzzo Chop-Chop. He had probably knocked a bitch on the inside, as he said with his pimpin' impeccable mouthpiece! He immediately called the number.

"Sup, Sirachi?" Chop-Chop answered.

"Damn, Big Cuh, like dat? I'm just posted, leaning back like a Mac! At da Clermont Lounge," Sirachi replied, bubbly.

"Cuzzo, send me sum pics to dis phone, and don't be slow playing and bullshittin'," Chop-Chop said eagerly.

"Man, I got cha pimpin', but wait till I go to Magic's or Strokers. You don't want none of these washed-up old hos. I'm just posted lo-key bleeding the bar…Oh and WTF is P-M-A-O?" Sirachi said curiously.

"Oh, Pimpin-My-Ass-Off! You kno all these thot hos are my minions, just like dem yellow 'Despicable Me' workers. They wild ratchet and out of line! I keep some minion hos working, pimpin'! I'm on these hos' heads for my bread, even in da Feds, ya dig, Cuzzo?" Chop-Chop said as he chopped and popped. Sirachi busted out laughing. His

Big Cuzzo was too much with a real pimp-or-die attitude.

Then he was interrupted by Tasha saying she was having back-to-back hard contractions. He told Chop-Chop he had to go and check on the baby and that Tasha just wanted some attention and for him to come over. He had been real distant lately now that she was big as a beached whale, but still sexy, though.

Sirachi told her he was out at the Clermont sipping and writing his new hit single lyrics. She sucked her teeth and hung up on him, swiping her phone to the left.

Teasing Tasha had hung up on Sirachi's bubbly annoying ass because she knew he was drunk and at the bar chasing hot thots. She was used to his routine. He barely came over and never fucked her since her last trimester of her pregnancy. She knew it was because her stomach was too big.

Her OBGYN doctor recommended sex to help her induce her labor or exercise, like simply walking, which she didn't have any choice because Sirachi wasn't complying with the doctor's order even after she repeated the doctor's order of sexing to induce labor.

So, she went to the Google app store to download the new Pokémon Go app, which was a worldwide phenomenon that made $17.3 billion in two days. She had been hooked on the game for a whole week, catching different Pokémon. She even named Sirachi one. He was the hardest Pokémon to catch in Atlanta.

The good thing about the game was it helped her get out and learn her way around ATL. She even knew how to use the MARTA trains and which ways and times they ran. In Chicago, they called the train the L, which she hadn't used since high school, especially since the Uber Chicago and Lyft takeover.

Suddenly, she had a hurting long contraction where

she couldn't move, then realized her water had broken as it wet up her pants and trickled down her legs.

She was scared and nervous at the same time. She knew this dreadful day would come. She couldn't take no real "D," so she really thought a baby was going to kill her. Especially if it was a baby boy with a big ol peanut head and hook like Sirachi's.

She called Sirachi with the news and he told her to stay right there. Big Tricky was around the area and would be there to pick her up and rush her to the hospital. Then he told her he would meet her at the Southwest Baptist Hospital, that he had to go pick up NaeNae first.

Teasing Tasha rolled her eyes and told him, whatever! She told him for what, all she going to do was be embarrassed from the baby looking like you regardless if it's a boy or girl, and told him to have Big Tricky hurry! She wasn't worried about Sirachi being in denial. She would make them into believers. She was worried about getting an epidural!

NaeNae got the call from Sirachi about the news and was told to get ready. He was on his way to pick her up and then shoot to Southwest.

NaeNae had been more confident lately with Sirachi being at home with her more, especially at night, but she wasn't relaxed. She kept watch on Michelle and Sirachi. Michelle went from hating Sirachi to liking him, too. Nae was paranoid. Her and Michelle went from having sex every day to 3 times a week. And they would ménage with Sirachi maybe once a week now.

She had told Michelle, "don't worry about Sirachi's dick, just worry about dis pussy" checking her quick. NaeNae wasn't exempt from kicking Michelle's ass out the crib, definitely over Sirachi! She had almost lost him once over her Tasha regrets.

NaeNae was so damn happy that Tasha was finally

about to drop that damn baby so she could get them talons out of Sirachi's neck and back. Beside her being bad and exotic with a vixen body, NaeNae didn't see how Tasha had bait trapped Sirachi's dumb ass. He knew he was damaged. She was going to tell Tasha, take her hot thot ass back to Chicago and all them possible baby daddies to the Bill Cunningham or Maury show.

By the time they got to the maternity ward of Grady Hospital, it was too late. Teasing Tasha had given birth to an 8 lb., 9 oz. baby boy, healthy. She named him a Junior after Sirachi.

Sirachi blamed his dogg Bigg Tricky for going to the wrong hospital! He said Southwest Baptist—not Grady where his Pops and a few day-one homies died!

He missed the baby's birth, if it was indeed his. NaeNae and he arrived outside the room to already hear a crying newborn with undeveloped lungs. This was the moment of truth. They both took a deep breath and exhaled nervously, anticipating whatever was behind the other side of the door. He asked Nae, was she ready? NaeNae was speechless and just nodded her head. NaeNae couldn't truly answer that question. She didn't know if she was ready. She walked in behind Sirachi and her mouth dropped.

"Sirachi—Sirachi—Sirachi…Dat's ya baby. OMG! You can't deny him. He looks just like you, Daddy!" NaeNae said, crushed, as Tasha handed Sirachi his son.

The baby boy was the same reddish complexion as Sirachi and shared the same exact nose, ears, hairline, and face of Sirachi. He had Tasha's Jamaican daddy's eyes.

NaeNae told him he couldn't lie or deny—no more. She couldn't believe it was really his baby. And the fact he got her pregnant at Coachella really hurt her. She the one that was responsible for seducing Tasha to come play their way with a lifetime of regret now. She had introduced them.

NaeNae wiped her eyes not wanting Tasha or nobody else to see her cry. She was heartbroken and crushed, thinking Sirachi was ruined and couldn't EVER have kids again. Period. In all of ATL, his M-thot ass never got a girl pregnant until Tasha came along.

She was jealous and hot, because even though she had a little girl that always was at her Mama's in Buckhead, she wanted a boy. And Sirachi's and her biochemistry never mixed. She wanted a little boy by him.

NaeNae sat quietly next to Big Tricky with her arms folded with an obvious attitude. She was ready to go and felt sick.. She couldn't take anymore. She'd seen their family's little bond now and Sirachi's overwhelmed look planted on his face when he handed Tasha back their baby gently and carefully, and then watched Tasha tell Sirachi to pour her a drink of cool water out of that tan hospital jug. She wanted to slap them both, ugh!

Teasing Tasha noticed NaeNae red hot in the face and watery eyes. She knew that bitch was sick and this baby just bumped her out her number-one spot back down to two. Tasha knew she would have more kids by Sirachi by telling him not to wear any condoms. She was lit inside and wanted to laugh at NaeNae and tell her she beat her ass and snatched her man, LOL!

* * *

Three weeks had past and NaeNae was still into her feelings and losing Sirachi to Tasha and the baby boy. She was sick of going over there to just sit in the car waiting for Sirachi to visit and drop off Pampers and formula.

She decided to go inside and squash their beef to call it a truce, even thought they'd both hold deep grudges. She felt it was only right for the baby's sake.

"Excuse me, Sirachi. Can me and ya BM talk, please?" NaeNae said in a slick tone.

"Talk! We all adults, right?"

"Bye—Sirachi, take ya son in the otha room, Daddy, please!" NaeNae replied.

"Girl, let's go to the back and talk, Tasha…away from Mr. Nosey Sirachi!" NaeNae snapped.

"Aiight, let's go…" Tasha agreed as they both walked off and shut the room door.

"OK, let me get this off my chest—Tasha, I kno you have feelings for my man…If not love him too as I do. And I kno y'all fucking and going to continue to do so. Plus, he's not ever leaving me, as you see. So, girl, I want to just squash the beef and I think it's better if we can get along for the baby, ya kno…and he is helluva handsome, too, with some fine hair. I've been knowing Sirachi for years now. He's a man and a dog at times that I don't mind cuz I love him for him, and accept all that comes with him, too. And my whole purpose of this convo is I kno you from O.T. and could use and need some help. Especially once Sirachi gets back out there in dem ATL streets and strip clubs all night long…" NaeNae let everything off her chest.

"Ya kno what, NaeNae, I appreciated the realness, but I'm fine, Jo!" Tasha declined.

"Well…Just kno that offers always stand and you could call me, girl. Oh…and I'm so sorry for shooting at you that day. You just don't kno me and that dude's history, man. But that's all, Tash, thanks," NaeNae said humbly.

"You kno what, Nae, I do forgive you and it's all good. But I'm gonna be honest with you, too. I do have strong feelings for Sirachi, and despite how the doctor says wait 6 to 8 weeks to have sex, me and Sirachi already have been, because he claimed he wanted to train me to take all his dick! And if you cool wit that, then I'm cool with you, too!" Tasha confessed.

NaeNae said, "Yes, I can be cool wit it."

The girls walked back into the front room and Sirachi Jr. screamed for NaeNae when he saw her as Sirachi held him up high in the air like Simba the lion king.

"Damn, girl, he likes you already! Hell nawh, son... no thots like ya Daddy chase. Please, don't take after ya sorry-ass Daddy!" Tasha said in a joking manner.

"He loves him some NaeNae and dis good red-hot hair, huh? Tell ya Ma-Ma!" NaeNae snapped back in a joking tone, too. Just like that they were cool again.

* * *

They had been kicking it tough. Every day NaeNae would go by her spot and take Tasha around with the baby for a week straight. NaeNae even started feeling some type of way on the low about Tasha. She wanted her again. Besides their beef and hating, Tasha was right. Her ass got phat and firmer. Michelle's ass was bigger but softer, the type to melt in your hands. Tasha's was more of an athletic firm track star booty.

Tasha never noticed NaeNae busting extra little moves or hitting on her once again. She was too busy blinded with the baby to see Nae hitting on her. She just thought NaeNae was being extra nice because of the baby, knowing babies had that type of effect on women.

Tasha's waist was still small and her baby gut was already gone. Her stomach was damn near flat once again like when Nae met her backstage, looking fine and sexy as ever. NaeNae click-clacked her tongue rings across her teeth back-and-forth as she did when she was wet and horny as she watched Tasha walk to the ladies' room.

NaeNae just wanted to treat Tasha out and get some liquor in her system to see if she could trick her out them panties, if Tasha ass was even wearing any. They were at Gladys Knight Atlanta Chicken-N-Waffles spot by themselves, no Sirachi, no Michelle, no baby.

NaeNae was brainwashed since she was a little thotler, the young fast girls not even in middle school and popping and twerking. Their Mamas usually egged them on, saying it was cute, but most of their moms were thots themselves or had mental issues. She didn't know how she developed an appetite for hot girls.

They came out the restaurant a little tipsy and hopped in NaeNae's pussy-pink two-door box on deuces. NaeNae secured her doors and went to spark the blunt up when she noticed a cat slouched down between cars in her rearview with his hand in his hoodie. Nae's heart raced but she remained calm and alerted Tasha as she grabbed her Glock out of the glovebox.

"Tasha! Girl, don't look back or make no sudden movements, please. Girl, I see one of Ant-Loc's goons back there behind your side. They kidnap me before, so if he try to creep, on three lean ya seat back, K?"

"Damn, NaeNae, you got me nervous, gurrl! Jo, I just left all that death back in Chicago! I got a son to make it home to! Just drive off, girl, before he gets a chance to attack—"

"Three! Three! Girl, three!" NaeNae cut Tasha off yelling at her to comply.

Bloch! Bloch! B-Bloch! Bloch! —DOOM! DOOM! Shots rang out, echoing thru the parking lot as fire was exchanged.

Tasha pulled the side lever and leant her seat back on the first three Nae had shouted. She was from the Go, but couldn't go!

NaeNae was a step ahead, which meant a step faster on the draw, and got off finally hitting her target, dropping him. His big caliber handgun sparked louder than NaeNae's and two bullets shot somewhere off towards the sky. Nae saw the surprise in his eyes and knew she tagged him, too, from his body flinching.

Teasing Tasha opened the car door to grab her phone she dropped leaning her seat back, thrown off balance. NaeNae was telling her to come on, bitch, let's go! She told NaeNae her phone! But never thought NaeNae just shot him dead.

She saw the victim sprawled out with the big black gun within feet from his body, eyes wide. She flipped out and damn near peed on herself. She recognized the victim and that damn gun. It was Ratchet Folks, Tina's little bro. She told NaeNae don't take her home, she didn't want to be alone, and Tina's Pops probably sent more killers from Chicago, especially after they sent Ratchet Folks, his only son, back in a box, too.

Tasha was petrified! NaeNae tried to calm her down and lie, saying he wasn't dead! And the ambulance was coming. She heard the sirens. NaeNae didn't trust Tasha and was afraid she'd snitch. So, she didn't mind her staying over with them at the Woodlake Drive Condo. She could monitor Tasha with a close eye.

However, Tasha knew he was 100-percent deceased. She knew a dead body when she saw one. And he died the same way as his sister, with their eyes wide open like the Angel of Death viciously ripped their souls from their eyes and neck. Tasha was paranoid. Now she couldn't EVER go back home, else she would be sleeping with the fishes, never to be found alive again or period. She wouldn't even have a funeral with no body or trace. Sirachi was unaware of the grave danger she was in, the K.O.S. they had out for his baby mom, or the price Denver JD had put on her head, too.

NaeNae took all the back streets, zipping thru neighborhoods and running all stop signs. She was curb checking, tearing them deuces up. She didn't care about them damn rims. Her life and freedom was way more important. NaeNae got to Riverdale and pulled the pussy-pink Chevy in the garage and shut it.

The girls broke in the house up the stairs, yelling. Sirachi was asleep with the baby on his chest. Michelle and he just got thru creeping 30 minutes ago as soon as NaeNae left to go pick up Tasha, Michelle went in their room in some white booty shorts. She was kissing Sirachi all in his mouth too like she was his real bitch. She was just another turned-out thot catching feelings.

The baby started crying from Nae and Tasha busting in the door screaming. Sirachi was hot at first, thinking they was fighting again. NaeNae told him it was AntLoc goon and Tasha claimed it was some nigga she recognized from Chicago. Either way, NaeNae ate his ass up. Tasha said he was dead. Nae claimed he wasn't.

Damn! His bitch done caught a body!

"NaeNae. give me the gun. I got to get rid of it. In the morning, report your car and gun stolen, like you woke up and they was gone."

Sirachi called Big Tricky to get the whip and burn it up in the woods, and they all agreed that Tasha would stay with them.

* * *

The four of them had all been shacked up in the condo for a week paranoid AF. NaeNae had her AR-15 in the front room locked and loaded. Tasha's nerves were still bad; she was scared and jittery. The crime rate in Atlanta was so high that the murder in the parking lot didn't even make the news. Michelle said she saw it online, though, and it was a John Doe with nobody to claim the body.

Michelle's head was all fucked up. She couldn't believe all this shit and the recent change of events, including her husband's bizarre death and her losing her kids to his evil family that hated and blamed her to this very day.

What really bothered her was this twisted double love triangle! There was Nae, Sirachi and her and then Nae, Sirachi, and Tasha. On top of that there was a baby boy now included in it all. She was living with her female lover, her lover, and his BM/lover. She never in life or on TV heard of a double love triangle that entwined two love triangles, let alone thought she would be starring in one. And Sirachi had some good dick, so yeah, she was guilty of creeping a few times with him behind NaeNae's back or when she was sleeping in the other room.

These three adult females in one house and all sharing one dick was going to cause problems and flare up a lot of emotions, especially if someone got caught fucking on the sneak creep, tippy-toes style.

Then it was very awkward that NaeNae and Tasha had got down before, too. Michelle disliked that and hated Tasha's exotic ass since day one. She knew that bitch was crazy, trouble, and bad luck. And she had to watch NaeNae's hot ass, too. She didn't trust her around Tasha, either. She'd been acting weird, too. Maybe it was from her shooting and killing someone? Michelle didn't have the heart to shoot or kill anything. She was a girly-girl. She still wore pink panties and played with hair all day. NaeNae, on the other hand, was straight hood. And Tasha was more of an ATL project bitch, even though she wasn't from no projects back in Chicago.

Michelle went to sleep with a helluva headache from all that thinking.

* * *

Riverdale, GA, OBGYN Clinic. At 7:40 a.m. Thursday morning, gynecologist Dr. Patricia Welch entered the room.

"Good morning, Miss Johnson. How are we doing today?" Dr. Welch greeted.

"Good morning to you, too. Oh, I'm fine! And I like ya hair, too," she replied.

"Oh well, thanks! OK, well, let's get straight to it. I have all your test results and I know you've been very worried about lumps in your breast, but your mammogram results came back clear. The x-ray showed no cancer spots, as you see," Dr. Welch stated.

"Thank God—Cancer free!" she replied.

"OK, now this is the part of my job I hate. I have some bad and good news, OK?" Dr. Welch said as she inhaled deeply.

"Uh…oh…OK, I guess? What's the bad news, though? I'm pregnant?" she said nervously and a bit intimidated, too.

"No—you're definitely not pregnant—Miss Johnson, you tested positive for genital herpes and tested positive for HIV! I'm so sorry to be the bearer of bad devastating news. The good news is you can still live with both. There is no cure, but if you take care of yourself, you can live a normal life," Dr. Welch said sternly. And 1 out of every 50 people in Atlanta had HIV, and clueless!

"OMG! OMG! No, oh God help me! This can't be… Oh, Dr. Welch, OMG! But like how? Why me? OMG! Lord, give me strength. Dr. Welch, I can't breathe…" she cried out, weak in the knees. It felt like she got hit by a freight train! She wasn't worried about the herpes, it was the HIV! That would surely take her to the grave.

"Just lay back, Miss Johnson, and take deep breaths. Do you know what partner gave you this or if you infected others? You had to contract this within the last six months. Your last results were all negative!" Dr. Welch said in a low tone, trying to comfort her.

She shook her head no. She needed to leave now and get some air. She left out the back clinic room to the waiting room with her ride.

"Damn, girl, you alright? You look like shit! What's the matter?" NaeNae looked at her, puzzled.

"Nae, I—I tested positive for herpes and HIV! My fucking husband was on the down low and gave it to me, that's why he really killed himself, and blamed me cuz he was into men! Dat's why my daughter kept saying Uncle Rayna!" Michelle spit with venom.

NaeNae's heart dropped! WTF? Could she get it from bumping or sucking pussy, too? Did Sirachi contract it? Did he use a rubber that night? Were they all infected?

THE END

Epilogue

Da hot thots had hot lives and dysfunctional, mainly from their impulsive sexuality.

Thot isn't a name or noun. It was an act, an action—a verb. The true and original definition for T.H.O.T. was That Ho Out There!

There was no doubt Teasing Tasha, Nasty Neesha, Notorious NaeNae, and Slutty Shelly were out there. Even Sirachi, as an M-thot, was way out there, too. Men have no excuses. There are such things as man whores, too.

This book shows you how to spot a hot thot! Caution... some don't come with red hair or thot flops warning signs.

Stay tuned for Hot Thots 2, and the highly anticipated Hot Wives!

"My Bitch Tropicana...Aye!"

"I'm in love with a thot...and I kno dat she hot...She twerking it soft...and she twerking it slow...and she twerk on the pole..."

Stay tuned for Sirachi's Soundcloud hits to redeem himself to his pipe dreams...

About the Author

Hitachi Choparazzi, is a New York City native, by the way of Omaha, who currently resides in Arizona.

Entrepreneur, tattoo artist turned author, Hitachi is the sole owner of Chop-A-Style Publishing LLC and Chatmon Sr. Literary Agency. He has written over 40 self-published books and currently is working on scripts for Netflix.

Hitachi prides himself on having his own signature Chop-A-Style where he freestyles all his books. They all rhyme with innovation and original storylines. Hitachi's tales are a breath of fresh air for all those who are sick of the same tired stories. Hitachi, who is currently incarcerated in a Federal facility in Arizona, writes prequels, sequels, trilogies, and more. He creates for the people who love to read and for those incarcerated in the United States and around the world.

"I do this for y'all. I love y'all and believe in y'all! I won't stop giving y'all the raw stories as God blessed them in my head. I have a hundred of them up there. Anybody that has a hot hand in writing, send samples to me or any comments, suggestions. Support incarcerated authors. Teflon Luv!" #FreeHitachiChoparazzi

E-mail: orders@chopastylepublishing.com

FB: Chop-A-Style Publishing

Pimp of da Ratchetts
Book I of the Pimp of da Ratchetts Series

Welcome to Baton Rouge, Louisiana, better known as BR. Young Twan, a fresh high school dropout, chose to ditch class, not for the street gangs, but to pimp! He took on one of the world's oldest trades. Twan don't believe in no such thing as ratchett. A hoe meant doe. He didn't care if they're ratchett or a damn runaway as long as they pay. He sees all hoes as cash cows.

All he wants to do is rep for the BR and put the Southside on the map. The only problem is his crackhead mama, Lela, keeps setting him back and his high school sweetheart refuses to let him go and chases him around the BR streets. Will Twan get trapped or cracked trying to pimp BR on the map? Stay tuned for this rare, exclusive page-turner. I promise you won't put it down, Pimpin'!

https://hitachichoparazzi.com/

Chop-a-Style Publishing and Productions LLC
Other Books and Scripts by the Author

Non-Fiction
How to: Rap; The Elementary Teaching of Hip-Hop
How to: Love
The Switch: A Social Awareness Self-Help
Nipsey Hussle Lockdown Society Dedication–Tribute
If Trayvon Martin Could Talk; Injustice

Fiction
The Eagle and Weasel (1-5 series kids' book)
She Go! (urban novel)
Reality Show 3D-HD (urban novel)
Hot Thots (urban novel)
Liqz (urban novel)
Paranormal Whisper (horror novel)
Pimp of Da Ratchets (urban novel)
Pimp of Da Ratchets II Vegas (urban novel)
Pimp of Da Ratchets 3 Orange is Da New Pimp (urban novel)
Hitachi (urban novel)
Penitentiary Pimp (urban novel)
Weasel Society (urban novel)
The Big Pepo and Plucker Story-She Go! Prequel (urban novel)

Screenplays/Scripts
Top Notch
Hot Thots
Pimp of Da Ratchets
Weasel Society
Million Dollar Games–A Secret Society
The Eagle and Weasel (animation)